The DOGGED DETECTIVE
A Lightning Bolt Mystery
Casey Swan

~

"The longer a case remains unsolved, the greater the chance there will be another murder."

Retired police officer Silas Chambers is in his forties and living on a pension half his old salary. He looks after the widow of a close friend killed in the line of duty, and is fiercely supported by his new girlfriend, but the rest of his life is a non-event.

Trouble builds quickly, and Silas cannot ignore the many cries for help. The old case of a murdered tourist and her family, who need answers, returns to haunt him, and then a local hunter disappears, followed by another.

Shot at, threatened, driven off the road and his car set on fire, Silas hides the people he cares about at an unlikely friend's motel. Then he uses his 'death' as a smokescreen to fight a bent lawyer and criminal mastermind.

This is a new kind of policing, with a hard edge he hasn't seen before. Using his friends in the police force, and his 'eyes and ears' – the Alcoholics Anonymous organization – he unravels the truth behind what has been happening.

Chapter 1

Penny was working at the kitchen table when she heard Maric's familiar knock. When she didn't answer he pushed the front door open and called out, "anyone home?" which was standard practice in the small seaside village of Ahipara.

Penny had deliberately not said anything, just so he would call out. She liked the sound of his voice, particularly when he put a bit of oomph behind it. It was the commanding voice of a leader, a voice that inspired confidence, and a voice she knew deliciously well.

"Come on through," she said, and closed down the work she was doing for Major General Wilkins.

"Ah, good, you're home," he said, and she raised her eyebrows.

"Where else would I be?" she said archly. "Your commanding officer has given me enough work to sink a ship! If you look under the table you'll see the chains that tie me to this chair," and he laughed.

"There's a lot on at the moment," he said apologetically, taking her hand. "It's a seasonal thing, so I hope you understand," and she nodded. He could get her to agree to anything if he took her hand and squeezed it like that.

There were two matters inside New Zealand that she was working on – one civil and one military – and a Lightning team would probably have to step in to sort them out before long. There was also one case she had just been given that originated offshore, and was about smuggled goods coming in through one of the New Zealand ports. It was her job to dig deep and come up with names and faces for the Lightning base, using the instincts she had developed in her previous life as a reporter.

"I hope you've got something planned for us for the weekend," she said, smiling winningly. "I could really use a break!" and he nodded, which made her day.

"What is it?" she said, feeling a little mean because she mostly left their romantic trips away to him – but he was so good at it!

"Wait and see," he said, and refused to say anything more. Oh well, she thought, a surprise was even better.

"I friend of mine needs your help," he said, which was a statement out of the blue, and she put both elbows on the table and looked at him.

"If you can't help him I doubt that I can," she said, a little confused. Maric had been elite military for most of his life, while Penny was barely competent with a pistol. She did have a knack with a sniper rifle, admittedly, and her self-defence wasn't bad, but the Lightning team were so much better!

"Not that sort of help," he said, and took a deep breath.

"Maybe I better start at the beginning," he said, and she nodded. This sounded interesting.

"I had a close buddy when I started out in the military," he said, "a guy by the name of Silas Chambers, but he went into the police force while I tried out for the SAS. We used to meet up fairly regularly for a while, but then he moved down to the centre of the North Island to get a promotion and we sort of lost touch – you know how it is," and she said that she understood.

"He contacted me last week," continued Maric, "and told me a story I could hardly believe. Part of it was what's been happening to him since I saw him last, and part of it was his belief that there's a twin-engined jet bringing drugs in from overseas and landing somewhere on his patch, and that bowled me over. It has to be the same drug cartel in Noumea that we came up against, right?" and Penny looked surprised.

"It looks like we didn't put much of a dent in their operation," he continued, with some annoyance, "and now they're pulling the same trick on the Volcanic Plateau in the middle of the North Island."

Penny was intrigued on both counts. Maric didn't say a lot about his early years, and maybe this old friend of his was a way she could get to know more about him. If she was honest, an old friend was of more interest to her than the annoying news that the drug cartel was up to its tricks again.

"Tell me about Silas," she said. "You mentioned that a lot has been happening in his life since you last caught up with him – could we start with that?" and he nodded. Then he looked at the ceiling, as if for inspiration.

"I was older than Silas," he said eventually, "and I remember I was 26 when I went into the SAS, so Silas must have been 21, or 22, when he went into the police force. He seemed to enjoy the work – at least when we were younger and met up regularly – but then two things happened. He had a good friend in the Tokoroa police force, Ian Findlay, who died in the line of duty, about the same time the station got a bad boss, a career jockey who didn't care anything for the boys and girls on the beat.

"Silas went to the station commander sure that he knew who had killed a Norwegian tourist whose body was found after the murder, but the commander said he didn't have enough evidence. It was all about cutting back on time and money, while the commander made a name for himself in the media, and that was hard to stomach.

"So Silas quit, and found himself in his mid-forties, after 25 years of service, with a police pension about half of his old salary. He was looking after Ian's wife Mereana, and their two boys, who definitely needed a man in their lives.

"I think he must have been searching for something to fill the void in his life when strange things started to happen around his little country town. He wasn't in the police any more, but he'd been a good investigative officer in his time, so he started to poke around. That's when he came across things that led him to believe someone was flying drugs into New Zealand from overseas."

"Well, we have to help him!" said Penny, when it seemed that Maric had wound down. To be honest the story was already captivating her, and it was far more interesting than the cases she was working on for Wilkins. There was also the chance she might be able to get Silas to talk about his early days with Maric.

"But I'm going to need a lot more information before I start digging," she said, and Maric raised his hands in surrender.

"You'll have to go to the horse's mouth for that," he said, "and it shouldn't be too hard to arrange." Then he promised that he would return with Silas' Skype address, and she could contact his old friend that evening.

"This isn't an official investigation," he warned her, "so you'll still have to do reasonable hours for Wilkins on those other cases, but if you can help Silas I'll owe you one.

"In fact," he said, getting up from the table so he could come around behind her and nuzzle her neck, "I'll owe you a complete set and an embroidered box to put them in!" which made her snort with laughter. Maric had a dry sense of humour, and it always delighted her.

"What am I going to tell him about us?" she said, when he turned up with the Skype address later.

"Nothing," he replied. "You're part of the Lightning base team, and you're on loan to him for a while as a favour to me. Let's not complicate matters.

"He knows I'm buried in some secretive part of the defence force, but he doesn't need to know about the Lightning teams. If we get drawn into this later on we'll reassess the situation then," and Penny nodded. It was a sensible answer, and she was mature enough not to read anything into it about Maric's attitude to her.

"An old friend of Maric's," said Ellie, as they were having dinner. "I bet you're going to pump him for as much information about your betrothed as you can!" and Penny rolled her eyes. Of course she was. Who wouldn't?

"And we're not betrothed," she said, narrowing her eyes at her sister. "You're always trying to read more into things than is there," and Ellie pasted an incredulous look onto her face.

"Oh, please!" she said. "Every other weekend away together, and you already treat each other like an old married couple! Well, okay, like an old married couple who are still very much in love. If that isn't betrothed then I don't know what is!"

Penny laughed, and decided that the main role of sisters was to wind each other up.

"So, what's this Silas like?" said Ellie, as she loaded runner beans onto her fork.

"I have no idea," said Penny. "Maric gave me a good description of the circumstances, but no idea of what he looks like," and they both shook their heads. Men had no idea about what was really important.

"But I think this is really important, Ellie," said Penny suddenly. "Maric wouldn't come to me about this unless it was important, but there's more in this case than smuggling drugs. Silas thinks he can find the person who murdered a Norwegian tourist, and while Silas didn't say anything, I got the impression that his friend's two boys are a bit of a handful."

She was right on both counts, and that night after dinner she listened spellbound as Silas went through everything that had led up to his current situation. He was a natural storyteller, and she was glad they were talking on

Skype. His face was very expressive, and along with the many hand gestures he used his body language added a great deal to what she was hearing.

Chapter 2

"I think it all started when Mereana thought she saw something as we were coming into Tawhiti," said Silas.

"No," he corrected himself, "when she saw something. I know better than that now.

"Tawhiti is a tiny place on the edge of the Volcanic Plateau," he explained, "not far from Tokoroa, and I've got an old villa just out of Tawhiti that I've done up," and then he stopped himself.

"But I digress," he said. "You already know that I do my best to look after Mereana and her two boys, Eli and Devon, after Ian Findlay got killed upholding the law?" and she confirmed that she did.

"Eli is now 19," he continued, "and a chippie with a building firm, but Devon, at the age of 16, is still a handful. I've had to haul him out of trouble a couple of times now, but I didn't know how bad it was going to get."

Then he seemed to catch himself getting off the topic again, and Penny waited while he relived a part of the story that she didn't need to know about.

Ian's death had started as a domestic call out, a de facto wife and baby held hostage in the front room of a rented house. No one knew the man had a firearm – he hadn't shown up in a search as having a firearms license – and Ian Findlay was trying to defuse the situation when the offender barged out of the house with a rifle in his hands. Ian had been unarmed, and his death had left a huge hole in Silas' life.

There were a lot of things Silas tried to think of as belonging to another life, another incarnation of himself, one that existed in a different time and a different place. The trouble was, he still lived in the same area, and those events had happened a few short years ago.

"Are you sure you don't mind listening to all this?" he said, and she hastened to reassure him.

"I've got all night," she said, "and besides, If Maric thinks we can help then I believe we can!"

"That man sure is something, isn't he?" said Silas. "I saw it in him way back when I was still on the other side of twenty."

Then he looked at the emotional nature of what lay ahead, and had second thoughts.

"I'm not sure knowing all this is going to be helpful, though," he said, and she gave him a few seconds before she answered.

"I used to be a reporter, and I know you were an investigative officer in the police force, but I might see something you missed by looking at it from outside the case," she said, and he seemed inclined to carry on after that.

"As I was saying," he said, "we were coming into the little township of Tawhiti, just me and Mereana out for a Sunday drive really, when she laid her hand on my aim.

"I had slowed the Outlander – I've got an old Mitsubishi Outlander – coming into town, and now I slowed it even further. Mereana's got a good eye for interesting things when we're driving around like this," he added, and then Penny just fell into the story. She was seeing it in her mind as he told it, and he could have been reading to her from a book.

0 ~ 0 ~ 0

Merana would occasionally have time free from her housecleaning round, and Silas hadn't really settled to anything after his sudden departure from the police force, so they would go for a drive on Sundays and end up at a coffee shop.

It was a friendship that was valuable to both of them, and it didn't go any deeper than that. She was still grieving, and he was unsettled, too young to be retired and too old to train for any other line of work. At least, that was what he told himself.

"Stodge wants to talk to you," said Mereana, waving at the veranda of a ramshackle old house to her left with a free hand.

"There's someone with him," she added, squinting to make out who it was.

Silas looked up as he approached the driveway leading to the old house, and saw Stodge in front of a big picture window, one hand raised, waving them in. The old man was upright, but he looked too low to be standing on the veranda. Silas wondered momentarily if he was kneeling.

A slim figure stood behind him, similarly diminished. It was a woman, with long blonde hair, and she was much harder to see. Silas rubbed his eyes as he changed gears on the Outlander, wondering why the woman looked so faded in the afternoon light.

Then Mereana's hand tightened on his arm. He looked at her face, and saw something there he had never seen before, and didn't want to see there again. Silas braked the Outlander to a stop, and she took her hand off his arm. He looked back at the veranda, but there was no one there now. The two figures had, impossibly, vanished in less than a heartbeat. A coldness settled over his heart.

"Stodge is dead," said Mereana abruptly, and her voice caught.

"There was someone with him," she managed, a moment later. "A young woman, with blonde hair, tall, and wearing a red coat. It was made of some kind of thick, fluffy material, and it didn't have sleeves."

"A puffer vest," said Silas, his hands tightening on the steering wheel. He was no expert on women's clothing, but Ella Brekken had been wearing a red puffer vest on the day she was murdered. There was no way that Mereana could have known that. None of the photos in the newspapers had shown Ella wearing the vest in which her body had been found.

The Norwegian tourist had gone missing on the edges of the Kaimai Ranges, not far from Tawhiti, and Silas was sure he knew who had murdered her. It had been shortly after Ian was killed, and normally the two policemen would have worked the case together.

Maybe that was why the failure to bring the offender to justice had hurt him so much. It was the one murder that still haunted him, and he had been unable to convince the station commander to take the investigation further.

Mereana looked back at him. "You didn't see anything, did you?" she said hopefully.

"No, nothing," he answered quickly. He wasn't going to open up that failure of his past for anyone, and certainly not on the strength of a vision supposedly brought to them from beyond the grave. If he didn't admit to seeing it, maybe it didn't exist.

Mereana had Maori blood in her, reflected in her black hair and light brown skin. Her mother, and her grandmother, firmly believed in the dead among the living, and she had inherited the tendency. Ian had told him about the things his wife had seen, and he claimed the information she provided was mostly right. Silas simply avoided the subject when he was with Mereana.

"A pity," she said, looking away. He could see the disappointment in her face. "I don't want to see dead people – in fact I would give anything to be free of the ability – but if other people saw the visions as well, I'd know at least I wasn't insane."

Silas smiled, and patted her arm. "You're not insane," he said, smiling, "and that's the official police position on the matter."

She didn't bother to remind him he was retired from the police force now. Instead she took her cell phone out of her purse.

"Rhonda?" she said, a few moments later. "You haven't got anything on a Stodge Graham, local resident of Tawhiti, have you? It would have come in today."

Silas could hear the duty officer at Tokoroa Station faintly. Rhonda had been a godsend when he was a Senior Constable there. She was a warm and concerned front for the police force when she was on the phone, and she had the experience to see that reports went to the right person, with the right degree of urgency, as they came in.

"Nothing?" said Mereana reluctantly. She paused, but there were no further comments. "Thanks Rhonda," she said, "I appreciate it."

Technically, reports that came into a police station weren't available to the public, but Mereana and Rhonda had been raising babies at the same time, and Mereana was a constable's widow. She was allowed some leeway.

"You don't mind if we stop, do you?" she said, as she opened the door of the car. Silas shook his head. As she walked away, to alert the neighbours on either side to look out for Stodge, he rolled the car forward and parked it in the driveway. Then he let out a long sigh.

There had been times he thought he was going mad in the last few years, and now something like this was happening. He had thought retirement would take the pressure off him, but it hadn't been the panacea he had hoped for.

At one stage he went to a counsellor. One session with her had been enough. She had started talking about unresolved issues, and Silas had found his own way to resolve them. He had decided to bury his 'issues' even deeper, where people couldn't see them and comment on them. The problem was, doing that was making things worse.

Then he wondered if Stodge had died of natural causes and was lying inside the house, but he figured Mereana would have known that. When he realized what he was saying, he almost slapped himself on the side of his face. Now he was taking her visions seriously!

Then he remembered the puffer jacket, and his heart sank. He couldn't explain that, no matter how hard he tried.

There were too many deaths in the last few years, and they weren't going away, and now, maybe, Stodge had been added to the list. It gave Silas a bad feeling that things were about to get a whole lot worse.

Chapter 3

_____

I told them I wouldn't speak to anyone but you, Silas, because I knew you'd give me a fair hearing. After this they can do what they like with me. I've been stupid, I know that now, and I'm sorry. Sorry I let you down too, man. You've done so much for me.

No, I'm fine. Well, considering. Ha ha, ha ha ha, eh? Yeah, it's not funny, is it.

How's mum taking it? Sure, I would expect that. Always admired her courage, should have told her so more often.

Yes, I understand the constable here has to be present. Yes, I give consent for this interview to be taped. Not really an interview though, eh? Just want to get this off my chest.

Yeah, in my own time. Thank God you're here, Silas.

Oh, my full name is Devon Alexander Findlay.

Well it started when Eli got taken on as a builder's chippie. After a year he moved out of the house and into a flat with some mates. He finally had a bit of money to spend, and his life was going somewhere, you know? But I was year 12 at school, and going nowhere.

Study has been a lot harder this year than last year, and the only place I've been shining is on the rugby field. It felt like all I had to my name was a tag – Devon 'Basher' Findlay, for some good blindside flanker work – but I was beginning to see that a name like that was more of a hindrance than a help in the real word.

Barnsey – Joseph Barnes – left school two years ahead of me, and the more depressed about my life I got the more I hung out with him. Two losers together, right? Come on, you must be thinking that. Yeah, well, I compare myself to him, even if you don't.

He had these ideas how a poor man might get ahead in the world, and in the end I listened to him. So that was where it started, Silas, in my heart. You always said people's problems start with a bitterness of the heart, and now I can see what you meant by that.

Barnsey said I could become part of the Devil's Outlaws Motorcycle Club if I did a job for them. They always find work for their members, and a man's never short of a dollar, that's what he said. He told me he'd done a few jobs for the Outlaws already, and things were looking good for him now. You know the Devil's Outlaws bought a house off the end of Papanui Street, right? Found a way to fiddle it past the district council. The council would have stopped the Outlaws from buying it otherwise.

My job was to drop a match inside the Royal Theatre on Campbell Street. That old dump hasn't been used for years, right? Hell, the side door wasn't even locked! Yeah, I should stop laughing at that, I suppose.

Barnsey said the Outlaws would set me up with an alibi if I was unlucky enough to be spotted near the place, and the deal itself looked sweet. Hell, it's an eyesore, right? I told myself I was doing my civic duty, like what you talked about sometimes with Eli and me. The duty of the citizen in a healthy society and all that. Um, I think I was full of civic shit, Silas, when I think about it now.

So on the Thursday night, that was the eighteenth, right, I turned up at the back of the theatre around midnight, like we arranged. Barnsey and some older dude were there, and we slipped through the side door and went around to the back of the stage.

Yeah, I wondered why they needed me when they could set the place on fire themselves, but it was like a test or something.

When we got to the back of the stage, there was an old man lying on the floor. He wasn't moving, and there was a lot of blood on the side of his head. I backed up real quick, because this definitely wasn't part of the deal.

Then this other dude said I had nothing to do with bumping the old guy off, so what was my problem? I was just there to burn the Royal down. He said the dead guy had got in the way of someone he shouldn't have, and the Devil's Outlaws had seen to it that he got what was coming to him. I figured the old guy on the floor was some criminal who had tried to put one over the Outlaws, and maybe it was justice. Pretty harsh, but I figured he'd got himself into this.

Barnsey said did I want to be in the Devil's Outlaws or not? He said one day the gang would be able to put up the Outlaws logo at that house off Papanui Street, and establish a proper headquarters. When that happened they would need lieutenants to run the show in the South Waikato, and those of us who got in at the start would be sitting pretty.

He promised that the Outlaws would look after me if anything went wrong, but it didn't seem like there would be any problems. A fire in an old wooden building late at night might have been the electrics, or maybe vandals, but a lot of people around here would be pleased to see the old place gone. Make way for the new, and all that. If the cops did manage to identify the dead guy, I reckon they'd be pleased another criminal wasn't around to bother the public.

So I lit the match. The curtains on the stage went up in minutes, and we had to hurry to get clear before the fire was spotted. Then it was congratulations all round, and I headed home and told mum the movie had been lousy. That way she wouldn't ask me any questions about where I'd been.

But someone saw me a few streets over from the theatre, heading away from the blaze, and reported the sighting. The police brought me in and kept questioning me about the fire, but what could they do? A young man out for a walk late at night? That could be a quarter of the town.

Then the Devil's Outlaws didn't come forward with an alibi, and Barnsey said just shut up and keep my head down, or I'd really be in trouble, and I wasn't having that! I might be stupid, but I wasn't going to be used.

Yeah, I know there wasn't a body in the rubble afterwards. Yeah, I know it couldn't have been burned up completely by the fire. No, I'm not making this up.

Goddammit! I need you to believe me on this one, Silas! I don't know anyone else who's got experience in finding things out, and you're the only one who might believe me. I had nothing to do with that body, the one that wasn't there later. Shit! You know what I mean. But that's the truth, and I swear it, so help me God!

Yeah, I know. I'm not helping the situation by getting angry. Sorry.

No, I've got nothing to add. No, there's nothing I want to change in what I said.

Hey, you think I can forget that old guy with blood in his hair? He was lying there like a waxwork dummy, cold and creepy. You think I can sleep at nights? Why the fuck do you think I came forward? I'm not playing with you about this!

Yeah, I know you will. Thanks, Silas. Get to the bottom of it, man. I feel like it was me that done it, killed the old man, you know, because I didn't stop it or something. Sure, I know I couldn't have saved him, but it doesn't stop how I feel.

Yes, you can stop recording now.

Chapter 4

"What do you make of that?" said Silas, once Devon Findlay had been led back to a holding cell. He pointed toward the squat electronic device that lay on the table beside him, the one that now contained the boy's confession. It sat like a question mark on the table between him and the constable who had 'officially' conducted the interview.

Asking Dave Tarrant for his opinion was a courtesy, really. Silas had handled all the criminal investigations in Tokoroa in his time, a police station too small to have its own detective branch, and his rank of Senior Constable back then would have trumped Dave's rank of Constable today. But Silas had left the police force two years ago to take early retirement, and Dave had stayed on. Silas didn't have any jurisdiction in Tokoroa Police Station now, and it had only been Devon's refusal to talk unless Silas was present that had got him into the interview room.

Both of the men had detested Marcus Billingham's approach to leadership when he came down from Auckland to take the top job as inspector. Billingham had made all sorts of changes, but they hadn't made any difference to the police on the front line. Tokoroa Police Station had gone 'online' for heaven's sake, but there hadn't been enough money for bullets for target practice when new weapons regulations had changed everything.

After two and a half mercifully short years, Billingham had gone on to be District Commander for Waikato, based in the Hamilton Central Station. To the men in the interview room, he was a career jockey who had done more harm than good in his time with them.

But Dave had played the long game, and put up with Billingham's third-rate leadership. The man had eventually gone, and Dave's patience had been rewarded. Silas, still hurting from Ian Findlay's death, and then taken off a murder case he knew he could solve, had quit. Plenty of people had told him he had an impulsive streak during his life, and his actions at the time looked like more evidence of it.

Dave swung his chair around to face Silas. Dave was a strong man just starting to run to fat, bulky next to Silas' tall, lean frame.

"The boy could have invented the body inside the theatre to distract us from his little act of arson," he said. "He might think we'll go easy on him because we need his help in a murder case, one that he knows will evaporate in time through lack of evidence."

Dave was right in one respect. Every confession the police looked at contained additions that were there to make the confessor look justified in his or her actions, or innocent of everything except being in the wrong place at the wrong time. Most of the changes were minor, nothing too easily checkable, but a body, now missing, wasn't a small change meant to distract. Not in Silas' mind.

"The police do have a missing persons report that matches Devon's description of the body," said Silas. Stodge's neighbors had put in the report two days after Mereana had asked them to look out for the old man. It had been upgraded to an investigation by the end of the week.

"Yeah, but the timing's off," said Dave. "The boy didn't mention any signs of decay on the body, but the old theatre was burned down ten days after the missing persons report was filed. Why would anyone kidnap an old man, and then kill him ten days later?"

Dave was right about the time delay. Murders hereabouts tended to be spontaneous, not premeditated, followed by a clumsy attempt to hide the body. But something from Devon's account of the incident at the theatre had stuck in Silas' mind.

"Not if the perpetrators had access to a freezer," he said. "Notice how the corpse spooked the boy? Sure, it was probably the first dead person he'd seen, but his reaction seemed like more than that to me.

"He said the body looked 'cold and clammy', and I think I know why. If the body had been taken out of a chiller, the face would have been covered in condensation from the air around it by the time Devon got there. The chiller would also explain the ten day time lag.

"I've seen bodies after they've been frozen and thawed out, and the process accentuates the veins under the skin so they come up as a web of blue lines. I think the old man might have looked like one of your comic book vampires about to rise from the grave. It would have spooked the boy all right."

Dave acknowledged Silas' point with a curt nod. It was possible. He was about to say maybe the boy felt bad about the old man's death – the last part of his confession – because he'd been involved in it. But he knew that Silas had been helping Mereana raise Devon, so he closed his mouth again.

After a while he said, "so you think his confession's a reliable account of what happened?"

Silas hesitated. He knew his opinion wasn't going to be on the form that recommended further action, Dave's was.

"Do *you* think the boy was telling the truth?" he said, parrying Dave's question with his own.

"Yes, I would have to say I do," murmured Dave slowly. "Going by my gut instincts. But that's what's so odd. Nothing else fits.

"The boy says the old man got offside with 'someone he shouldn't have'. How? He wasn't moving in any powerful circles. And why hire the Devil's Outlaws for the hit? Sure, I can imagine them taking a contract killing, but the old man wasn't into methamphetamine, home invasion or prostitution, and I can't imagine the Devil's Outlaws moving too far outside their areas of expertise.

"You knew Stodge Graham," he continued, looking across at Silas. "If it actually was him in the theatre, do you know of anything he might have done that would get him into trouble like this?"

"No," said Silas slowly. "He stuck to himself mostly, drank a bit, and did a lot of deer hunting. He's been known to go out after deer in all weathers and stay out for days. I can't think of anything else he was involved in.

"And there's no body, Silas," said Dave, with an air of finality in his voice. It was enough to tell Silas what would be in the report. No further action on the body, and Juvenile Court for a boy from a good background who had no previous convictions.

Silas wasn't convinced it was the right call, all the same. There was much more than what Dave saw in Devon's confession, and Stodge would want him to follow it up. There was every chance the death of an old man who kept to himself, with no unusual circumstances, would gather dust as an unsolved case.

That glimpse of Stodge on the veranda of his house in Tawhiti, beckoning Silas in, still burned the tall man's soul. He kept telling himself it was a product of stress, and his growing restlessness these days, but telling himself he should believe that wasn't working.

He'd lied to Mereana about it too, which he couldn't remember doing before. It felt like he was turning into someone he didn't want to be. Maybe solving Stodge's murder, as he was fast becoming sure was the case, was the only way to redeem himself.

His mind started to tease the case apart as Dave rose from his chair, on his way to write up his report. Silas' old investigative skills, having lain fallow for so long, were making suggestions. If Stodge hadn't been directly involved in anything that led to his death, then the old man must have been indirectly involved.

That meant he had heard or seen something he wasn't meant to. Killing him for something that minor seemed over the top though, if that was all the old man had done.

Stodge, my old friend, he wondered, what did you get yourself into? And Dave was right. Where was the body?

Chapter 5

Silas and the two women looked around Stodge's living room. It was – surprisingly for an old man living alone – clean, and generally tidy. Especially if they discounted the boxes and assorted items stacked along one wall. Stodge had called himself a 'collector', and Silas figured the other rooms in the house would be piled high with the rest of his 'collection'.

The tall man had travelled the short distance into Tawhiti on a rough gravel road from his block of pines in the hills behind the village. Mereana had climbed the 14 km from her home in Tokoroa on a dead straight, two-lane, sealed road through poor farming land and plantation forestry. She had known before Silas did that Stodge's sister had arrived in Tawhiti, and gone to help her settle in.

It was typical of Mereana, and even though she was struggling to come to terms with Devon's problems she still had time to help someone else. She'd managed to get Devon transferred to home detention until his trial date in four weeks time, and that had lifted some of the weight off her shoulders.

Silas had never heard Stodge talk about a sister, but Mereana's summons to meet up at Stodge's place reminded him of the fierce efficiency of the small-town grapevine, distributing news and gossip as soon as it became available. He already knew that the sister's name was Emily, she lived in Dunedin, that a taxi had picked her up after a bus had dropped her in Tokoroa, and she would be staying in Stodge's house for a while. She had also, apparently, taken some time off work.

"Did you know my brother well, Mr Chambers?" Emily asked, looking around the room sadly. Silas figured she had already accepted the fact that after two weeks Stodge wasn't coming back.

"Off and on for a long time," said Silas warmly, "and please, I'm Silas to everyone in Tawhiti."

Emily nodded, and took a seat in the armchair opposite the television set. It would have been Stodge's favourite chair. She ran her fingers along the worn fabric, as if she could pick up some reminder of her brother's presence. Mereana and Silas shared the three-seater next to the armchair.

Emily stirred herself, and belatedly offered them some tea, as if pleasantries could be dispensed with when her world had just been mauled by news of her brother's disappearance. Mereana and Silas declined.

"Why do the people hereabouts call him Stodge?" she asked suddenly. Her head snapped up as she did so, and Silas wondered what she did for a living. She was clearly used to asking direct questions.

"Oh, that," he said. "He collected everything, and never really settled to one or two areas of collecting. He seemed to know an awful lot about every type of collectible, to be honest. His collection was a strange mixture, a 'stodge' of so many unrelated things mixed together, like leftovers in a pudding. The folks around here didn't mean any disrespect by the name."

She nodded, as if this was reassuring to know.

"Well," she said, "his name is Ernest, Ernest Graham. Rather old-fashioned perhaps, but then I'm Emily Graham, so that tells you something about our parents. Ernest is 16 years older than me, a mistake by our mother. She didn't marry the man.

"Ernest always looked after me when I was a young girl," she said, her voice trailing off, and Silas saw her blink back tears.

"Mereana says you used to be in the police," she said, recovering, and looking at Silas. He nodded. "I'm a legal secretary at a small firm," she continued, "and we work with the police sometimes. I'm a solo mother, one child, and the two of us are doing okay. Ernest and I just drifted apart over the years, and then there's the distance from Dunedin to Tawhiti.

"No need to kill him for his, ah, collection, in case you're wondering," she said, smiling ruefully.

Silas smiled back, his eyes twinkling. Mereana must have told Emily that he used to be an investigating officer. If anyone thought he was wondering about Emily having a part in Stodge's disappearance, she had deftly caught the serve and fielded it back to him. He liked her immediately.

"My brother's story is one of riches to rags," she said quietly, staring out a window into the distance. Silas said nothing. He had always found that good listening skills encouraged people to talk.

"He did well at school," she went on, "and there was no doubting he was a natural scholar. Then, in his last year at High School, he had his first manic episode. Others followed. He was soon diagnosed as bipolar, and the medication back then had some unpleasant side effects. Continuing with academic study was out of the question.

"Then, in his middle years, he managed to dig himself out of the mood swings and the constant unemployment. He used his brains to keep track of how he was doing each day, and took steps to centre himself again when he needed to.

"He eventually stopped taking the medication, replacing it with a very rigorous self-discipline. He never took on anything stressful, so he never achieved much in the eyes of the world, but I would call him a success story, wouldn't you?"

Silas found himself nodding in agreement. It was a great lesson about not knowing who someone really was. He watched as Emily's eyes travelled slowly around the room, lingering on the stacked boxes, and he sympathized. If Stodge were dead, it would be her job to dispose of a lifetime of collecting before she sold the house.

Mereana stepped in to make arrangements for Emily's stay in Tawhiti. She offered to ferry her to the supermarket in Tokoroa some time in the afternoon, and help her with anything else she might need. A neighbour had already invited Emily to dinner that evening. The neighbour had found a couple of unpaid bills in the mailbox, and Emily would take care of them when Mereana took her into Tokoroa.

Stodge's sister had a week off work, and then she would be returning to Dunedin. Mereana suggested that she and Silas return the next day to help out, and then Silas found himself asking a question he would have asked in his police days.

"Did Ernest say or do anything unusual in the weeks before he disappeared?" he asked. Emily hesitated, then shrugged her shoulders.

"I would normally consider this private," she said, "but I guess that's not important when he's gone missing.

"There was one thing. Sometimes I wouldn't hear from Ernest for months, but lately he's been in touch every other day. I wondered why, and eventually he told me he could help my daughter, Eva."

Emily looked around the room again, gathering her strength. It seemed this was not an easy topic for her.

"Eva was in a car crash when she was six, and I was driving at the time. I survived fairly well, but the crash did a lot of damage to the bones in her face. The doctors said they could restructure the area, but it would have to wait until she finished growing.

"She's sixteen now, but hospital budgets keep getting cut these days. I've been worrying she'll get the most basic of treatment when the time comes, or none at all.

"Ernest finally stopped hinting that things might be looking up for me a few weeks ago, and said he had all the money I would need to make Eva look normal again."

She glanced across at Silas and Mereana. Silas in particular would want to know where Stodge could possibly get so much money from.

"He said, and I quote, 'the money is all arranged, we just have to sit tight and wait now.'

"I'd already told him how much it would cost to have it done privately. Close to a hundred thousand dollars, spread over three operations and a year of follow up work, but that made no difference to him. He insisted he would soon have the money.

"It didn't seem like one of his manic episodes, but it's hard to tell sometimes."

Silas filed the information away in his brain under motivation. Many a person had been killed for a lot less than that.

"I would like to know what happened to Ernest," she said, "and if you can help me with that, Silas, I would be eternally grateful."

Silas hesitated. His main interest in Stodge's disappearance was getting Devon's sentence reduced. The more he knew about what had happened at the theatre, the more persuasive Devon's defence lawyer would be.

Mereana looked at him pointedly. She had been making suggestions over the past year that he needed to get back into some sort of work. This would be ideal, from her point of view.

"I could pay some of your expenses," said Emily, who seemed to have made the judgment that Silas had been good at his job – which he had been.

Silas dismissed the idea of money with a wave of his hand, but it forced him to decide how much he was prepared to help her.

"I'll keep you in the loop," he said quietly. "I can't promise anything, but I know a lot of people in this area. Whatever I find out can also be fed to the police to speed up their investigation into Stodge's disappearance."

Emily smiled gratefully.

An hour later the two women headed for the supermarket in Mereana's car, and Silas took the opportunity to look through Stodge's house. He had Emily's blessing, and moved methodically about his task. The key to the gun cabinet was hanging with other keys near the back door, and Silas shook his head with a smile. Trying to keep firearms locked away was only as good as the owner's idea of security.

All the rifles were present. At least, there were three vertical compartments and they held a short pig-hunting rifle, a 22, and a lightweight Ruger, ideal for deer, that had been well used.

Silas didn't hurry as he looked through the rest of the house, but it didn't help. Answers wouldn't come. His mind chewed away at what it knew about the case, but he didn't have enough pieces of the puzzle.

In the end he was no nearer an answer to his question. What had Stodge been part of that got him into so much trouble?

Chapter 6

———————

Dave Tarrant rang Silas the next day.

"Got a few things I thought you would want to know," he said, without preamble.

"You off duty?" said Silas, before the constable could continue.

"Not exactly," said Tarrant. "Tidying up a few loose ends from a recent run of break ins. Same M.O. on all of them. Some self-righteous little shit who thinks the world owes him a free ride.

"But don't worry, no one can hear me talking to you," he said. "I'm alone, and a long way from the station."

Silas had left Tokoroa Station under a cloud. He had made it clear he thought Billingham wasn't the right man for the top job, and he didn't know if the man had soured his successor, Matthew Flynn, against him as well. Technically, Silas shouldn't have access to any information relating to a live case, the same as any other member of the public. Rules could be broken, but that depended on how Silas was viewed by the higher ranking officers at Tokoroa Station.

"Just watching your back, Dave."

"Appreciate it. Now shut up and listen."

"We brought Joseph Barnes in," said Tarrant, "but he's a right little crim. Only 19 and someone's already schooled him in what not to say. He denies anything to do with the theatre fire, and claims he can produce two alibis for the time it was burning. We're following up on that, but I figure the Devil's Outlaws will be able to provide witnesses saying anything they want them to say."

"So Devon's story isn't going to hold up in front of a judge," said Silas. It was bad news.

"At least he's back home now," said Silas, with more feeling. He kept thinking he should have watched the boy more closely, picked up on what was happening in his life, but everything had seemed normal recently. At least Devon was still 16, just, and couldn't be sent to prison for crimes against property.

"The boy only gave a vague description of the older male at the scene," continued Tarrant, "which is not surprising in the dark, so we've drawn a blank there too. Barnes of course claims the older guy doesn't exist, wasn't there, that sort of thing – which is interesting, as Barnes says he wasn't in the theatre to see that.

"At least Devon was able to tell us about a new Devil's Outlaws base in Tokoroa. I bet Barnes' handlers are unhappy he let that slip. I've leaned on a few members of our local drug fraternity, and they say it's an old four-bedroom house on Baird Street, off Papanui. Someone is selling narcotics out of the place, but it's small-scale stuff so far.

"The house appears to have three inhabitants. A Sergeant-at-arms for the Devil's Outlaws who goes by the name of Maloof, about as common an Arabic name as you can get, and two runners, Luke Matto and Terz Lahude.

"The last two are both New Zealand born, with a charge sheet as long as your arm but nothing major. A bit of digging told me they were involved in a major drug bust in Auckland a few years ago, and got off because of gang-related alibis."

Silas nodded to himself. "That was when they were recruited," he said. "The Devil's Outlaws would have said, 'we can free you from a long prison sentence, but we own you body and soul in return.'"

Tarrant agreed, and then he carried on.

"The name on the title deed for the house says Edson Mackay. We're trying to track him down, but his address turns out to be a corner dairy in Auckland, which is another dead end.

"And that's about all we've got so far," said Tarrant, pausing for a moment before he plunged on.

"Now here's the deal," he said briskly. "I'll keep you in the loop, if you stay out of the charges against Devon Findlay. We're doing everything we can to get the boy off lightly, Silas, since Mereana is a constable's widow and its a first offence. But I know you, and you'll want to be all over this case.

"You're not part of the police force any longer," he said sternly, "and I can't protect you if you do something silly. Look, you trained me up on investigative work, so trust your own training, and let me do my job!"

He gave Silas a moment to think about it before he said, "do we have an agreement?"

Silas almost smiled. Dave didn't want to know about Stodge's disappearance, at least until there was a body. He was only interested in Devon's part in the theatre arson, and that suited Silas well enough. He could continue trying to find out what happened to Stodge.

"You drive a hard bargain, amigo, but consider it done!"

There was a moment's silence, and Silas wondered if he had given in too easily. Tarrant would know how much he wanted to be involved in the theatre case, how much he wanted to help the boy.

"All right, then," came the reply. "I'll check in again when I've got more to report. Got to get back to work now."

Silas wished Tarrant well, and was about to slide his cell phone back into his pocket when it rang again. Someone, he figured, had been trying to get through while he was talking.

"How's the warthog?" said the chirpy voice of a young man on the other end. Silas had to smile.

"Better than the meerkat," he said, "skinny little dude looks like he was rolled together out of lion poop."

"Easy, hey, easy!" said Gords, from the other end of the connection.

It was Silas' unofficially adopted son. Gords was only 13, and living in the garage of a house occupied by a totally dysfunctional household, when Silas rescued him. He had taken the boy from a gang member and some wannabes who were growing marijuana at the back of Silas' 70 acres of pines. That was a serious mistake on their part, though they probably thought they were in the huge commercial pine forest next door.

Silas had set an electronic eye across the track, and gone in to arrest the perpetrators when they came back to look after their crop. He should have phoned it in, but this had been his family's land for many generations, and he needed to deal with the threat himself.

The two gang prospects had fled, but the gang member and this scrawny kid had stayed. The gang member had fancied his chances, but Silas had laid him out cold before hog-tying him face down on the forest floor.

Somewhere in the confrontation the kid had given the gang member a right proper bollocking for growing dope on private property, which could lead to the land being confiscated from the owner. Silas had taken a knife cut across his ribs in the process of subduing the gang member, but he'd also taken a liking to the mouthy youngster.

Silas had registered Gordon, soon universally known as Gords, with the Ministry for Children, but the first attempt to place Gords, with his mid-twenties aunt, had ended badly. She wasn't in the permanent relationship she claimed, and she was mostly after the benefit money that came from being a foster parent.

From then on Silas had hidden the boy at his place, setting him up with a trapping line for possums and taking on the task of home schooling him. Then he set up a homework system at the Potter's Rest tea rooms in Tawhiti to help with socialization. It was open for a couple of hours each day after pupils got back from the two high schools in Tokoroa. It must have worked, because Gords was now in the last year of his electrician's apprenticeship, flatting in the sprawling city of Hamilton while he studied.

Gords had needed a lot of discipline, and a lot of love, before he came right. Silas had put bolts on the outside of his window, and on the door of the boy's room, and sometimes thrown him bodily in there before locking him in.

On the other hand, Gords was 15 before he stopped watching old Disney movies each Saturday night with Silas, as if he was trying to catch up on a childhood he never had. The Lion King was one of his favourites, and they would often take on the goofball characters of Pumbaa the warthog and Timon the meerkat in their conversations.

"Back at the villa Saturday morning?" said Silas, and Gords agreed that he would be making the drive to Silas' place as usual. The 21-year old still needed to return 'home' regularly to confirm he had a reliable base in this world. It might just reflect his difficult beginnings, but it pleased Silas no end.

"You might want to drop in and see Devon while you're here," he said, and they talked for a while about the boy's situation. Silas wondered if Devon would have turned to Barnes if Gords had been still living in Tawhiti. The two had been close once.

That was the problem with early retirement, decided Silas, he had too much time to think. He could see the fine lines of cause and effect that made and unmade lives. A nudge in the right direction early on could stop a fully-fledged disaster from happening later.

Chapter 7

Silas pulled up outside Julian McCabe's law office in the early afternoon. He told himself he was investigating Stodge's disappearance and presumed death, and his visit had nothing to do with the recent burning of the Royal Theatre. The same set of questions could probably be asked in either investigation, but that was coincidental. The distinction was important to Silas, it was a matter of keeping his conscience clear.

"Ah, the redoubtable, and now retired, Senior Constable Chambers," said McCabe, after his secretary had kept Silas waiting for twenty minutes. "I do have that right, don't I? You are retired, and you leave all matters of justice to the appropriately appointed agencies of law and order?"

McCabe was laboring the point, and Silas wondered why. He nodded his head agreeably as McCabe motioned him toward a chair opposite the broad expanse of his desk. McCabe followed suit, settling into a top-of-the-line office chair that looked a lot more comfortable than the sturdy frame and minimal padding Silas was sitting on.

McCabe was older than Silas, but not by much, and he looked fit. Silas figured he worked out. The tautness to his body, and the expensive suit he wore, were intended to convey to the world that here was a man of power and substance.

"Nothing to do with the agencies of law and order," said Silas, opening his hands and lifting them up to show there was nothing in them. "I'm rather pleased to have some peace and quiet, to be honest. The police force takes it out of you over the years."

McCabe seemed to relax when he heard that.

"So, you want my help to buy a property, or set up a trust fund for that boy you adopted?" he said. "Though the land you've already got would surely keep you busy." His eyebrows went up. "You're not thinking of selling up and moving into Tokoroa?"

Silas was surprised McCabe knew so much about him. His life wasn't a secret, but the two men had rarely met outside of Silas' police work, and had little in common. On the other hand, Silas knew a great deal about Julian McCabe.

McCabe had arrived in Tokoroa as soon as he finished his studies and been given a practicing certificate from the New Zealand Law Society. It had been about the same time Silas had taken up his first post as a policeman, in a town nearby. Silas had once looked up where McCabe was born – a small town called Hanmer Springs in the South Island – but there was little in the public record about his activities before he arrived in Tokoroa.

From that point on, though, he had been a man on a mission. A mission that had elevated him to the highest possible social standing in the South Waikato over the last 25 years. He had offices in all the towns around Tokoroa now, and a number of lawyers working for him. None of them were partners in his business, and Silas figured none of them ever would be. McCabe wanted to be a big fish in a small pool, and not the other way round. That was why he hadn't set up his practice in a much larger center.

The lawyer gave large sums of money to community projects, particularly if they lifted his profile in the public eye. He had a new house, several new cars, and a trophy wife. Silas wondered if McCabe would ever feel he had arrived at his destination – whatever he was trying to get out of life.

Silas looked around the office. It had been tastefully furnished. It was part of the substantial old brick building McCabe had bought and set up as his law offices. It was one of the best buildings Tokoroa had to offer, but Silas suspected it wasn't enough for the man's ever-expanding idea of his own importance. Nowhere near enough.

"I wanted to check something," said Silas, "make sure my recollection is the same as yours."

McCabe smiled confidently. He was a lawyer. His recollection was always correct, and if it wasn't he had the vocabulary and semantic skills to make others realize how mistaken they were.

"We both sit on the Tokoroa Chamber of Commerce," said Silas, "though I think my welcome is wearing out since I no longer represent the police. But that's beside the point.

"You made an offer to buy the Royal Theatre about a year ago, didn't you? You wanted to build yourself a new office on the site, and you offered to turn half the land into public amenities. Whatever the chamber wanted, a squash club perhaps?"

McCabe's face froze over for a moment, and Silas knew he'd hit a nerve.

"The absentee owners had already agreed to the deal, but the building had a covenant on it, as I recall," he pushed on. "It was protected as a category two heritage building, by virtue of the Building Act and the Heritage New Zealand Act.

"You pushed for the Chamber of Commerce to have the covenant lifted, which Heritage New Zealand will sometimes do if it's the clearly stated wish of a united community, but the Chamber turned you down."

"Yes," said McCabe smoothly, as his face became more mobile again. "It was a thank you to my adopted town, in fact. I've done a lot to help the community around here, but not enough apparently for the Chamber of Commerce to see things my way on this one.

"We have to go forward, Mr Chambers, I'm sure you can see that. If this town doesn't have the money to restore an old building, what's the use of having a piece of history we can point our fingers at but not use for anything?"

Silas pretended to be pondering the argument. He could already see that the morality of the situation, in this case the people's point of view, was an unknown concept to McCabe. Since Tokoroa had a population of fourteen thousand, that was a lot of hopes and aspirations and futures and opinions to ignore, but people like McCabe had turned that part of their brain off long ago.

The lawyer thought he had done enough for the rich and powerful to buy a favour of this magnitude in return. It was business ethics. You scratch my back and I'll scratch yours, and any damage that may occur to bystanders is an uncounted cost of doing business.

"So, and I'm just checking here," continued Silas, "your offer to the absentee owners still stands?"

McCabe smiled for some time, and Silas could sense the irritation the man felt. He had been backed into a corner by someone who no longer had any power in this town. A nobody who dared to speak up.

"The deal has already gone through, Mr Chambers," he said at last. "Why wait? I actually hurried this thing along so that the good people of Tokoroa wouldn't have to look at a pile of burnt timbers any longer than necessary.

"And now if you'll excuse me, I have a lot of work to do," he said abruptly, pushing himself upright in his chair.

"I also find your interest in these matters to go far beyond that of a concerned citizen, and I shall be contacting the inspector at the police station about it. He cannot, of course, censure you, since you no longer work for him, but I'm sure he could make your life uncomfortable if you persist with these questions.

"And now that we understand each other, perhaps you could show yourself out."

McCabe touched a button on his desk, and his secretary opened the door to his office.

"Mr Chambers is leaving," he said, already seated and perusing a document that had been lying on a folder in front of him.

Silas was back in his Outlander before he had a chance to go over the meeting in his mind. He knew he would never be able to have a conversation like that with the lawyer again. McCabe had thought he could handle Silas, now his power as a constable was gone, but he had discovered that a formidable investigative mind still remained.

It had been wise not to ask McCabe if he knew anything about the theatre burning down. The man would have thrown him out at once, and it would have been a pointless fishing expedition on Silas' part.

What he did know as a result of the interview, and he would stake all his years of experience on it, was that McCabe had put out a contract to have the old theatre destroyed. There was nothing like a face to face meeting to show up a suspect's body language. The problem now would be proving that McCabe had done it.

The 'how' of the contract was easy. McCabe had represented enough people on criminal charges to know who to turn to. He would know who had the contacts for a job like that, and who was capable of keeping their mouths shut.

The Devil's Outlaws probably didn't know who had ordered the arson. The instructions would have gone through a number of intermediaries, each one suitably motivated to deny everything if they were asked about it.

Then one day McCabe would have heard about the fire, and smiled to himself. A sum of money would have left one of his trust accounts almost immediately, triggered by a code. Then he would have buried the transaction so deep it could never be found.

But other parts of the case weren't so clear to Silas. There was an overlap between McCabe's business and the Devil's Outlaws, that much he knew. The Devil's Outlaws must have thought it was a great opportunity to get rid of the evidence from a contract hit when they were told they had a building to burn down. A charred body held no clues. But then, why had they later removed the body? Silas couldn't think of anyone except the Outlaws who had the opportunity to do that.

Silas had agreed to leave Dave Tarrant to follow up on any part of this that related to Devon's case, and he thought he was keeping his part of the deal. But he hoped Tarrant was leaning on the Devil's Outlaws already. If they admitted that one of their associates was present at the theatre, on some minor and dismissible charge, a judge would be able to read between the lines, but it would add to the possibility that Devon was innocent. His sentence might then be home detention and community work. It was the best outcome Silas could hope for.

He looked at the time. It was mid-afternoon, and he needed to be back at Stodge's house soon. Mereana would be there already, helping Emily through the grief of Stodge's disappearance. Sometimes, he thought, women just needed other women.

The Outlander pulled out onto the quiet side street next to McCabe's offices, and headed for State Highway One, which was a block over. A short dogleg delivered him onto the side road to Tawhiti.

Chapter 8

Penny stopped Silas when Ellie stuck her head around the door and asked if she wanted any supper – a cup of tea perhaps? After Ellie had left with Penny's request, which was a cup of tea and one of those shortbread biscuit she had baked yesterday, she tried to get her head around the story Silas was telling her. The fact she felt like a piece of shortbread with her tea was the most obvious sign of how much it intrigued her. She wished she was right there beside him and working on the case.

"Do you want to take a break?" she asked, and he shook his head. When she looked at the time she discovered that an hour had gone past, and she could see that one night was not going to be enough to hear the whole story.

"I need feedback from someone who looks into these things professionally," he said, and she understood that he felt awkward asking for help.

"In the police force we would normally investigate something like this as a team," he continued, "and it feels odd to be on my own. As you've heard, it has already involved someone who I think of as an adopted son, and as I get deeper into this I worry about the lives of those who are dear to me," and she knew what he meant.

When you take 'the King's shilling', as had happened with her and the Lightning base, and Silas and the police force, you knew you might be putting your life on the line, but you didn't expect those you cared about to be in danger as well.

"Maric says you've solved some difficult cases up your way, and you have an impressive work rate," continued Silas. "If you're involved in whatever hush-hush thing he's got going up there, I would really appreciate your outlook on this."

Penny felt a little guilty. She wasn't part of a Lightning team – though Maric seemed to keep putting her on the front line with his troops. But then

Major General Wilkins seemed to appreciate her investigative skills, and she knew she had contributed quite a lot to the Lightning ops.

"I don't think you've put a foot wrong so far," she said, quickly going over the shorthand notes she had taken. "You've appreciated the fact you're no longer part of the police force, and there are boundaries you can't cross, and you're right to be worried that Stodge's disappearance might never be solved if you don't take up the case.

"The police position is likely to be that an old hunter has had a heart attack in the forest somewhere, which means no further action, but Devon tells a different story. According to him it's likely that Stodge was at the theatre, and the old man's death is tied up in this in some way."

Then she took a deep breath and made a decision. There wasn't any sign of a twin-engined jet smuggling drugs into a high country topdressing strip yet, but Silas had told Maric it was there, and she would wait for the story to unfold.

Silas, though, needed to get all this out in front of someone else – since he was so much on his own down south – and she did want to be in on the case, despite the heavy workload that Wilkins had given her.

"I think every detail might be important in a case like this," she told him, "where there's no obvious connection between the parts of the puzzle, so I think we should continue as we are.

"To be honest I lose concentration after a couple of hours taking in new stuff, so we might not get this finished tonight. We can carry on tomorrow evening if that suits you though," and Silas sounded hugely relieved.

Penny had a short time to sip her tea and think that shortbread must be one of the cooking world's greatest inventions, and then they were back into it.

0 ~ 0 ~ 0

It was two days before Silas decided to continue his investigation into Stodge's death. Matthew Flynn, the new inspector at Tokoroa Station, hadn't called him in to give him a roasting, and that surprised him. McCabe would have called the inspector and complained about Silas and his questions, there was no doubt about that.

Now Silas stepped out from the shadows under the overhanging roof of an abandoned dairy on Papanui Street, and waited for the approaching figure to close the gap. Fortunately Barnes had an ear bud in each ear, and was lost in some retro punk album that had been laid down before he was born. He kept tapping at the battery-powered device in his pocket with a partly closed hand, and it made him look like someone with palsy.

Silas reached out a long arm and pulled one of the ear buds free. Barnes came to an immediate stop. He was momentarily confused, but then he swung his body toward Silas, ready to throw his weight around. When he saw who it was, he stopped cold.

Silas had perfected a knowing smile over the years. It was his way of dealing with difficult people. It was a show of confidence that suggested the recipient was about to be on the end of some very unpleasant news.

"What you doin' here, man?" hissed Barnes. "I caint be seen talkin' to you. Shit, the Outlaws will think I'm stitching them up!"

"That's why we should walk round the back of the dairy, and have a quiet little conversation no one can hear," said Silas. "It's either that, or a ride down to the station."

Barnes wavered. Silas thought his target might make a break for it, and that would have been awkward, but the thought of a ride in a squad car drained Barnes resolve. The Devil's Outlaws recruit was the weakest link in the theatre case, and Silas intended to exploit that fact. Barnes probably thought retired police had special powers they could still exercise if they wanted to. Silas was depending on him having such misperceptions.

The dairy wasn't far from the new Devil's Outlaws property, and Silas had been running surveillance for a day and a half before he managed to arrange the meeting. Fortunately, Barnes was a creature of habit.

The back of the dairy morphed into a standard suburban house, but no one lived there any more. This area was the closest Tokoroa had to a slum, and renting out the house wasn't worth the risk of the place being trashed. There was a BBQ area on the back patio made out of concrete blocks, and three raised wooden beams that surrounded the front of it. They were intended as seating. Silas took the end of one, and motioned for Barnes to take the end of the next one.

"I weren't at the theatre," said Barnes defensively, as soon as he sat down, "an' I've got witnesses! Don't you try to make me say nothin' else!"

"I'm not interested in the theatre, Joseph," said Silas quietly, "I want to know who the old man got on the wrong side of."

Barnes face went through a whole range of emotions while he considered all of his possible responses, and which of them would put him in the most favourable light. Then he remembered he wasn't at the theatre, at least that was the story.

"Weren't there, man. Din't see nothin', don't know nothin'," he said at last.

"Sure," said Silas. "Maloof tell you to say that? Told you to stick with the story and the police would eventually go away? How's that working out for you?"

He got a bout of sullen silence in reply.

"Look," said Silas, "I know you didn't kill the old man. You aren't high enough in the Devil's Outlaws for that. It was Maloof, wasn't it, or his two offsiders, Luke and Terz."

Barnes looked surprised when Silas mentioned the gang members' names, but the sullen silence soon returned.

"Yeah, well, a hardened crim like you would know better than to answer that question," said Silas, and Barnes looked up with something like pride.

"You got that right," he snapped.

"Which is why I'm not asking that question," said Silas. "I'm asking you what the old man did to piss somebody off. No names, no dates, nothing to tie him to the Devil's Outlaws."

Barnes seemed to honestly consider answering the question, for one second.

"Why should I help you!" he spat. "Next time you meet me you'll stop me for drugs, or no rego, or whatever you can think of!"

"Come on, Joseph," said Silas, chiding him, "we both know speed ruins families and fries people's brains, given enough time, and we both know the Devil's Outlaws sell the stuff. You have to do your job, and I have to do mine. We can't complain about the way things are."

An argument about the balance between good and evil in society was too much for Joseph Barnes. He didn't bother trying to understand what Silas was saying.

"Anyways," he retorted sharply, "no one calls it speed any more. It's ice, or meth, these days!"

"I think we've got off the point, Joseph," said Silas quietly. "Either you tell me what you know about the old man – and of course you weren't involved in his death in any way – or I'm about to become your new best friend.

"I found you easily enough today, didn't I? Where else do you hang out, Joseph? I can be there too, not a problem. I can be waiting for you even when you're just out taking a walk.

"There isn't anywhere I can't be, and you know that. You've got Devil's Outlaws business to attend to now and then, so you can't stay in the headquarters all day. What are the Outlaws going to say about you associating with the police? It looks like a no win situation to me, Joseph. What does it look like to you?"

Barnes was nearly doubled over on the wooden bench. He rocked from side to side, his body twisted up, as he tried to make a decision. It was his coping behaviour, the place he went to when things were spiralling out of control, and Silas figured he had learned it before he was five.

Some people never got a chance in life, but that wasn't Silas' problem. His job was to police the law as it currently stood. Or it had been his job, but he was having a hard time turning that part of himself off at the moment.

"You'll say you never talked to me?" said Barnes, and Silas assured him his name would never be mentioned.

"I don't know much," said the miserable-looking figure. "Maloof don't talk about things like that, and he tells the others not to either, but they's got to brag sometimes."

Silas nodded encouragingly.

"There's this important dude the Devil's Outlaws are tight with. I think they're in business with him. The old guy was snooping around on this dude's land, and he must have seen too much.

"The Outlaws went an' found out about the old guy's family, and tol' him what would happen to them if he din't forget what he seen. It was okay for a while, an' then the old guy tried to make a deal or somethin', I don't know what, but he had to be silenced."

"I don't know more'n that, honest!" he said, looking up imploringly from his twisted position until he could see Silas.

"I need a name, or a place, Joseph," said Silas, holding the young crook's gaze intently.

"I don't know a name – an' I wouldn't tell you anyway!" said Barnes, a little of his earlier fire returning. "But it's a big place, like a farm, or bigger, but not all farm I think. Pretty rough country, on account of a few things they said. Up on the plateau maybe, I don't know."

He looked at Silas sullenly. The retired policeman decided that this was about all he was going to get out of Joseph Barnes today.

"Thank you, Joseph," he said. "You're free to go, and you won't see me again – unless you're leaving out something I ought to know."

"No way, man, that's it, I swear. Everything I know!"

Silas nodded, and Barnes scurried across the patio and down the side of the abandoned dairy.

Chapter 9

It was a 64 kilometre drive to Hamilton along State Highway one, through the rich farmland of the Waikato, and after that Silas had to find a parking space near his destination. He hadn't called ahead, and he took a deep breath as he entered the Police Prosecution offices on Bridge Street. Somehow his luck was in, and Tracey Donovan came straight to the front desk when she was called.

She was older than Silas was, and she power dressed in a way that showed her age and experience. A business suit incorporated a skirt in the warmer weather, and her legs were well toned. She looked good.

"Senior Constable Chambers, retired," she said brightly. "What can I do for you?"

Silas asked for a private room so they could discuss a case that was pending. As a member of the public he was pushing his luck, for a whole lot of reasons including 'trying to pervert the course of justice' as it was called. He tried to keep his voice firm and his tone reasonable.

Senior Prosecutor Donovan raised an eyebrow, but when he wasn't forthcoming with any details, she led the way to a conference room.

"What's this all about, Silas?" she said crisply, once they were seated. She steepled her hands on the table in front of her, and watched him with a mixture of curiosity and caution.

Silas outlined Devon's case, including the mystery of the disappearing body. He asked her to delay the court date until he could show that there had, in fact, been a murder, and the Devil's Outlaws' involvement had been a material influence on Devon's actions at the theatre.

She sat up straighter, and folded her arms. That wasn't a good sign.

"The Tokoroa Police Station will be looking into this," she said, "and they won't want you involved. They've got a new investigative officer now, ah, Tarrant isn't it?"

"Yes," said Silas evenly. "I trained him. The trouble is, an old man who kept to himself might not get the attention he deserves, especially when there isn't a body."

Silas looked down at the table. "He lived in Tawhiti, and I knew him well."

Donovan leaned forward on the table. "You're not with the police any more, Silas, and you're emotionally involved in the case. You know what you would have said about that when you were in the force."

Silas nodded. It was the worst possible combination, and emotional involvement was guaranteed to get in the way of the proper authorities doing their job. When he didn't say anything else, she leaned back in the chair and looked up at the ceiling. She sounded exasperated as she spoke.

"You were a damn fine investigative officer, Silas, and I don't know why you quit. I heard it was bad blood between you and the inspector at the time, but you should have stood back from the situation and not taken it personally. Hell's teeth, that's the first rule of investigative work, isn't it?"

Silas nodded. He wasn't sure how they had got onto his personal situation from Devon's case. The discussion wasn't going well, but at least she hadn't told him to stop wasting her time yet. Then she slammed her elbows back on the table, clasped her hands together and looked him straight in the eye.

"And on top of that you've got a hell of a nerve. I asked you to check on certain lines of inquiry a long time ago when a friend of mine got dragged into a fraud case. It was not long after I became a police prosecutor. She couldn't prove what she was saying, but I knew she was telling the truth.

"In the end she was lucky. She got a fine and a suspended sentence, but that's on her record now, Silas, and it's not helping her banking career!"

Silas waited for Donovan to calm down a bit. A large part of his investigative success had come from knowing people. All he could do now was wait until she was in a more receptive frame of mind.

"Sue Downs, I remember her," he said, "and I will always regret the fact that I didn't help you. I hadn't been a Senior Constable very long at the time, and I was an officious prick in those days. Oh, and I'm sure you could add that I was a bit of a jerk as well. I've got a few more miles on me now."

He saw the corners of her mouth turn up in the slightest of smiles. That was good, but then she looked intently at him once again and frowned.

"I know," he said, "that it would be very unfair of me to ask for a favour now, when I was so ungenerous in the past. But I care about a young man who's a little short on guidance at the moment. That can't be wrong, can it?"

There was a strained silence in the room, and Silas racked his brains to think of something else to say. He had always admired Donovan. She could easily have made more money in another job, but she was a senior prosecutor because she wanted to see criminals brought to justice. There were too many important cases being thrown out of court on technicalities, and poor presentation of the evidence.

"I can't do it, Silas," she said at last. "Not because you let me down long ago, but on the strength of what you're asking. I have some leeway in these matters, but I can't justify delaying Devon's case on the evidence you've put before me. It would be too damaging to my career if I was challenged on it.

"If you had the body of the old man, then maybe. A murder case trumps an arson any day, and minor offences can be shuffled around to get the best result for a more important prosecution.

"So that's my advice – bring me a body if you want to help Devon."

She was right, of course. It was the decision Silas had expected, but he had also known he had to try and get an extension. He was rising from the chair when she stopped him with a question.

"How old are you, Silas, mid-forties?"

He froze where he was, and nodded.

"You've got skills that need to be used," she said, "and it will haunt your old age if you don't. Take those skills as far as you can while you've still got time, and that's good advice!

"It doesn't have to be the police. Most government departments have an investigative branch these days. Hell, go private if you want to, anything from insurance fraud to setting up as an investigator for yourself.

"But get registered, get the law behind you. All I can see at the moment is friction between you and everyone else trying to understand what happened with those two people!"

Silas was surprised – and annoyed. Why was everybody on his case? First Mereana, and now Donovan. Was he that much of an open book? He just needed some time off from policing, that was all, and why did people feel the need to give him advice? He could read that for free in the agony aunt columns.

"Thanks for giving me some of your time," he said calmly. "I appreciate it. I'll try to keep out of everybody's way, but I have to keep working on this. The boy's depending on me, and I want to see justice done for the old man. Those two things aren't negotiable."

Donovan lifted her arms, and let them drop in resignation. "Let me know if you find anything new that might change things," she said, "and I'll do what I can."

Silas nodded, and walked down the corridor back to the front desk by himself.

Chapter 10

It wasn't far from Bridge Street to Annabel Kirsk's place in Hillcrest, but Annabel wouldn't be home from work yet. Her workplace varied day to day. She was a specialist nurse in pain relief, and could be anywhere in Hamilton or a long way outside it. On this particular day she was based at the main Hamilton Hospital.

The two of them had met through a friend of Silas'. Aunt B ran the Potter's Rest tearooms in Tawhiti, and she had invited Annabel to one of Silas' occasional dinner parties for his friends at his old villa. She had done so over his protests, but Aunt B was hard to put off when she had her mind set on something. Now he was glad she had railroaded him into it. Very glad in fact.

Annabel was a tall woman, and she was solidly built. Not fat in any sense, but she had a physical presence that didn't stand for nonsense. It must have been a great asset as a nurse. She was pretty, and she liked men unreservedly.

It was this last fact that had engaged Silas' attention. She seemed to revel in his intense interest in her, body and soul, as the relationship deepened. Maybe it was something about him that kindled the devotion in her, pondered Silas, but if so he didn't know what it was. Women were something of a mystery.

Since he had a little time, he went shopping for a gift he could take her later. He didn't know enough about Annabel's taste in music to make a choice from the selection in the small music shop he had happened upon, and he moved to the shop next door, which contained a well-stocked delicatessen.

At one stage the two of them had downloaded a series of cartoon images – not unlike emoji – they could text to show how they were feeling. Silas had sent her an image of a dishevelled artist looking at a blank canvas earlier in the day, which he thought captured his lack of progress in his investigation, and she had sent him a belly dancer in full shaking mode.

Normally that would have delighted him, but recent events had left him subdued. Fortunately there was a lot of give and take in the relationship, and he knew she would understand if he was less than enthusiastic in his texts today.

A suspicion that he should make the relationship more permanent kept nagging at Silas. His father had left all of his son's big decisions up to him, but his father had also been fond of saying, 'if you're going to bed 'em you might as well wed 'em, it saves a lot of time and money in the long run.' That saying might not be as relevant today as back then, he thought, but the old man had also said, 'we all need someone who knows our story,' and that was ageless wisdom.

The trouble was, Silas couldn't summon up the necessary enthusiasm – and courage – for a proposal when he had Devon's court date and Stodge's disappearance in front of him. He wondered if he would always find excuses not to broach the subject. He squashed that thought by promising himself he would talk to Annabel as soon as the present mess was over – if she would stick with him for that long!

Annabel turned into her driveway as his Outlander cruised down the same street, and he smiled to himself. Perfect.

"What's this?" she said, when they were sitting at the kitchen table with the jug on, and he had pecked her on the cheek. He pushed the loosely-wrapped parcel toward her. "Open it," he said warmly.

When she saw it was cheese, she bent down and sniffed tentatively at the excised wedge. Her eyes widened.

"Asiago d'Allevo," said Silas, "a hard cheese from Italy used for grating, apparently. Great over food with a red wine alongside. That's all I know, but I thought you might like it."

She nodded appreciatively. Annabel liked to try out new recipes, especially when Silas was staying over, and he reciprocated with the large dinner parties he held occasionally at his villa. He would slow-roast the meats, and his friends would bring side dishes.

Aunt B always turned up with something interesting from the Potter's Rest to complement the other courses. Annabel happily admitted that there was a competition going on between her and Aunt B. There was nothing like trying to outdo each other over a man to stir up a woman's blood, even if Aunt B fell into the 'best friend' category, rather than a lover.

"I haven't started cooking yet," she said, looking apologetic, "and I haven't decided what to make."

"Let's just pick up something easy from nearby," said Silas. "A lot has happened in the last few days, and it's not the sort of stuff I wanted to talk about over the phone.

"Do you have any free space in that busy brain of yours for other people's problems?"

She looked surprised, and then she nodded.

Five minutes later they were sitting in the lounge, two cups of tea on the coffee table, and Silas was talking about Devon's predicament and Stodge's unexplained disappearance. What was left of the tea was cold by the time he had finished.

"Oh, that poor boy!" said Annabel, clenching one hand tightly against her lips. Her deep capacity for the pain of others was what had led her to become a pain relief specialist. Silas nodded at the comment. Devon would be accused of mindless vandalism if Silas couldn't show that the Devil's Outlaws had drawn the boy into it.

"You're going to get involved, aren't you?" said Annabel, after a moment. "Despite the fact it will probably ruin any chance you have of getting back into the police force."

Silas nodded, more slowly this time. Hearing it said out loud made the possible consequences more real for him. It didn't change his mind though. Then he told her what Mereana Findlay and Tracey Donovan had said about getting his life back on track.

"You're not trying to get me back into a 40-hour week as well, are you?" he said cautiously, with his eyebrows raised.

"Of course not," said Annabel, and he relaxed a little.

"But they're right," she said, "absolutely right. You need to be using your skills, but there's a difference between their attitude and mine. It's my job to support you in whatever you decide to do. It's their job to bring the obvious to your thick-headed attention."

Silas almost choked. "Gee, thanks," he managed, after a while. She curled up around him, and kissed him firmly on the mouth.

"I can be very supportive," she said, coming upright and straddling him, knees either side on the couch. He laughed out loud at that.

It was much later when Silas got back to the house with some Indian food in plastic containers, and Annabel had the dining table set up and a bottle of wine opened.

"Special occasion?" he said, noting the wine. She nodded.

"The occasion of you having some investigative work to do, even if it is unpaid," she said. "You need this, Silas. You've been a bit lost over the last year."

He accepted the comment without reacting. It felt like it was true, but he hadn't taken on the cases to keep himself busy, or to stop himself being 'lost'. Devon and Stodge needed him, and he wasn't going to let them down.

"I got Gordon to take the three-pin plug off the power board behind the TV," said Annabel, as they sat back on the couch after dinner. "He cut the end off the cord, where it was worn, and put the plug back on."

Silas wasn't surprised. Gords had been surrounded by older women in Tawhiti, especially when Silas had first taken the street kid under his wing. His adopted son was used to running errands and fixing things for his many 'aunties'. Annabel had welcomed Gordon as part of Silas' extended family when the two of them got together, and she and Gords were often in touch now he lived two suburbs over.

Silas had to give the Tawhiti 'aunties' a lot of credit for the way Gords had turned out. The young man now had the right sort of friends, and he would be making good money as an electrician soon. It was hard to believe it when he thought of the skinny, argumentative thirteen year old who had first come to live with him.

Then he told Annabel about his talk with Joseph Barnes. It was the only bit of information she didn't already have, and he had left it until last.

"So Emily's story about her brother checks out," said Annabel. "Ernest came across something unusual going on, run by someone with wealth and power, and thought he had a chance of leveraging it into some money to help his sister. From what Barnes said, that was enough to get Ernest killed."

Silas nodded.

"What really concerns me is his description of a big place up on the plateau," he said. The fertile plains of the Waikato to the west, and the Bay of

Plenty in the east, swept up to a volcanic plateau in the middle of the North Island. Tawhiti was on the very edge of it.

The plateau was composed mostly of soft pumice gravel from the volcanoes in the middle of the North Island, and it made poor soils.

"The area above Tawhiti is mostly reserve and regenerating bush," he said. "I don't remember any big spreads up there, none that are economically viable anyway. Maybe Barnes got that bit wrong."

"But you're going to check it out anyway, aren't you," she said softly.

He didn't reply, already thinking how he might search the title deeds quickly and easily. Fortunately Annabel was used to him being distracted like that. Then she steered the conversation along a new line of thought.

"Barnes said the gang threatened Ernest with retaliation against his family if he talked about what he knew," she said, "and that must be Emily and her daughter. Do you think they're still in danger?"

Silas shook his head.

"I'm certain that Ernest is dead now," he said. "Devon described someone like him in the theatre, and Mereana says she saw his . . . ghost, on the veranda at his place. The Outlaws don't need to threaten a dead man."

Annabel put her hand on Silas' arm, and he jumped. It was the same thing Mereana had done before Silas saw the apparitions she had been seeing.

"Easy, big boy," said Annabel, with a smile. "That vision unsettles you, doesn't it? Do you think she really has the power to see supernatural things?"

Silas shrugged. "Ian thought so, before he died. He said the things she described checked out more often than not."

"But that's not all, is it, Silas," she continued. "What's really going on?"

He would normally have made some excuse, but this time he paused. He had just admitted to himself what the relationship with Annabel meant to him, and how much he hoped she would stay with him through all this. She deserved more.

He let out a long sigh. This was worse than having his teeth pulled. He hoped sharing his innermost thoughts and feelings got easier with practice.

"I saw Stodge on that veranda, the same as Mereana did," he said, looking away from her. Annabel's grip on his arm tightened.

"It was after Mereana laid her hand on my arm, something like you just did. I think it made me see what she was seeing."

Annabel put her arms around him, and pulled him close. It took a while but he finally relaxed in her embrace, and the unease flowed out of him.

Telling her stuff wasn't so bad, he decided. Maybe it wouldn't kill him after all. Maybe he could do worse than share everything that happened in his life with this woman.

Chapter 11

Inspector Matthew Flynn regarded the retired Senior Constable coolly across his work desk. Silas kept his face impassive, and stared back. The new inspector at Tokoroa didn't attend the social functions for his staff, and Silas wasn't sure what that said about the man. What it did mean was that Silas had only met him twice, briefly, and shaken his hand once.

"This, Mr Chambers, is a complaint from a local lawyer, Julian McCabe," said the inspector, picking up a sheet of paper from his desk.

"Our eminent citizens don't like being harassed while going about their legitimate business, or, as Mr McCabe says in his complaint, 'doing their best to improve the lot of Tokoroa and its inhabitants.' What on God's green earth did you think you were doing?"

"McCabe has wanted to buy the Royal Theatre for over a year now," said Silas tersely, "and he tried to get the Chamber of Commerce to change the heritage classification on it to speed up the process. I was there when he made the proposal, and it was turned down.

"Now the place has burned down, and it turns out he's already paid for the pile of rubble that remains. Paid with, I might add, a rather handy drop in price. He confirmed the change of ownership to me personally. That is a sufficiently avaricious motive for arson in my book."

Matthew Flynn didn't say anything. He got up from his desk, and walked over to the window in his office that looked out over Logan Street. When he came back to his chair, the look on his face hadn't changed. He was not happy.

"How should I handle this, Mr Chambers?" he said, looking at Silas thoughtfully.

The retired Senior Constable wondered what he meant. Flynn couldn't seriously be asking him how to run Tokoroa Police Station.

"Area Commander Billingham insists it was a mercy you left the police force when you did," continued the inspector, "so he didn't have to remove you. A number of others at Hamilton Central seem to share his views.

"On the other hand, every officer I've met who has worked with you says you were a diligent investigator, and at times brilliant. A modern day Sherlock Holmes, if they are to be believed."

He left a space for Silas to make a comment, but the man on the other side of the desk kept his silence. Though his heart rate had doubled, and he hoped that didn't show on his face. It looked like Flynn was interested in both sides of the story, and the opinion of a good man who would look at both sides meant a lot to Silas.

"A cynic might say that Billingham and his little coterie are all tarred with the same brush – career focused men and women who would do anything to further their own interests," said the inspector. "I must say, I do find these to be cynical times, Mr Chambers."

He seemed to be expecting something, so Silas cleared his throat.

"As do I, Sir," he said.

"I'm told you're interested in both the Devon Findlay and Ernest Graham cases," said the inspector, and Silas nodded.

He wondered who Flynn's sources were. He didn't think Dave Tarrant would have said anything, the constable was too open to disciplinary action for helping an ex colleague. Then he realized it must have been Tracey Donovan from Police Prosecution. He wondered what the connection was between her and Flynn.

"It would seem to be easier all round if you were re-instated into the police force," said the inspector. "Tarrant needs a guiding hand if he's to reach the standard you set before him. I take it you still feel some loyalty toward Constable Tarrant's training?"

Silas nodded. It appeared that Flynn took an interest in how his staff were progressing, and that was also a very good sign. At least it was in the way Silas viewed leadership. The inspector would probably encourage local knowledge as well – his constables getting to know their community. Nothing beat having your ear to the ground in Silas' opinion.

"A reinstatement would also avoid any, shall we say, duplication of efforts?" continued the inspector.

"Reinstatement would take too long, Sir," said Silas. "These cases need action now, and undoing a bad call later is a lot more difficult than getting it right the first time. I also feel there's something, ah, bigger at play here."

Flynn looked at him with eyebrows raised, and Silas realized he was going to have to give the inspector something.

"I believe Ernest Graham died because he stumbled onto some form of organized crime," said Silas, "and I believe it involves a powerful individual, or group of individuals, in this area."

Flynn was listening intently, and Silas found himself saying more than he had intended. "These people work in the shadows, Sir," he said, "and I feel my best chance of bringing them down is to go looking in the shadows myself."

All of which was true, but he wasn't ready to rejoin the police force yet. There were a lot of trust issues he had to work through. Somehow he had to trust life itself once more, when it had taken a good friend and left a widow and children behind, and he also had to regain his trust in the people above him in the police system.

"That's a very big call, even for an investigative officer," said Flynn. "Are you sure you can justify it?"

Silas didn't have a lot to go on, when he looked at his 'evidence' in his mind, but he found himself saying he would have the evidence he needed soon. Flynn didn't speak for a long time, and then he seemed to come to a decision.

"If you decide to work alone on these two cases," said the inspector, "then I can't protect you. You won't have the power of the uniform behind you."

Silas nodded. "I understand, Sir," he said firmly. Then he realized what Flynn was doing. "And of course, Sir, I fully understand I have been cautioned against interfering in police work as a citizen."

Flynn almost smiled. Silas was watching his back. The 'retired' investigative officer in front of him didn't want anything he did to tarnish the inspector's reputation.

"Yes, Mr Chambers," he said loudly, "impersonating a police officer is a punishable offence, and I hope I don't have to talk to you about getting involved in police matters again!"

"No, Sir, absolutely not, Sir!" said Silas, playing his part. He felt a pang of guilt as he remembered how he had let Joseph Barnes believe he had all the power and authority of a police officer, but he hoped he wouldn't have to set up another play like that.

"And I take it you will have no reason to go anywhere near Mr McCabe in the future?" said the inspector. He was asking Silas if he had all the information he needed from McCabe at this stage, and Silas quickly nodded.

If Silas could prove McCabe had engineered the arson, it wouldn't help Devon's situation directly. He had to prove the Devil's Outlaws were connected to the burning of the theatre, and Devon had been led in his actions. He needed the middle men as well.

"Good!" continued the inspector. " Then I can reassure our local dignitary that you have been duly reminded of the lines you should not cross.

"I think that's all, Mr Chambers," he said, after a pause, and rose from his desk. He reached across to shake Silas' hand as the retired policeman rose to leave. Silas was almost at the door when he heard the inspector's final words.

"You be careful in those shadows, now."

Chapter 12

The sound of young men laughing burst into the kitchen of a three-bedroom family home on Noel Street in Tokoroa from outside. It was a warm Saturday afternoon, and Mereana had the kitchen windows open. She looked up at Silas and smiled. Gordon and Eli were busy making Devon forget his troubles for a while.

Silas nodded. He understood what she was smiling about. Then he turned his head to look out the window, and saw Eli and Devon pass a soccer ball back and forth before a makeshift goal in the back yard. They jockeyed for position until Devon fired the ball past Gords, low and hard on his left. There was a round of self-congratulations and derisory name calling.

Juvenile Court tried to get a hearing for those brought before it as soon as possible, but once Devon had been given home detention his case had been demoted from urgent to routine. That meant the date of his hearing was still more than two weeks away. Mereana had confided to Silas that her son was getting noticeably down in the dumps on those occasions when no one was around to cheer him up.

Ian Findlay had been alive when Silas adopted Gordon off the streets. Gords had been five years older than Devon, and a year older than Eli. Finding time for the boys to do things together had brought Ian and Silas close together, on top of the time they spent each day in the police force. The friendship had been very informative for Silas in those early days, and he still remembered their long discussions on parenting.

Silas had been hard on Gords – he'd needed to be, since the boy had been so poorly socialized – but Ian had convinced him that boys needed affection too. Silas had learned to roughhouse with Gords, and then give him a hug for no reason. The combination had, eventually, worked out well.

"Emily coming round later?" said Silas, and Mereana nodded. Stodge's sister would be around for a few more days yet before she returned to Dunedin.

"I'll pick her up in an hour or so," she said. "I invited her to stay for dinner, hope you don't mind."

Silas shook his head. He had already asked what he could bring for the meal, and been told he wasn't to bring anything. This was a thank you for doing so much for Devon. Silas had moved his usual Saturday night arrangement with Annabel to Sunday.

"Emily goes back to Dunedin on Monday, right?" he said, and Mereana nodded. It was disappointing there was still no news of Stodge's whereabouts, and Emily would be returning home with the same sense of unease they all felt about her brother's disappearance.

Mereana got up from the kitchen table and flicked the tab on the jug to the on position. She passed Silas on the way back to her chair, and laid a hand on his arm. He flinched, and she pulled up short at the sudden movement. They both began talking at once, and Silas let her continue.

"I was going to say how much I appreciate everything you've done for me and the boys since Ian's death," she said. "I'm not sure I could have made it through without your help."

"I know that," said Silas, smiling, "and it's what we do for friends and family, at least when we're close. You would have done the same for me."

There was a long pause and then she let go of his arm and took up her previous position in the chair alongside him. Silas looked at the floor, then at the ceiling, and ended up looking anywhere but at Mereana.

"What is it," she said. "Get it off your chest. You're about to tell me you're moving to Australia for a change of climate?"

Silas laughed out loud. It was too hot in the Waikato summers already, without adding more heat.

"No," he said. "Not that. The thing is, I owe you an apology."

She waited for him to continue.

"I saw Stodge on the veranda," he said quietly, "when you put your hand on my arm. That's why I jumped just now. Every time you do that it brings the experience back."

She looked shocked, and he hesitated before he continued. "I also saw the woman that was with him. I think she was Ella Brekken, a Norwegian tourist killed in the car park at the start of a tramping track along the

Horohoro escarpment. That's on the way to Rotorua. You described her puffer vest perfectly, and her killer, or killers, have never been found."

"I remember that one," said Mereana, nodding. Murders in the area were rare enough that they made it to the front page of the newspapers, and became a topic of conversation.

"You told me you saw nothing," she said, accusingly.

"Yes, well, that's why I'm apologizing," he said. "We're friends. We shouldn't lie to each other."

She paused for a moment, and then seemed to accept that.

"Why was it I could only see Stodge when you put your hand on my arm?" he asked, curious now.

Mereana shifted in her chair uncomfortably.

"It's the way my Maori grandmother trained me," she said at last. "She wanted me to become a matakite, a seer, in the same way she was. But I was like you at first, I could only 'see' things when she had a hand on my forearm, or an arm around my shoulders. Then later, the ability grew stronger, and it came and went of its own accord."

"You're saying the more it happens to me, the stronger it will get?" said Silas hurriedly, not at all taken by the idea.

Mereana nodded, reminiscing. "It was a strange thing to happen to a child. I was only twelve when my grandmother started showing me these things. I remember a pouwhiri on our local marae, when I saw a host of faded people in old-fashioned clothing waving fern fronds and mouthing words of welcome. They were arranged in lines behind the living, as the visitors came in. I got used to seeing the dead do things like that eventually.

"I still try to avoid old slipways where my people used to run canoes down to the sea," she said. "You wouldn't know where they were now, but I can see them. Maybe the faded shapes I see are fishermen who never came back, maybe they're warriors from the war canoes who died violently, I don't know."

"So that's why you live in the middle of the North Island," said Silas, with a smile, and Mereana waved a dismissive hand at him.

"I live in the middle of the North Island because I married a good man who happened to live here, Dumbo," she said. "Let's get our feet back on the ground!"

When she had finished berating him she came back to the question of seeing spirits.

"The ability to see the dead has to be in you to begin with," she said. "Some of your ancestors would have had the ability."

Silas wasn't aware of any, but then he had never asked.

"The real question," said Mereana, "is why Ella and Ernest appeared together. That only happens for a reason, and I think you should find out what it is."

Silas sat up straighter in his chair. Could this help him solve the mystery of Stodge's disappearance?

"Does it mean the two of them were killed in the same place?" he said, cautiously. "Does it even work like that? Do spirits stay near the place where they died? And why should we see them at Stodge's house then?"

Mereana shook her head. "Ernest has been missing for two weeks now, but no one has reported anything strange on the hunting or tramping tracks, or at the car parks, right? So I'm guessing Ernest was killed somewhere different to Ella, who was killed at a car park at the start of a tramping track."

Mereana had a good point. Tarrant hadn't phoned him with anything like that, and he would have passed on the news. Even if it was only because he remembered that an old man had turned up so bizarrely in Devon's confession.

"And the dead aren't bound to the place of their death," said Mereana, "though they may be seen there more often than other places."

So what's the connection between Ernest and Ella? wondered Silas in frustration. Then it struck him what the answer was.

"The same killer," he said, softly, looking across at Mereana.

She thought about it for a moment, and then nodded.

"There is a strong connection between people who are seen together after they die," she said. "It's usually a positive connection, such as love or bravery, but I don't see why it can't be a negative one as well.

"We might have seen Ella and Ernest together because they were killed by the same person," she finished.

Chapter 13

Silas continued reworking the case in his mind. At the time of Ella Brekken's murder he had thought her killer was a man named Tarek Assoulin, the son of a wealthy Syrian immigrant. Assoulin had lived briefly in the Tokoroa area before going back to Auckland. The disappearance of Silas' main suspect was part of the reason Billingham had closed the case down.

Was Assoulin back, wondered Silas, and why would he come to a rural heartland like South Waikato? There had been no sightings of him that Silas had heard about, but then, the police weren't looking for the man.

It would be a good idea to scour the Tokoroa area for Assoulin, and Silas had just the private army to do that. He was also going to need a photograph of Assoulin to circulate, and wondered if Tarrant could help him with that.

Mereana was thinking about ways to work the Ella and Stodge connection as well. "We could ask Ella how she died," she said, looking speculatively at Silas.

That thought made her friend's blood run cold. On the other hand Mereana's sighting of Stodge had accurately predicted his disappearance, and almost certain death. If the two of them learned something from another vision, it might save Silas a lot of time and effort.

"Sure," he said, trying to sound more confident that he felt. "But how do we do that?"

"The car park at Horohoro," said Mereana. "I have to pick up Emily in an hour or so, and we can collect her on the way back from the car park. Eli and Gords can entertain Devon until we return."

"Wouldn't it be easier at Stodge's place?" said Silas, thinking the house was a lot closer.

She shook her head. "Ella was 'riding on Ernest's coat-tails' when we saw her there. If we want to talk to her, it will be easier at the place where she died. There will be no other energies in the way."

Silas shrugged. What did he know about it? She was the one with all the experience of these things.

Half an hour later they were in the car park. The native bush around the edges looked magnificent, and the summer hum of cicadas was just starting to fill the air. The massive limestone escarpment of the Horohoro reserve towered above them, and a white hatchback and old pickup truck shared the car park with Silas' Outlander.

"We should move away from the car park," said Mereana, "but not too far."

They found a spot in the shade of an impressive rimu tree. Mereana leaned back against the trunk, and then put her hand on Silas' arm. He tensed immediately, but then forced himself to relax. Mereana had emphasized how important relaxing was to the process.

After a while he realized her hand was trembling on his arm.

"She was killed here," said Mereana, "and it was an accident. They didn't mean to kill her, not in the beginning.

"There were three of them," she continued, "and Ella wants you to know about the leader. He was a dark man, foreign to her. She had trouble distinguishing him from local Maori, a race she hadn't met before, but she thinks he wasn't a New Zealander.

"They wore Halloween masks," she said, "and they were taking whatever they could find in the cars. They weren't smashing windows, they were, maybe, picking the locks?"

Silas understood at once. They were sliding a piece of fencing wire down beside the windows, and hooking up the latching mechanism.

Car parks at the entrances to reserves and national parks were the occasional target of thieves, particularly teenagers who were just starting out on a life of crime. This approach sounded more organized than that, if the thieves wore masks, but stealing from cars was a poor choice from a criminal point of view. There was too little reward for the level of risk.

"Ella surprised them," said Mereana. "It had been an easy tramp for her so she had run the last few hundred yards, keeping to the moss on the edge of the track. She was on her own, and there were none of the usual sounds of a tramping party to alert the thieves. She burst out into the car park to find them breaking into the car next to hers.

"She was young and fit, but there were three of them. They soon had her kneeling beside her car, hands tied behind her back with the sweatshirt she was carrying.

"Then they went around her car smashing the headlights and tail lights and denting the panels, trying to get a reaction from her, but she stayed silent. She's proud of that now, proud of the fact she didn't let them get to her."

The car was probably a rental, mused Silas, but the important thing was how she was taking control of the situation. The thieves wouldn't have liked that. Criminals lived pointless lives on the fringes of society, and they craved influence over others. He had learned that in Criminology 101 during his police training, and found it to be almost universally true.

"They started to push her around," said Mereana. "Then one of them pulled her head back and showed her a knife, like he was going to cut her throat. They wanted to see her panic, see her beg. They were laughing and giggling. She remembers that, high-pitched giggles like a boy soprano would make."

Mereana opened her eyes, and looked at Silas. "Are you getting any of this?" she said.

Silas shook his head. "Sometimes I get an image, like a still photo," he said, "but it goes too quickly. I can hear voices now and then, but they're too faint to make any sense of."

He tried to figure out what he could do to improve things, and came up with some answers. "The more I still my mind, the more I feel 'tuned in'," he said, finally.

"We're all too busy being emperors in our own make-believe palaces to listen to what the world is actually telling us," said Mereana, ruefully, "and it's getting worse with today's busy lives. It will take you a lot of practice to hear things clearly."

Silas was surprised at her thoughts on modern life. In hindsight, though, he agreed with her. Then she closed her eyes again. After a while she continued with the story.

"There was a scuffle," she said. "The leader hauled Ella to her feet and pushed the point of a knife through the clothing over her heart. But in the scuffle she was able to work her hands out of the soft material of the sweatshirt.

"She reached up and pulled his mask away, more instinct than thought, and that was when she saw his dark colouring.

"The knife went in a little deeper, and she grabbed his wrist to stop it. One of the others was beside her, and he shouldered her as the leader tried to pull his mask back up.

"She slipped, and they both went to the ground. She landed on the knife, and the point entered her heart.

"The thieves panicked, and left the body where it lay. They had come out to the car park in a stolen car, and they dumped it as soon as they could, setting it on fire."

Silas remembered this well. Mereana was bringing the case back to life for him. He had done a solid search of the burned-out old Nissan for evidence, but come up with nothing.

The fact the thieves had panicked was interesting. He doubted they had killed before. Now, if he was right, they were part of the Devil's Outlaws gang and they killed for money, or status within the organization.

He mused on that fact for a moment. So this car park had been where their descent into inhumanity had started.

Then Mereana was silent for a long time. "Ella wants to bring something else to your attention," she said at last. "It's especially for you, not for anyone else.

"You have to find a small, bronze, mm, paperweight perhaps. It has something to do with horses. Someone wants it returned. No, her family must have this back for reasons that are very important to them.

"Yes, she's happy now she has managed to get that idea across."

Mereana waited for a while longer, but then she opened her eyes.

"Ella is gone for now," she said. She stepped away from the tree, and seemed to have trouble focusing her eyes. Then she looked at Silas.

"How much of that means anything to you?"

Silas nodded. It meant a lot, but he couldn't trust himself to speak at the moment. He pointed towards the Outlander, and they started in that direction. On the way to pick up Emily he was able to explain what Ella's words had told him.

"I had a suspect in the murder investigation," he said, "the son of a Syrian immigrant, but I was stopped from pursuing the case any further by my bosses. The man was dark, and foreign, so I think she's pointing me towards him.

"The bronze object you mentioned is the flat part of a stirrup from Norway, made in the 11th or 12th century," he said. "It's only two and a half inches long.

"Ella was a horse fanatic, and she chose the bronze piece when her parents asked her what she wanted for her 21st birthday. She wanted to own an artefact from Norway's past. After the funeral, which was conducted here, her parents asked me if we had found that bronze piece. They wanted it back, to remind them of their daughter.

"We hadn't found it at the time, which surprised me, and we still haven't. Her killers would not have known what it was, or that it was valuable, but maybe one of them wanted to keep a memento of their first kill."

He paused. "She got the artefact for her birthday, six months before she came to New Zealand as part of a trip around the world. We certainly understand the big OE for young people here in New Zealand. It's a terrible pity that it all went so wrong."

Mereana reached across and put her hand on his shoulder as he drove.

"It looks like you've got some business to tidy up from the Ella Brekken case," she said.

Silas added it to the Devon and Stodge cases he already had, and he didn't mind doing so. It looked as if they were all connected in some way. But how exactly was that, and how was he to find out?

Chapter 14

———

Tarrant rang the following afternoon. Silas saw the name come up on his cell phone, and wondered what his old work colleague was doing calling him on a Sunday.

"We've got the body," said Tarrant, and for a moment Silas didn't understand what he was saying. Then it dawned on him.

"Where?" he said sharply.

"In a swamp beside a forestry road, off State Highway One and not far from the turn-off to Rotorua. It's an active logging site and the gate is not usually locked. There is a forestry sign at the entrance and a 'no trespassing' notice, but that's all.

"A forest ranger went up to mark out a stand of pines for his logging crews to start on tomorrow, and he saw the body."

"What condition is it in?" said Silas, and heard Tarrant say the body looked remarkably fresh. It appeared to have worked its way out of a muddy hole where a side stream entered the swamp. It couldn't have risen to the top more than a day or two ago.

"There was a rope around its chest," said Tarrant, "but it wasn't attached to anything. Maybe the body was weighed down originally, and it worked its way loose. There was a fair amount of rain a few days ago, and the run-off from the side stream could have disturbed it."

Or maybe it was meant to look that way, thought Silas. Throw a rope around a corpse, roll it in the mud a few times, and leave it somewhere over the weekend so it's discovered on a busy Monday morning. Except someone turned up on Sunday.

The freshness of the body supported Silas' theory that it had been kept in a freezer after Stodge was killed. The first time it had been kept until it was taken to the Royal Theatre, and a second time so it could be 'discovered' at the swamp. But why freeze a dead man?

"I ran some crime scene tape along the edge of the road," said Tarrant, "though I don't see anyone from the logging gangs coming out to the site today. I've just finished taking photos, and I can send them to you from home this evening. I don't want them to be traced back to the devices I use at work."

Silas thanked him for that. Then he asked Tarrant to hazard a cause of death. His friend wasn't sure.

"I can see lacerations on the side of the head," said Tarrant, "but there are stab wounds on the torso as well. So, no clear cause of death at this stage."

The damage to the side of the head supported Devon's account of matted blood on the side of the old man's head at the theatre, but the boy hadn't mentioned stab wounds.

"When will the autopsy be done?" said Silas. Tarrant, as the investigative officer, would have the autopsy report from the coroner's office two days later. Faster if he went to the coroner himself, but Silas didn't want Dave calling in favours on his account.

"The autopsy will be done on Monday," said Tarrant. "There's nothing major on at forensics at the moment. That means the body will be released to the next of kin on Tuesday. Do you want to come down and do the identification?"

Tarrant knew Stodge by sight, but mistakes had been made that way before. It was protocol to bring in someone from outside the police force, who was a member of the family if possible. Tarrant was assuming Stodge was a loner, so he wouldn't have anyone closer than Silas to identify him.

Silas explained who Emily was, and promised to bring her to the forensics department in Hamilton as soon as he was contacted on Monday. The body would need to be cleaned up before she saw it. After that she would have to start planning a funeral.

Tarrant promised to make a copy of the autopsy report for him, and Silas let him get back to work. Tarrant would have a constable working with him in a situation like this, and the officer must be running an errand if Tarrant felt free to talk to Silas. The two officers would run through a site examination, and collect anything Tarrant was interested in for analysis. Then the body would be bagged up for its ride to Hamilton.

Silas put his cell phone back in his pocket, and hustled to the coffee caravan parked nearby. He came back with two takeaway coffees. Annabel was waiting at one of their favourite spots beside Hamilton Lake. Maybe later they would take a dinghy out on the water.

Silas realized, all over again, how lucky he was to have her. He could talk dead bodies with Annabel any time, and he couldn't do that with most women. The two of them made a great team.

"Should we ring Emily now?" asked Annabel, once Silas had explained that Stodge's body had been found. She was unsure of police procedure in cases that required notification of death.

"Emily was due to fly out to Dunedin on Monday," she continued. "I expect she'll stay in Tawhiti now while she gets the funeral organized." Silas shook his head when she had finished. He had someone else in mind to contact Emily.

"I'll ring Mereana shortly," he said, "and get her to drive out and break the news. I don't think it will come as a surprise. Dave Tarrant's the investigative officer, and he'll be making an official visit to Tawhiti to talk to her on Monday morning."

He turned and saw the question in her eyes.

"It's okay if we beat the police to it," he said. "It's better if it's someone known to the person."

Then he turned his head away. Annabel had got used to him doing that in the middle of a conversation. It meant he was thinking. His eyes would focus randomly on an object some distance away, but she knew he wasn't seeing anything.

"I need to look at the big picture," said Silas slowly. "The place and time of Stodge's death is fresh information, and there must be some way it helps my existing understanding of the case."

Annabel was used to the changes in the way he spoke as well. When he started talking about 'the big picture' she could almost see dozens of possibilities being checked against hundreds of facts, with some kept for further analysis and most discarded.

It was something like the way she diagnosed an illness, except illnesses ran through a limited range of symptoms and bodily reactions. Silas had to check a behaviour, or a motive, against the whole gamut of human existence, and that often led him into areas that weren't within a normal person's range of experience.

"So Devon was right about the old man," she said, "but we knew that already."

Silas nodded. "The problem is the stab wounds. They weren't there in the theatre, and it doesn't make sense to kill a dead man all over again. Unless it's misinformation."

She looked at him questioningly. "It makes sense if someone is leading us towards a conclusion they want us to draw," said Silas, by way of explanation. "A conclusion from false premises that benefits them in some way."

"And you need to know who 'they' are, before you can guess at the games they're playing," said Annabel softly.

Silas nodded. "I'm still confused as to why someone would want a body to appear twice, in two different locations, some time after death has occurred."

"It's like a magician using a loud bang and a puff of smoke to take our eyes off what's really happening," said Annabel.

Silas smiled. She really was quite good at this.

"I think we should ring Mereana," said Annabel, seeing that Silas had come to a natural close in his thinking. "It would break into our time together, but we could volunteer to make the drive to Tokoroa, and go with her to see Emily."

It was an hour's drive, and it probably meant Silas should carry on to his villa afterward, while Annabel came back to prepare for work tomorrow.

"You would do that?" he said, and she nodded.

"Soon," he said, lying back on the grassy bank. She put her coffee down and rolled herself against his side, her arm across his chest.

Soon, he said to himself, but not right now. Then he decided lazily that coffee, and understanding women, were two of nature's finest inventions.

Chapter 15

Silas ran Emily over to the autopsy lab at Hamilton hospital late on Monday morning. Mereana had to catch up on her house-cleaning round, so she didn't join them. Silas had offered to ID Ernest himself, sparing Emily the task, but she was adamant it should be her. He figured it was a combination of wanting to see him one last time, and a sense of family duty.

They were back from Hamilton around 1 pm, and Emily wasn't talking much. Silas let her process the image of Ernest lying cold and still on the metal table in her own way. He was pleased when she made them some lunch, figuring it was good for her to keep busy.

He headed for the Tokoroa library on Mannering Street not long after she had rung around and chosen a funeral director. She was half way through making the rest of the arrangements as he waved and left.

Silas had a cadastral map of the properties on the Volcanic Plateau sitting on a library computer within a few minutes of arriving. One of the librarians told him she could find the owners from the District Council rates data if he wanted. That was a definite bonus.

Silas could have done all this easily if he was still in the police force, but he didn't have access to those databases now. He also didn't want to ask Tarrant to find the information for him. The man was busy, and he had already gone out of his way to help.

Silas was looking for a large ranch, or a forestry plantation, somewhere up on the plateau behind Tawhiti. Of the two possibilities, he didn't think it would be a plantation. The rich and powerful didn't make their money from pumice-grown pine. He printed off an A3 copy of the map at a good resolution, and sat down at a table to mark out the likeliest properties. From there he would look at the district rates information to find the owners.

Three hours later he had a list of candidates that wasn't promising. Maori land, Queen Elizabeth II covenanted land, holding companies for plantations, swampy areas that came under Regional Council control, and historic trusts from the early railway and logging days. There were farms around the edges of the plateau, and up some of the valleys that led into it, but none of them seemed grand enough.

Discouraged, Silas thanked the librarian for her help and headed back to see how Emily was getting on with Stodge's funeral. She looked exhausted, and Silas figured it was the emotional strain of the funeral as much as the details. Mereana arrived an hour later with Devon, and Silas drove the ten minutes to Tokoroa to get some pizzas, or 'happy food' as he called it, for dinner. He didn't want Emily feeling she had to make them something.

Silas made an excuse to leave about seven fifteen, and drove back to an old scout hall on the outskirts of Tokoroa. There was one car in the parking lot, and the lights inside the building were on. He nosed the Outlander in beside the existing car.

The cadastral map and the data base from the council's rates system hadn't provided Silas with any answers, but what did they know? Data wasn't a connection, and knowledge wasn't wisdom. Silas was about to tap into the most powerful source of local knowledge he knew.

He sat at the back of the hall, as he always did. He was opposite the door, where he could have a quiet word with people as they came in. If they nodded in agreement, he handed over a photo of Tarek Assoulin. Tarrant had come through with a copy from the Ella Brekken case files, and Silas had run off twenty more.

Assoulin had been in his early thirties then. He was three years older now, but that shouldn't make much difference to his appearance. It was rare for Silas to ask the people in the hall to look for a specific person, mostly they just reported in when they saw or heard something they thought might be interesting. It was surprising how often those snippets of information had tied right in to a case Silas was investigating.

Then the chairman called the monthly meeting of AA to order. It was one of the few meetings open to the public, and Alcoholics Anonymous in Tokoroa knew that Silas would attend most of those. The leaders had quickly seen the meaning Silas' involvement in the meetings gave to the sometimes fragile lives of their members.

Keeping eyes and ears open, and relaying information back to the senior constable, helped restore self-esteem and give a sense of purpose. The twelve-step program of AA took the same approach – though Silas didn't think of himself as a Higher Power – and what he was doing fitted right in.

When the meeting was over, Silas waited until most of the members had left, and then he tapped Gummy Watkins on the shoulder. The old man in a thick checked shirt and worn jeans looked up at him, and nodded. Silas met him outside.

"What do you know about hunting up on the plateau?" he said, as they leaned back against Silas' Outlander. Gummy's face looked craggy in the crossed lighting from the bulb inside the building and a street lamp nearby. He snorted at Silas' comment.

"What don't I know about that area," he said dismissively. "Why? What are you up to, Silas? You got that look you get when you're following a lead."

"I'm trying to track down what happened to Stodge," said Silas, and Gummy sighed sympathetically.

"Heard about that, crying shame. He had some good years left in him, and no one has the right to make you leave this world because it suits them.

"But," he said, lifting his eyes to look straight at Silas, "that's a whole different question. You want to know where Stodge did most of his hunting on the plateau, right?"

Silas nodded.

"Lately," said Gummy, "he's been over on the far side, where it slopes down toward Lake Rotorua. Want me to show you the area?"

Silas smiled. The old man was always keen to get back into the forest, and he loved having someone tagging along. But he also loved company at any time.

The news that Stodge had been hunting on the far side of the plateau explained a lot. It explained why Silas hadn't found what he was looking for during his cadastral map search. And it explained how Stodge might have run into trouble.

There were some big spreads on those far slopes. Some of them were making good money, and not all of it was legal. There could be something hidden away there that the owners wanted to protect, and Stodge could have been a casualty of that.

"Can you say where he was hunting, exactly?" said Silas. "I can get the owners' names for the properties if I can whittle it down to a small enough area."

"Sure can," said Gummy, launching himself off Silas' Outlander and making his way to a battered twin cab nearby. He had bought the vehicle off the company when he worked for New Zealand Forest Products at Kinleith, ten minutes south of Tokoroa. Now he was retired he spent half his time keeping the ancient beast going. He pulled a map out of the glove compartment and was soon back.

"There," he said, pointing to an area more south-easterly than Silas had been expecting. It was close to the far end of the Horohoro escarpment, and Silas felt his blood tingle. In his many years as an investigative officer, he had found that there was no such thing as a coincidence.

"Perfect!" he said to Gummy. "I can find the details now I know where Stodge went, but I'll want to take a closer look at the area at some stage, and I'll need a guide then."

"Count me in," said Gummy, with a huge smile.

Silas was about to climb into the Outlander when he got a text from Annabel. It was a cartoon image of a woman down on her knees, hands clasped together and begging. Silas laughed solidly at that. He'd had a busy day, full of new developments, and she was eager to know what had been happening. She would want to know how Emily was holding up too.

Silas sent a text back that showed a young man in his best suit, looking hopeful, with a bunch of flowers in one hand as he rang a doorbell. Annabel had work tomorrow, but he could be in Hamilton in fifty minutes if he pushed it. They needed to have this conversation face to face.

Chapter 16

Silas was back at the Tokoroa library on Mannering Street as soon as it opened for the day. He was humming to himself as he pulled up another cadastral map on one of the library computers.

Then he realized what he was doing. He was not a humming man by nature, but Annabel had been adamant he stay the night, and that had to be the reason for his high spirits. The lively discussion about the volcanic plateau at her place hadn't generated any new leads, but he was much more optimistic about making headway now. Long may it continue.

The librarian who had helped him the previous day was, once again, an invaluable ally. The area Gummy had pointed to on his map was a much smaller area to investigate, but there were still several variables he had to factor in.

He was still getting too many hits if he excluded small holdings, and included only properties in private ownership. He didn't have access to the police database any more, but his librarian ally cross-referenced the land holdings against newspaper files, and made a judgment call if she discovered any police involvement.

The breakthrough came when Silas only looked for properties that had changed hands in the last three years. His instincts told him that the people behind the theatre arson, and Stodge's death, and possibly Ella Brekken's death, were a new threat to the area. Silas knew every notable case in the South Waikato in the last fifteen years, and none of them fit the profile of the new killings.

When he eventually found a landholding that matched every one of his requirements, it turned out to be the biggest on or near the plateau. Aldous and Irena Huxton had bought the place eighteen months ago, and they had moved to the area from California. Aldous was in his early fifties, and his wife was much younger.

He had been in the film industry, and had spun together a career lasting several decades, mostly from minor acting roles. A closer look at his life told Silas that the money for the ranch had come from producing films. Aldous' role in film production seemed to have tailed off a few years ago, and it looked as if he had then retired to a life of comfort and ease. Silas would bet anything the man had a farm manager on the property to look after it for him.

A satellite image gave Silas a better idea of the ranch. The lower slopes looked like they were well maintained and were used for farming animals, but much of the ranch ran across the top of the plateau. Much of that was reverting to native forest, but some of the sheltered valleys were still maintained for farm use. Silas memorized each feature as he crawled the database over the ranch at high resolution.

When he had finished, he felt his resolve harden. He had a name now, and a location, and he only had to find a motive. It wouldn't be long before Gummy would guide him into the area, and he could get a first-hand idea of what he was dealing with.

Ernest Graham's funeral was the next day, and Silas wanted to attend that so he could say a few words. He had forced himself to put together a speech for Ian Findlay's funeral two years ago, and it had been the hardest thing he had ever had to do. This time round it was easier, but he wanted to take the time to do Stodge's life justice. He wanted to honour the old man in front of Emily, and the residents of Tawhiti.

When the time came, he didn't use the background information on Stodge's early life that Emily had given him, even though Ernest had overcome his mental problems. What he did do was point out Ernest's ability to discipline himself when he needed to, and his understanding nature. He brought these characteristics out as he told stories of Ernest's life in Tawhiti, and he thought it went well.

"Thanks for talking about my brother so touchingly," said Emily, when the coffin had gone to the crematorium and the guests were next door in the supper room. "I knew a little about the latter part of his life, but you gave me a more rounded picture of him."

Silas smiled. "Good," he said, "and I'm sure we can make up a scrapbook for you and Eva, so she has some idea of who her uncle was."

Emily looked like she was about to burst into tears at the thought, and Silas wished for a moment he hadn't made the suggestion.

"That is an excellent idea," she said a moment later, regaining control of her feelings with an effort, and patting him on the arm. "I'll take some photos to add to it before I leave."

Emily had moved her return flight to Dunedin back to Friday, and that gave her a couple of days extra to organize anything that needed doing for Ernest around Tawhiti.

Mereana turned up on the other side of Silas. She had appointed herself the person in charge of catering, and taken on a number of other tasks as well.

"You must come back to Tawhiti sometime and visit us," she said. "Silas is always rattling around in that old house of his, or you could stay at my place in Tokoroa. Maybe when you can bring Eva with you as well."

Emily nodded, but Silas could see that her thoughts were far away.

"I suppose it's a mercy you were still here when Ernest's body was found," he said, thinking it had saved her a journey back to Tawhiti the moment she arrived in Dunedin.

"Nothing about this is a mercy," said Emily fiercely. "Eva and I are the last of our family now. We have friends, of course, but I let the gap between myself and Ernest grow too wide, and I should never have done that!"

Silas could see she was blaming herself for the lapsed state of the relationship, and the best thing he could do was listen.

"Eva needs an uncle, or a grandfather," she said sadly, "and neither of those options are available to us now."

Mereana stepped in to talk about families, and Silas stepped away to take a call that was on vibrate in his back pocket. When he saw it was from Tarrant, he stepped out of the funeral parlour and down a path beside it, trying to lessen the noise of cars passing on the street.

"Have you got that autopsy report already?" he said, surprised.

"No, not yet," said Tarrant flatly. "Actually, Silas, I'm not calling about that."

There was something in Tarrant's voice that stopped Silas cold.

"We found a wallet on Stodge," continued Tarrant, "and a few things in his pockets, and a hunting knife in a sheath on his belt. I sent them away to be tested on Monday, standard procedure, and they've just come back."

There was a long silence at the other end of the phone, and Silas didn't dare break it.

"Stodge was stabbed with his own knife," said Tarrant, at last, "though it's hard to tell if it was that, or the blow to the head, that killed him."

Silas didn't say anything. He could tell that Tarrant was building up to something that was very, very important.

"Devon's fingerprints were on the knife, Silas, two full matches and a partial. He wouldn't have been in the police system at all except for the theatre arson, but it was a positive ID.

"Youth officers picked him up an hour ago, from home. We tried to contact Mereana first, but a murder charge moves him into the adult justice system, and the rules there are quite clear. We don't need to liaise with family."

Silas was speechless. Mereana had left Devon at home because the boy had enough to worry about without a funeral bringing up the question of his own mortality. Eli was back at his chippie job in Hamilton, so one of Mereana's friends was minding Devon. The friend was there to meet the home detention requirements, and for company. Silas was surprised the friend hadn't rung, but Mereana must have had her cell phone switched off for the funeral.

For a moment Silas wondered if Devon had actually done it. Stabbed the old man and killed him. That was what totally unexpected news did to you. It reshaped your reality, and the mind tried to fit new information into a shape that made sense.

Tarrant had asked if Devon's confession at the first interview – that he wished he could have stopped Stodge's death – was a cover for his part in the murder. Could Tarrant have been right?

But a quick check of what he knew about the boy, the support he knew Devon had, and the lack of a possible motive, convinced Silas that Devon was innocent. The fact that Tarrant had rung with this startling news didn't change what he felt Devon was capable of, and it wasn't murder.

"Where's Devon being held?" he asked, as calmly as he could.

"The youth justice residence in Rotorua," said Tarrant. "At least the system is taking his age into account while he's waiting for trial."

Tarrant said he would send Stodge's autopsy report through as soon as he got it, but that seemed of little consequence now. The stakes in the game had just been raised through the roof, and Silas was trying to figure out what he should do next. He told Tarrant he appreciated the call, and rang off.

Now he had to find Mereana and speak to her in private. He needed to break the news that Devon's situation had just got a lot more difficult, and it was going to be the worst possible news.

Chapter 17

Penny got Silas to stop for the evening at that point. For one thing concentrating on such a complex story was tiring, but more to the point she could now see where the farm, the topdressing strip, and the twin-engined jet would come in. The Lightning team had stopped the drug cartel in Noumea once, and to know that they had come back to try again in New Zealand infuriated her.

She knew that Maric would give Silas all the help he needed, and more, but first they had to have a date and time when the jet would be arriving next. She had to admit that Silas was doing an excellent job of investigating the case on his home turf, and she was confident she could leave the detective work to him until help was needed.

"You've come to the right people," she said firmly. "We want the criminal organisation behind this stopped as much as you do, and it looks like you've got some other crimes involved in this that need solving as well."

"There isn't a lot more that I've done on the case so far," he said, "and another hour tomorrow night should bring you up to speed."

"Maric speaks highly of you," said Silas, and Penny wondered how curious he was about her and Maric.

"I can't do what he does!" she said, deflecting the question, and Silas seemed to accept that.

When the call had ended she was left with a little glow of satisfaction. So Maric didn't just speak highly of her to her face, then. And, of course, he couldn't do what she did in digging up names and faces and making connections, she realised, and felt a little more confident about being part of the team.

0 ~ 0 ~ 0

The youth justice residence at Rotorua wasn't that bad. It could have been a cross between a school and an outdoor camp, if you ignored the high chain-link fence around it.

Silas had difficulty getting access for Mereana when he came to visit Devon, and he eventually understood why the system limited time with parents. Most of the youth held at the residence had learned their dysfunctional habits at home.

Eventually Silas pulled the 'police inquiries' card, but that just got him stonewalled. Then he was told the meeting could go ahead, because someone had phoned in on his behalf. He wondered if it had been the new Tokoroa inspector, Matthew Flynn.

"How are you feeling?" said Mereana earnestly, as she released Devon from a hug that had looked like it was never going to end. Silas ushered the three of them toward some chairs that were placed around a low table.

"I'm okay," said Devon, once he was seated. "I kind of like it here. Everything is run on a routine, and that includes our free time outside the dorms, the dining room, and the school. Oh yeah, they have school stuff for me to do, and some kind of teacher to help. There are team sports, and games, if we like, or solitary stuff. Gym if you want it."

He was in his own clothes, which seemed to be standard in the residence. Silas had also been told the inmates had single rooms, and he could see the sense in keeping the boys busy. Some were just waiting for a trial date, and some had been sentenced and were trying to build themselves a better future. None of them would benefit from being alone with their thoughts.

Devon looked nervously at Silas, and the man who had been trying to help him reached across and grabbed the back of the boy's hand.

"Yeah, it's looking bleak, Devon, but you were led into this by others. Don't think too badly of yourself."

Then Silas lowered his voice, though there was no one else around to hear. "I've been finding out how the Devil's Outlaws gang got involved in the theatre fire, and it's looking like they were not acting alone. You were set up, Devon, and I'm going to prove that. You just hang in here, buddy, and we'll get it sorted."

Devon smiled crookedly, the sort of smile that was only there to make someone else feel happy. Silas wasn't surprised. The boy was terrified of what his future might hold.

"Now, I have to ask you some questions," he said. "The police will have asked you some of them already, but I need to hear the answers from you, okay?"

Devon nodded.

"You know about your fingerprints on the knife that killed Mr Graham, right?" he said, and Devon nodded again. "Can you think of any way those prints might have got there?"

Devon's face twisted in anguish.

"I've been so stupid, Silas," he said. "Everything that seemed so free and easy was just a trap to draw me in and set me up, to make things look like they were something else!"

"Easy, boy," said Silas, using his best voice for calming skittish dogs and horses. "One thing at a time. What do you know about the knife?"

"It was Barnes," said Devon, sitting back miserably in his chair. "I thought he really liked me. Thought we were like, going into business together once I'd finished school. He had these cool things, and one of them was a collection of hunting knives.

"We used to throw them at targets, and sometimes we made bets on who could stick the points into a lump of wood at like, ten paces. Now that I think about it, I realize he let me win. Mum was so careful with money, and then suddenly I had some extra cash to spend. It felt good.

"All part of the trap," he continued, "now that I look back."

Silas pursed his lips. Barnes didn't have the brains for it, but someone had wanted Devon's prints on those knives. It meant the Devil's Outlaws, or their powerful and wealthy partner, had an end game in mind long before Stodge's death.

It also made Silas remember what Tarrant had said. Stodge's knife had been taken from his belt and used to stab the old man. But that was an assumption. What if it was a knife very similar to Stodge's knife, one from Barnes' collection? That would explain how Devon's prints came to be on it.

"Think back to the body in the Royal Theatre," he said quietly. "Can you say for sure Mr Graham was dead at that point?"

Devon nodded. "He was like, blue and white, and his eyes were closed. There was something wrong with him, like he wasn't there any more. I stared at him for a while, and I couldn't see any sign of him breathing."

He paused. "Ah, dammit. I can't think of anything else about him!"

That was good enough for Silas. It meant the stab wounds were added latter, to implicate Devon, and that was another sign of forward planning. He realised it didn't matter who was caught in the trap. Had Barnes tried to 'recruit' other young men or women? Was Devon just the first, or the easiest to sway?

"I'm going to talk to the police prosecutor," said Silas, fairly certain that Tracey Donovan would be taking the case, "and I'll try to get some idea of the court date. I'm sorry, Devon, but it will be a month or so after the date you were given for the arson hearing. You're going to be in here longer than we first thought."

Devon shrugged his shoulders. "I figured that," he said.

"But it will give Silas more time to find out who's trying to put the blame on you, and why they're doing it!" said Mereana. Her hand closed firmly on Silas' upper arm, and he could feel how much she wanted him to crack this case.

"That's a good point, Devon," he said quickly. "I've got some people helping me with this now, and we're making progress. But for the moment, you just have to believe we can do it. Okay?"

Devon smiled bravely. It was a much better response than the previous one, when Silas had first tried to reassure him.

Families were only allowed to visit the residence at set times over the weekends – with some very stringent rules – and Mereana worked out when she could see Devon again. It was heart-rending to see her face when they left the boy, but Silas steeled himself to smile and wave to Devon. Then they were outside in the parking lot, and Mereana wasn't saying much.

Silas' Outlander had covered half the distance to Tokoroa when red and blue lights began flashing behind them. Silas looked in the rear view mirror, and waited for the police car to pass, but it didn't.

He sighed, in the long suffering way of all motorists, and pulled over. He had the window rolled down when the man in blue walked up beside his car.

"Silas Chambers?" said the police officer, and Silas nodded. That was quick work, he thought. The officer must have read Silas' number plate from a distance, and pulled up the vehicle details.

"Message for you," he said, and looked away into the distance. Silas was mystified. Who would send him a message by cop car? And he had a cell phone in his shirt pocket didn't he?

"Tarek Assoulin dropped out of sight in Auckland six months ago," said the officer, "and he was under surveillance for drug-related crimes at the time. Any information leading to his whereabouts would be greatly appreciated, especially by the Criminal Investigations Branch in South Auckland."

Silas digested the information. The time line fitted.

"Are you stationed at Tokoroa?" said Silas, looking up at the officer, and the man noticeably straightened. He must have known Silas had once been a Senior Constable there. "Probationary Constable Stephen Foy, Tokoroa police station," he said crisply.

Probationary would be right, mused the tall man. The constable might have been in his late twenties, but he looked just out of police college to Silas. He was also enjoying his little game of clandestine messages far too much. Once he had seen the mess that was left after a head-on car crash, and helped a battered wife to hospital, that attitude would change.

Mereana leaned over from the passenger seat. "Stephen's the one who helps Dave when there's investigative work to do," she said, and waved briefly at the young man.

Silas wasn't surprised. Mereana knew everyone in Tokoroa, and she was still, unofficially, very much part of the police force there. Foy must be new, thought Silas. He hadn't come across the young constable before.

It also meant that Probationary Constable Foy would have been the one helping Tarrant when Stodge's body was discovered in the swamp south of Tokoroa. So it was Tarrant who had sent his new apprentice out with a message. Tarrant was the only one who knew Silas had made a connection between the Ella Brekken case and Stodge's death, and Assoulin had been the prime suspect in the former.

Tarrant had also known where Silas would be this afternoon, so that fitted. It was a small thing to send Foy out on the main road to Rotorua to get some practice at traffic infringements, and look for the distinctive Outlander at the same time. That way there would be no electronic trail to show that Tarrant was helping Silas.

Still, his old friend must have had a connection in the South Auckland Investigative Branch to get this information. Assoulin had fled to Auckland when the heat from the Ella Brekken case got too much for him. If he had disappeared from his Auckland haunts, then it was very likely he was back in Tokoroa.

Silas thanked Foy for his time and trouble, and the Probationary Constable went back to his patrol car with his shoulders squared. He had completed the task Tarrant had entrusted him with.

Mereana turned and looked at the retreating figure. "I think he'll make a good police officer," she said, and Silas nodded.

He couldn't bring himself to tell her he had that strange feeling again, the one he had when she laid her hand on his arm, and he saw and heard things – only this time it was his policeman's instincts. There was something wrong about Stephen Foy.

Then he eased the Outlander back onto the highway.

Chapter 18

Silas didn't have to wait for another AA meeting to learn that one of the members had matched a face to the photos he had handed out. He heard his cell phone chirp just after lunch, and flipped it open. The text read, 'Got a hit,' followed by a name.

Silas knew where the sender would be, and half an hour later his Outlander pulled up outside an old hall in Tokoroa. It had been a scout hall for generations, before the numbers attending dropped and the two scout groups in Tokoroa merged.

Now it was a Men's Shed, where the retired, or unemployed, or those with a love of power tools, could work on projects. There were over a hundred of them across New Zealand now, and they all came under the umbrella of MENZSHED New Zealand.

The AA member who had sent the text pointed towards the back of the building, and Silas followed him outside.

"Got a good look at him a week or so ago, and I'm sure it's the guy you want," said Silas' companion, once they were seated on a bench by the back door.

"He was having an argument with the dairy owner at the north end of Papanui Street. You know it, the Rainbow Dairy, run by an Indian family.

"The owner was sending him packing, right furious he was. Your guy had that look about him, you know, 'I'm coming back with some friends'. Got to give it to him, though, that Indian feller stood up to the aggro right properly!"

Silas made a mental note to ask Tarrant to follow up on the incident. One of the town patrols could drop by the dairy every other day for a while too. A police presence should scare Assoulin away from the area.

He wondered what the man – a son of Syrian immigrants – was trying to achieve. Was it the old protection money racket? Scams like that were almost unknown in New Zealand, but Assoulin might have thought the Indian owner was new to the country. He might have thought the man expected to be shaken down occasionally.

What interested Silas most though was the location. The dairy was just two blocks from the Devil's Outlaws' new base. He would bet pounds to pennies that Assoulin was passing himself off as Maloof. It was a nice bit of misdirection, designed to keep the Ella Brekken investigation buried. It would have worked too, if Silas hadn't pulled up an old photograph from the police files, and got eyes on the streets.

"Got's to get back inside," said his companion, pointing towards the back door. "I'm helping a young guy build toys for his kids. He's unemployed at the moment, and this helps him keep his head straight."

There was so much pride in that statement, and the AA members were often looking for ways to put things right, having got it wrong for so many years. Silas thanked him for keeping a lookout for the man in the photo, and stayed on the bench as the other went inside.

Assoulin, or Maloof, had two gang members working with him now, and they were from Auckland as well. Silas didn't remember either of them from the original Ella Brekken case. But then, Mereana had told him there were three men when Ella ran out into the car park at the start of the Horohoro track.

Were they Tarek Assoulin and his two apprentices in crime, Luke and Terz? Had the two junior gang members come down from Auckland three years ago, but returned to the city as soon as the Ella Brekken case became a murder inquiry?

Some of the pieces were starting to fit together, but there were many more scattered around the table. It was some kind of frustrating jigsaw puzzle.

Silas decided there was nothing more to be gained here at the moment, and retrieved his cell phone from his pocket. It took a while before the front desk at the Police Prosecutor's office got an answer for him.

Yes, Tracey Donovan would see him this afternoon, and was four thirty a suitable time? Silas agreed that it was, and walked around the Men's Shed premises to get to his Outlander. For once it would be a leisurely drive to Hamilton.

"I thought you would be pushing for Devon to have the earliest court date possible," said Donovan, leaning back in her chair. She had been waiting when Silas appeared at the front desk.

"That wouldn't work," said Silas. "Nobody pushes Tracey Donovan into anything."

She smiled at that.

"Besides," said Silas, "the boy's in a good holding pattern for now. He's settled in okay at the Rotorua youth residence, and they have an on-site school. I think he's getting more one-on-one teaching time there than he did at his regular school."

They both took a moment to think about that. It was funny where government money went.

"I'm getting somewhere with my investigations," said Silas, "but I need as much time as you can give me. You said 'bring me a body', and you've got one now, but it's landed Devon in ten times as much trouble."

She nodded at that, but she didn't say anything. Silas sighed. She wanted to know why she should help him.

"I've tied the main suspect from the Ella Brekken case to the Ernest Graham case," he said. "The suspect is currently living in Tokoroa, and that gives me a name, a location, and two bodies, and I'm working on a motive. I think it could be this.

"The Devil's Outlaws push a lot of methamphetamine around Auckland because of their Triad 14K connections, and I think they want to expand south.

"The gang has recently established an 'unofficial' base in Tokoroa. I have a lead on what may be a new player, with money, who's working with them. I think they're putting together something really big."

That was all he had, so he fell silent. Donovan came out of the recesses of her chair like a clockwork apparition rising into the light. She had been aware of the flood of 'ice' coming into New Zealand from Australia through 14K channels, but she hadn't known the rest of it. It was a personal mission of hers to put such people away.

"Silas Chambers," she growled, muscles tensing, "tell me you've shared what you know with the Tokoroa police, or so help me I will have you arrested right now!"

Silas wasn't sure she could do that, and he knew his lawyer would have him out in less than a day, but he understood her frustration.

"Flynn agreed I should work from the shadows," he said. "I wouldn't have got this far if I'd followed procedure. I think there are going to be more bodies, and I haven't got time to debate the ethics of policing with you."

He couldn't afford to get on the wrong side of a senior police prosecutor, but his firm rebuttal of her position seemed to work. Or maybe it was the fact he had mentioned the name of the inspector at Tokoroa. What was it with those two?

It took a while for Donovan to settle back into her chair.

"The only reason I'm helping you," she said eventually, "apart from your excellent past work, is that your lady friend was a godsend to someone close to me recently."

Silas had no idea that Donovan knew Annabel, and he wondered what the connection was. He presumed that was who Donovan was speaking about. Annabel would be amused to know she was his 'lady friend'.

"A motorcycle accident left my nephew with a number of broken bones, and unremitting pain," said Donovan. "Ms Kirsk was the only one who managed to control the pain well enough to get him into a rehabilitation programme. At least without pills fogging his brain.

"He's almost back to normal now, and the family is delighted that he's started light duties at his old workplace."

Silas had heard people say things about Annabel's work as a pain specialist, but here was concrete proof. The world was a small place it seemed, and everyone knew someone you would least expect.

The problem was, Tokoroa and Tawhiti were small places too, and Silas should have uncovered a lot more useful information by now. He was angry with himself for moving so slowly. But he didn't think he was missing anything in the details he already had, which left only one possibility.

He was thinking too small. There was something really big going on here, and he wasn't seeing the full picture. It made him feel inadequate, and unworthy of all the help people were giving him.

Chapter 19

Two days later Silas talked to a different AA member about her sighting of Assoulin, which gave the first report more credibility. Then Gummy rang him again about making a trip up onto the plateau, if he was still keen. Silas knew it was time that he did so, but he had been busy trying to track down Assoulin's handlers in the Devil's Outlaws.

The man's connection to the gang looked straightforward. He was a gang member and he would do what he was told to do. The Outlaws ran a business model based on the sale of drugs, and it was unlikely to lead to contract killings. So why had they got involved in Stodge's death?

The 14K Triad in Auckland were more likely to order a killing, especially if it would expand their area of influence, but they used Hong Kong nationals for anything like that. It also looked like Assoulin didn't have any direct connections with them. Silas found it puzzling. Why were people dying? What was he missing?

He was getting out his tramping gear at first light the next day when his home phone rang. That was odd. He mostly kept it for older folk in the area who hadn't made the transition to cell phones and monthly plans. It was a relic really, of little use now he was no longer in the police force, but having it supported the community.

"Silas, thank God it's you," said a familiar voice. "You've got to come quick, they're turning the place over and I don't know what's going on!"

Gords was one of those who did use the home phone occasionally, and Silas figured he'd made a subconscious decision that home was where the help was, and Silas was a great guardian to have.

"Whoah, Gords," said Silas, "slow down. Where are you, and what's happening?"

"I'm at my flat," said his adopted son. "The police are here, and they're flashing bits of paper saying they can search the place. Simon is home, but Di is still at her boyfriend's place. Why are the police here? And what are they looking for?"

Silas knew the routine well. It was a weekend raid, hitting early, not long after dawn. But why a student flat? All three of the flatmates were sensible people. Two of them were studying, and one was working. The most likely cause was a drugs bust, but that didn't make any sense.

"I'll be there in fifty minutes," he said. "I'll get our family lawyer in on this too. You remember Dennis? Good. Stay out of it, mate. Go outside, take Simon with you. Don't let it wind you up."

There was an affirmative, and Silas grabbed a few things before he hustled to the Outlander.

Forty-five minutes later he pulled up at the curb behind two police cars. He could see a police van, fitted out to carry suspects, in the drive. That wasn't a good sign. He couldn't see the much lower profile of the dog patrol vehicle, so the sniffer dogs must have been and gone already.

"I'm sorry, Sir, this is a police operation," said a figure on the veranda, as Silas came down the driveway. "No one is allowed on or off the property at the moment."

"I'm Senior Constable Silas Chambers, recently retired from Tokoroa," said Silas, though the 'recently retired' was a big stretch. "I understand it's irregular, but my boy flats here. Could I have a few words with your boss?"

The task force leader came out of the house a few minutes later. He was a Senior Constable, the same rank that Silas had held, and he hoped he could trade on that to get some concessions. He introduced himself, and they shook hands.

"I know you can't make a statement tying anything you've found to an individual," said Silas, "because of the civil rights issues involved, but could you let me take a quick look at what you've discovered, while it's still in situ? I used to be an investigative officer, and I want to see my boy gets a fair hearing."

The Senior Constable looked at Silas for a while, then seemed to make a decision. He turned and walked down the side of the house. "We found this," he said, stopping beside the gully trap for the kitchen, and pointing underneath.

Silas got down on his hands and knees, and peered under the side of the house. A short distance in from the edge was a snap-lock bag full of marijuana heads, stapled to the underneath of a bearer. It was more than the amount allowed for personal consumption, and the penalties for being a dealer could run as high as eight years imprisonment.

Silas had driven hard to make Hamilton in record time, and his gut had clenched and unclenched all that way as he worried about Gords future. Now, for the first time since the phone call, he started to smile.

"Thank you, Senior Constable," he said, smoothing his face over as he dusted off his hands and knees.

"I have no jurisdiction in this case," he continued, "but I would like to advise. Would that be possible?"

Task force leaders often got the opinion of an investigative officer, and Silas was hoping he could have a similar input on this case. The Senior Constable looked hesitant, but then he nodded. He didn't have to take Silas' recommendations, so he had nothing to lose.

"Snap-lock bags are used because they can be rubbed down with methylated spirits and made free of odour," said Silas. "It's a way of neutralizing the effectiveness of police dogs when the bags are hidden in wall cavities or ceiling spaces.

"You noticed the staples holding the bag to the bearer?" he added, and the Senior Constable nodded. Silas had counted nine or ten of them, far more than was necessary to hold the bag in place. It looked like a rushed job, and he thought he knew why.

"They suggest that the bag was meant to be found. The staple holes would have spread the odour and drawn a dog straight to it. There is also the question of why an amount slightly more than the maximum for personal use is secured here. Everyone knows the limit, why not play safe and have just less than that amount? Why take the extra risk? Everything is adding up to this being a plant.

"There is also the question of mold spoiling the product. You can see the bag is secured on the dampest side of the house, and the ground under it isn't covered to stop ground moisture."

He took a deep breath. "If that could be in your report, the prosecutor will be able to put all the possibilities before the judge. I would also appreciate it as well."

"I can't promise anything," said the Senior Constable, and Silas nodded. It was up to the man's discretion now. Silas would check with the prosecutor later, whether it was Donovan or not, and put in a statutory declaration about the bag if he had to. It might be the only way to get his point of view into the courtroom.

"The occupants of the house will have to be processed as normal," said the Senior Constable, and Silas nodded again. He wasn't asking for any favours – that would really turn the police officer against him – he just wanted to make sure the truth was heard.

"My lawyer should be here any minute," he said. "We can wait for him to arrive, or you could give me a bit of time with the two young men you've got in custody."

Silas got to have a few words with Gords and Simon straight away. He couldn't promise them anything, but if he could convince the prosecutor's office there was a good chance the marijuana was planted, both of them should be out on home detention within 48 hours.

It would be an unusual decision, but one of the flatmates who was present was in his last year of an apprenticeship, and the other was working, and the absent girl was studying. They all needed to attend their places of study or work, and that would help their cases.

Gords was not at all happy, even with a good chance of home detention, and Silas could sympathize. The young man felt victimized, and none of this made any sense to him. Timon the meerkat, Gords other persona, would have found the deepest burrow his meerkat family had excavated and dived to the bottom of it.

Once Silas could safely leave Gords with his lawyer, he eased his Outlander away from the curb, and drove the short distance to Annabel's place in Hillcrest.

Chapter 20

Silas plugged in an earpiece, and put an urgent call through to Annabel as he drove. She wasn't at home, but she would meet him there. Ten minutes tops, she said. As it turned out he was waiting on the pavement when she pulled into her drive. It took a moment for her to walk across and open the front door for them, and then they were inside.

"Don't," she said, as words came out of his mouth in a jumble. She laid her head against his chest, and put her arms around him. Then she held him tightly until his breathing slowed. They hadn't even made it to the lounge, but it was what he needed.

"Sit on the couch and work out what's most important, and tell me that first," she said, as she moved quietly about the kitchen. She wasn't far from him, just on the other side of the breakfast bar, and that felt good. She was making coffee.

Silas was embarrassed at his emotional state, and pleased at the same time. He knew that people like Mereana, Gords, and now Annabel, had stopped him turning into a machine over the years. An investigative monster with no thought to the consequences of his actions. It also meant that she saw him when he wasn't at his efficient and police-trained best, and it had taken time for him to feel okay talking about his emotional workings.

He gave Annabel a brief run down on what he was thinking as she waited for the jug to boil. Stodge murdered and he didn't know why. Devon talked into arson and then framed for murder. And now Gords caught up in a drug bust with planted evidence, a fact Silas couldn't get his head around.

"Am I cursed, or what?" he said, when she came back to sit beside him on the couch. "Do shit storms always come in threes?"

"You're still not mentally where you need to be," she said, taking one of his hands. "You're talking in cliches. That's not the investigative master I know, the one that would look at the facts."

Silas was shocked into silence. When had she become his counsellor when he was confused, his guiding star when he wasn't sure of the direction to take? He waited for that thought to worry him, and was intrigued when it didn't.

"I hadn't even met you when your friend Ian Findlay died," she said, "and then you left the police force, but it looks to me like you've been searching for something to believe in ever since then. Sometimes you're a different person, as if you're trying on a new personality, and I guess that's part of it.

"But through it all your mind has continued to shine brightly as you tackled your share of life's problems. It's been an education for me, I can tell you!

"I've learned from you, Silas," she continued. "I do the same things to other people now. Asking them why, getting them to list their options, saying the answer could be something else entirely, knowing that of two possibilities the simplest is the most likely to be true. And keeping in mind your guiding axiom, 'there is no such thing as coincidence'."

"So it's not only my body you want, then," said Silas, when he had recovered from this intense personal analysis into who, and what, he was.

"No, you idiot," she said, hitting him on the shoulder. "But as the saying goes, you have ruined me for other men."

He laughed at that.

"I want Silas the investigator back," she said, "and you need him back too, or someone out there is going to ruin your life!"

That sobered Silas all right. It was a startling thought, but he could see that she was onto something.

Silas had been too young to be retired, but he had tried to live as though he was. He hadn't wanted to go back into the police force, where good men and women could get shot by mindless egomaniacs over nothing. But if someone didn't take on that role, and live with that risk, then a lot of innocent people would die.

He used to go in hard after the facts in his investigations, and he wouldn't back off until he got an answer. Now, though, he knew that searching for the truth could get you killed, maybe in the way Ian Findlay had died. It took him a moment to realize he already knew the answer to this – it was better to die doing something worthwhile than to live an empty life.

The understanding shocked him, but then it started to firm his resolve. He needed to go after this case with everything he had. He would gain nothing by hanging back.

There were other things involved too, and good leadership helped. There had been something terribly wrong about the previous inspector, Billingham, something that triggered every anti-authoritarian bone in his body. Maybe he would have to look into those feelings one day, he thought, but Matthew Flynn was a totally different type of man. Silas knew he could work with the new inspector. He trusted the man already.

"Why did you take up policing in the beginning?" said Annabel, gently prompting him. He acknowledged that his desire to help others hadn't gone away, it had just got buried under the accumulated tragedies of the last few years.

"So I should get back on the horse then?" he said quietly.

She grimaced at another cliche. "If you can put that in more authentic terms," she said, "then yes, following what was a genuine vocation back then, something you loved, would make a lot of sense."

Silas was convinced, but it was still a big step to take. Flynn had opened the door with his offer of reinstatement into the police ranks, and it felt like the right thing to do. But there were a number of complicated things to be sorted out before that could happen.

"You are a hard woman to please, Annabel Kirsk!" he said, with a smile.

"Then it's a good thing I've got a soft spot for you," she said, drawing him toward her.

An hour later they were back on the couch and thinking about an early lunch, but it didn't work out that way. Annabel mentioned idly that Mereana was in regular touch with Emily in Dunedin now, and perhaps Silas could let her know how the investigation was going. That was enough to re-awaken the murder case for him.

"How can I connect Stodge, Devon, and Gords?" he said, as he got up from the couch so he could pace up and down Annabel's living room. She sighed resignedly, and went to make them another cup of coffee. There was nothing else she could do when Silas' brain started chipping away at the problems in front of it.

"What do you think connects those three people?" she said, standing in the kitchen with her arms folded. He looked across at her.

"I don't know," he said. "I'm missing something. I've felt there was a difference about this case from the beginning. It's part of something bigger, and I can't see it."

Annabel poured the hot water to make the coffee.

"You're too close, Silas," she said. "You're emotionally involved, and it's clouding your thinking."

Silas could hear the exasperation in her voice.

"You know what it is, don't you?" he said, suddenly. "You've thought of something that ties them all together."

She looked at him, neither confirming or denying.

"Well, spit it out, Annie," he said. "I'm not too proud to accept help. God in heaven this is Gords' and Devon's future we're talking about!"

Annabel brought the coffees over and sat down beside him. He only called her Annie when he really needed her help.

"The connection is you, Silas," she said. "All these things are aimed at you. Someone doesn't want you poking your nose into this. It's all been set up to keep you occupied, and get you worried and anxious because it's family. The whole point is to take away the time you might have used to look at their activities."

The idea completely derailed Silas, but it made sense. Tarrant was a new investigative officer, Tokoroa was a small station not used to the complexities of city crime, and the only threat in the area was Silas Chambers. A man at the peak of his investigative powers with time on his hands.

"Start thinking, Silas," she said, leaning back into the couch. "This is personal. Someone knows how good you are at what you do, and they want to sideline you. Think about the cases you were working on before you left the police. Who knows you that well?"

She was right. Assoulin would have seen how fast Silas moved once he got onto the scent, how quickly he unravelled the lies to find the truth. That meant the Devil's Outlaws would want him out of the way, and maybe the 14K Triad as well, but it still didn't feel like the right answer. There was no one in either gang with the sophistication, or resources, to put together a series of misdirections as complex as this.

Was Aldous Huxton already involved in the Outlaws crime network, he wondered. That was possible, but there was nothing tying a ranch on the far side of the volcanic plateau to Stodge in Tawhiti. At least, not yet, but Silas needed to make a trip across the top of the plateau to look at the ranch for himself.

First, though, he would talk to Inspector Flynn. Someone must have phoned in the tip-off that led to the dawn raid on Gords' flat, and everything about this part of the case seemed to lead back to Tokoroa. He wouldn't be surprised if the tip-off came from there too.

Chapter 21

"I understand you phoned reception, Mr Chambers, something about setting up a neighbourhood watch in Tawhiti," said Inspector Flynn. "There appeared to be some urgency to the matter."

"Yes, that was the cover story," said Silas, dropping into the chair the inspector indicated, the one opposite Flynn at his desk.

The inspector raised his eyebrows, but said nothing.

"There was a drug raid in Hamilton on Saturday morning," said Silas. "It was in Frankton, and I'm supposing it came from a tip-off. I would dearly love to know where that information came from."

Flynn seemed to be having a lot of trouble with this one. He steepled his hands together, and looked off into the distance.

"A member of the police force cannot act in such a way as to hold himself, or his family, subject to a different law from the one he or she applies to the public," he said, eventually.

Silas understood at once. Flynn had read the report on the Frankton raid and noticed Silas' involvement. He was now asking whether Silas wanted special treatment for his adopted son. If that was the case, Flynn wasn't prepared to answer any questions Silas might have.

It was the sort of question that made him want to hit something, because it suggested he didn't know the rules. His knuckles grew white on the arm rests of the chair. Perhaps he was wrong about Flynn. Didn't the man know he was as straight as a truckload of rulers?

"Which is how it should be," he ground out. "I wasn't asking that question to gain an advantage for myself, or my family!"

The silence between them continued to grow for a full thirty seconds.

"As paranoid as it may seem," he said, more calmly, "I have enough information now to suggest someone is targeting me personally. I believe they are doing that because I'm getting close to them and close to their operation. I know I'm onto something big, Sir. I just don't know what it is yet!"

Flynn got out of his chair and walked to the window looking out over Logan Street. He had done the same thing when he talked to Silas about the complaint from the local lawyer, Julian McCabe.

"It isn't a bad idea, you know," said Flynn, looking out the window. "Forming a neighbourhood watch in Tawhiti."

Silas had to scramble to keep up with the change of topic.

"There's no need, Sir," he said. "I already have an effective system in place, and another one here in Tokoroa. It's unofficial I'm afraid, due to the nature of the participants, but I'll bring you up to speed when I'm back in uniform.

"If I live long enough, or don't ruin what's left of my career," he amended cynically.

Flynn stood stock still for a few seconds, then turned back toward his chair.

"Glad to hear it," he said, as he sat down. Silas figured he was glad to hear both things. The news about an effective neighbourhood watch, and the fact that Silas intended to rejoin the police when the time was right.

There was a moment's silence, before Flynn reached a decision.

"Despite the fact I have a – shall we say – better understanding of your reasons for requesting a name behind the tip-off," said the inspector, "it is still police policy to keep information that comes from the public confidential."

He followed that up by deliberating for some time. Silas knew he couldn't pressure the inspector on this. The decision on how much he could reveal lay with Flynn, and Silas didn't interrupt.

"However, the policy on confidentiality refers only to individuals, as I recall," said Flynn, "which leaves me free to disclose that the information came in on a Chamber of Commerce letterhead."

"Then it has to be McCabe," said Silas, sitting up in his chair. He was surprised at the revelation.

"When I was the police representative on the Chamber of Commerce," he continued, "I saw McCabe push them to lodge complaints on a number of occasions. It seemed to stroke his bloated ego to get his dirty work done in a way that was 'for the good of the community.'"

Silas sat for a while as he worked out what this new information might mean for him, and for Gords.

"McCabe has done enough work as a criminal lawyer," he concluded, "to know who to pay if he wants to plant evidence. And then he can back up his informant's claim through an official complaint."

It was too much. "God damn the man!" he cursed.

But still, McCabe had slipped up. A named tip-off by an individual would have been bound by the police confidentiality rules. Getting the Chamber of Commerce to back the informant's complaint had left an opening. It meant that Flynn had been free to discuss the matter.

"I'm not in a position to offer an opinion on McCabe's character, of course," said the inspector, "but I have noticed he is the motivating force any time the Chamber of Commerce brings up a concern with the police."

That was a yes, realized Silas, behind the convoluted language. It had been McCabe who had tipped off the police that his informant had claimed there were drugs to be had at a certain address in Frankton.

"Whether he was instrumental in causing false charges to be laid against a citizen, or citizens, for his own ends, is another matter," said the inspector. "It would be no more than speculation to go that far."

He was smiling now. Silas could see that the man enjoyed the word games.

"If I may ask," said Silas, "did the inspector at Tokoroa before you ever confide why he didn't support my line of inquiry in the Ella Brekken case? I thought my evidence at the time was strong enough to proceed, especially against the prime suspect."

"You mean Inspector Billingham, of course," said Flynn. "I never spoke to him personally about the case, but I have read everything on file about it.

"I have also, I might add, read everything on all the unsolved cases going back at least five years. It's always useful to know which matters might become active again at a new station."

In a way, Flynn's memory of the file was even better than having the file itself, thought Silas. The head of each police station had to justify their decisions in high profile cases, and Billingham would have written down his thoughts about the case generally, and about Silas' recommendations as the investigative officer.

"Inspector Billingham didn't shut down your inquiry, Mr Chambers," said Flynn, "Julian McCabe did."

Silas sat there pole-axed. McCabe hadn't been the prosecuting officer at the time, Donovan had been. McCabe wasn't even eligible to be a police prosecutor. Why had Billingham listened to McCabe?

"McCabe was representing Tarek Assoulin," said Flynn. "He made a strong case that nothing could be proved against his client, and a prosecution would be a waste of public time and money."

This was news to Silas. He hadn't known that Assoulin had a lawyer when the case was closed down around him. Assoulin had disappeared back into Auckland soon after, but that wasn't a problem. He could have been tried and convicted in his absence, and the police would have found him eventually.

It was McCabe again! Silas was beginning to suspect the lawyer was acting for the crime bosses he was up against. That made McCabe a bent lawyer, paid with dirty money.

He ground his teeth. Crime reached a whole new level when it was able to operate through a respectable figure in the establishment. Then he had another thought. Was Julian McCabe Huxton's lawyer? Was that the connection? And if Assoulin was still being advised by McCabe, was there a connection between Assoulin and Huxton?

It gave Silas a small sense of satisfaction. It felt like he was closing in on the people behind the murders. Maybe everything would fall into place when he knew more about Huxton and his wife, and what was happening at the ranch on the far side of the volcanic plateau.

He thanked the inspector for his help, and rose to leave. Of course, if anyone asked, the only reason he had made an appointment at reception was to talk about starting a neighbourhood watch group in Tawhiti.

Chapter 22

It was time. It was 5.30 am, and Gummy's twin cab had rolled in beside Silas' restored villa. Gummy wanted to do some hunting up on the plateau before they reconnoitred the Huxton ranch. The old hunter hoped to catch a few deer in the open, enjoying the first rays of the sun.

It wasn't clock time that Silas was thinking about, though. It was time he followed up on his only promising lead in this case, and found out more about Aldous Huxton and his wife Irena. Gummy would take him to the ranch, because it was the area Stodge had been hunting before he died. They were the same place, though Gummy didn't know it yet.

The twin cab shuddered and hiccuped for a while after Gummy turned it off. He said it was carbon deposits inside the heads of the cylinders, acting like a glow plug on a diesel engine. Silas just shrugged, and took his word for it. Apparently Gummy would fix the problem one day.

Then Silas had made his way outside, and was loading his lightweight pack into the back seat of the twin cab. Gummy started the engine when Silas slid in beside him in the front, and the pickup truck lurched forward. It was still dark when they reached the end of Forestry Road Number Three, and the beginnings of native forest.

"You just keep up now," said Gummy, when they were ready to head off, "and watch where you're putting your feet. Deer can hear a bolt slide home at fifty paces, and they can certainly hear us crashing about if we're not careful."

Silas nodded. He was decades younger than the old hunter, but he knew he would be pushed to keep up. His police fitness, checked every two years in the physical competency test, had gone downhill since he left the force.

It was a hard first hour, walking steadily uphill on a rough track, but then they came out onto the plateau itself. The physical demands eased off as Gummy worked his way along the edges of more open ground, looking for deer. He waved Silas over when he hadn't found anything by eight thirty.

"Might as well brew the billy," he said. "The deer will be off the open patches by now, and it's hard to spot them among the trees. Once we've had a cuppa we'll cut across the plateau to where Stodge was hunting last."

Silas watched the old man set a fire in minutes, and cut a length of branch and a stand to hold the billy over the flames. New Zealand still had a number of these experienced woodsmen. A new breed of hunters and trampers was coming along nicely too, but they relied too much on high-tech equipment for Silas' taste.

Gummy's story was interesting. He had taken on some poor land near Tawhiti, and started planting it in pines in the eighties. Forestry was all the rage back then. It made sense for him to join the trend, since he was a forestry worker in the vast Kinleith forests. The sticky pine gum from pruning his trees got into his clothes and onto his hands, and that was how he got his nickname.

Then Gummy lost his family to a drunk driver, and swore off any form of alcohol. That was why he came along to AA, where he'd eventually progressed to being a mentor.

The old man spent a lot of time stalking deer, and occasionally wild pigs, and Silas had seen him do amazing things with a rifle. He had often thought Gummy could bend bullets to their target with the power of his mind.

The following hour consisted of flat tops and occasional gullies, all covered in increasingly dense forest. Gummy seemed to have an unerring sense of direction, and plunged on when Silas couldn't see any signs of a track. Then the two men came out at the edge of a cleared valley that climbed onto the plateau from the Rotorua side. It was sheep-cropped farmland and well fenced.

"Stodge was hunting the forest edges around these valleys," said Gummy. "There are a few more of them on our right, and a cleared area in the forest a bit further over. Where do you want to start?"

That fitted the picture in Silas' mind perfectly. He could see the satellite map as if it was in front of him. Four fingers of farmland that hung on to the top of the plateau by their tips, and an irregular cleared area on the top itself. It was the top half of Huxton's ranch.

"Let's get a good look at them all," he said, and Gummy led him across the top of the first clearing and down the side to a handy vantage point. Silas looked for anything unusual in the farm tracks, fences and gates, hay barns and water systems that lay spread out before him. He found nothing, and it was the same at the next valley, and then the last two.

The open area further into the plateau was more difficult to get a good look at. The two men had to skirt around most of one side of it to find an unobstructed view of a broad central valley.

"What do you make of that?" said Silas, as they lay on a mossy ledge under trees, and searched the shallow depression beneath them with binoculars.

"That middle section has been a topdressing airfield at some stage," said Gummy. "I can see where a bulldozer cut and filled a section in the middle from the hill behind it."

Silas nodded. Topdressing planes were small and powerful. They had to carry close to eight tonnes of lime or superphospate these days, and take off from incredibly short grass runways.

The airfield wasn't being used now though. A hay barn sat in the middle of it, and several fences ran across it at an angle. A rusting bulldozer sat near one end, with a pile of rotting logs beside it. Lifting his eyes, Silas saw that a gravel farm track ran out of the forest opposite and down to an old cottage that looked like it would house staff when they were needed. There was no sign of anyone living there at the moment though.

Silas sighed. He didn't know what he was looking for, but he had thought he would know it when he saw it. He started to lift himself to his feet, and felt dizzy. He dropped back on one knee, but flashes of light started up behind his eyelids, like a slide show set too fast. A background hiss developed into a pulsing roar, and Silas could have sworn there were words in it.

"You all right, man?" said Gummy, crouching down beside him. His firm grip on Silas arm helped, as he pushed himself to his feet.

"It's nothing, Gummy," he said. "Just a bit of inner ear trouble. I get it from time to time."

Gummy seemed reassured, but it wasn't inner ear trouble. It was the same odd sensations Silas had felt when he was with Mereana, and she had seen Stodge and Ella. Mereana believed the feelings would get stronger as he was exposed to more of them, and the thought of that happening gave Silas an uneasy feeling.

This time, though, Mereana hadn't had her hand on his arm. If Stodge was trying to contact him, it might mean this place had something to do with his death. Silas didn't like it, but the feelings he was having might be the only way to find the truth. He forged on ahead of Gummy, and his senses returned to normal as the two men plunged back into the forest.

It wasn't long before they found the first 'No Trespassing' sign. There seemed to be one every hundred meters or so as they skirted the big central valley. The signs promised hidden cameras, and suggested offenders would be arrested and dealt with on the property. That wasn't legal in New Zealand, and Silas wondered what strange Californian customs the Huxtons had brought with them.

Gummy turned onto an old logging track. He assured Silas it would take them back toward the road end where his twin cab was parked. There were more 'No Trespassing' signs along the track, promising swift and unpleasant punishment. It seemed excessive, until Gummy triggered an electric eye beam across the track.

There was a tiny flash of light from the undergrowth, and Silas pulled some branches back to reveal a piece of high-tech security equipment.

He wrote down the maker's name, and some technical data he found on the back of it. They were about to carry on down the track when Silas heard an engine start up. It sounded like a pickup truck, and it was coming from the valley they had just left.

Silas figured the vehicle had been behind the cottage, and he hadn't seen it. Triggering the beam had alerted someone, and now they were headed this way. Silas did a rapid evaluation of risks and benefits, and decided they should stay where they were.

"Let's see what they want," he said, and Gummy nodded. The old hunter flicked the bolt back on his rifle, and then slid it home. It now had a bullet in the firing chamber.

"Insurance," he said, when Silas looked at him.

That was all right with Silas. The two men waited until an overpowered off-road vehicle came tearing down the track toward them, destroying the mossy surface as it came.

"They sure as hell aint from around here," said Gummy, tightening his grip on the rifle.

Silas agreed, though he was more intent on watching the vehicle as it slid to a stop, and two burly men in security uniforms tumbled out of it.

"What are you guys doing here?" said the first one sharply. Silas heard an American twang in his speech.

"Can't you read the signs!" snarled the second one, and Silas placed his accent somewhere along the east coast of America.

"Just turned back," said Silas. "The first sign we saw was that one down there," he added, waving vaguely down the track in the direction the vehicle had come from.

"Yeah, well that isn't good enough," said the grumpy one, and he leaned forward aggressively, his hand going to the butt of a holstered handgun at his belt.

Any form of handgun was illegal in New Zealand, unless carried by police. Silas figured Huxton had brought his own security people with him, and they had not adapted well to New Zealand ways.

"Is that right?" said Gummy, bringing his rifle round to the port arms position.

"What are you going to do, old timer?" said the man. "I can put a bullet though your heart before you fire a round from that old rifle you got there."

"Try me," said Gummy.

Silas could see how Stodge had died now. He hadn't been put off by the signs, or maybe he was just following a roaring stag, but he had discovered something in this valley that he felt he could blackmail the Huxton's over, and it had ended his life. What Silas needed now, though, was a way to extricate himself and Gummy from a tricky situation.

"McCabe sent us," he said. "He wanted to check security after the problems they had last time."

It was suitably vague, and Stodge's death had to count as a 'problem'. The two men looked at each other.

"That weasel of a lawyer's always pushing Huxton to keep things tight," said the first guard, and the second one nodded. "Typical of him to test our defences, and spring it on us as a surprise!" he added.

"Anyway, who the hell are you two," said the second man, still holding an aggressive stance.

"B team," said Silas. "We take care of problems with the locals. You guys don't have the right accent, and you wouldn't understand how the people around here think anyway. We split the work. You do the heavy lifting up here, and we make sure no one gets out of line down on the flats."

"I thought McCabe had Assoulin for that," said the first man, and Silas nodded. "Tarek's good in some situations, but he's got no finesse. We come in when people just need to be reminded what their obligations are."

The use of Assoulin's first name seemed to convince the two men. Still, they didn't leave. They intended to stay and watch Silas and Gummy walk away down the track. Gummy motioned Silas over beside him, and then turned sideways as he vanished into the trees. Silas followed.

"Wasn't going to turn my back on those fellas," said Gummy, after they had gone a hundred meters along an old animal trail.

"Good call," said Silas, finally beginning to relax.

Chapter 23

"And that brings Silas' story up to date," said Penny, as she sat with Maric and Ellie at the kitchen table in the Bolt residence. Ellie had made them all a cup of tea, but it was too early for cake. Penny had been surprised at that, she didn't realise there were rules for cake, like 'the sun has to be over the yard arm' for a pre-dinner drink.

"Man alive!" said Maric, in astonishment. "He told me just the basics, and I had no idea there were so many other people involved, and so many crimes to be solved." But then he grew thoughtful.

"That was probably why Silas went into police work while I felt drawn to the military. I don't know how we knew, but we've both ended up in jobs that suit us. The military has definite objectives and streamlined rules of engagement, I don't think I could cope with all the dead ends and side issues that Silas is now faced with!"

"We love you just the way you are," said Ellie, punching him playfully on the arm. "Some of us more than others," she added, looking at Penny and rolling her eyes. Penny tried not to let a flash of embarrassment show on her cheeks, and fortunately Ellie's little comment went straight over Maric's head.

"But I can see problems ahead," said Penny earnestly, and the other two looked at her.

"It's clear that Silas intends to deal with this problem himself, with maybe the help of some locals. He feels it's his problem, on his turf, and he can't go to the police about it after leaving the force."

"Inspector Flynn sounds like he's prepared to listen," said Ellie, and Penny nodded.

"That's the one good thing I can see about the situation," she said, "but Silas would have had access to an Armed Offenders Squad if he was still a Senior Constable, and now he doesn't.

"He did the right thing by contacting you, Maric, as soon he could see that this was an international conspiracy with a lot of power and money behind it, but you and your team are up here and he's down there. My biggest concern is that things will get out of hand, and Silas won't have any backup.

"He probably thinks there's a limit on how much he can call on an old friendship, and then there's the distance to consider. Add that to the fact he doesn't want to bring ordinary police up against these armed thugs, and the fact he no longer has the clout to call in an Armed Offenders Squad, and we could be looking at one very dead Silas."

Maric looked at Ellie, and they both nodded. They could see that Penny was right.

"He was always like that," said Maric, reflecting on the past. "I had to bury my emotions deep to get into the SAS – where it was all about objectives and risks and even acceptable casualties – but I think that was what drew Silas to the police. Changing people's lives for the better, or at least getting them justice and maybe closure.

"I don't think we're going to change his attitude, but at least we can be well-informed. He trusts you, Penny, so I want you to make him promise to Skype here every evening, and every time he makes some sort of breakthrough," and she nodded. She would press Silas for all the details, too.

"There's an Armed Offenders Squad in Rotorua, which is the nearest big centre," said Maric, "so I'll be giving them a heads up that they may be involved, and they're going to need choppers.

"I want them to arrive when Silas is in trouble as fast as possible, and I'll pull a few strings to make sure they have something fast and roomy that can fly in at a moment's notice if they don't have the right sort of choppers at Rotorua."

It was a plan, if not a perfect plan, and all three of them were now seriously worried about Silas' chances of surviving the next few weeks.

"He's good at what he does," said Maric reassuringly, "and he used to give me a run for my money when we were doing martial arts together. I think he'll sense danger well before it happens," and the others looked reassured.

"It's just a matter of how much trouble he's going to get himself into," said Maric, which kind of flattened the moment again.

Penny put through a Skype call that evening, and managed to get Silas at home. She explained the way she wanted to run things – which she called the new rules of engagement – and Silas agreed. She sensed that he might even have been a little relieved. It must be lonely for him out there in the field without the backup he would normally have had in the police force, she reasoned, and then they logged off.

There wasn't much to talk about for the next few days, and then the old intensity was back in Silas' voice as he recounted new developments.

0 ~ 0 ~ 0

"How much information did you get about Huxton's security detail?" said Silas, and the voice at the other end of the call snorted derisively.

"Everything," it said, "right down to the type of flies they use when they're trout fishing."

"They fly fish?" said Silas, intrigued.

"Figure of speech," said Tarrant. "Really, Silas, try to keep up!"

The retired policeman had to stop and laugh at that. Tarrant was blossoming into his investigative role now that Silas had left the police force, and Tarrant had taken over. He carried on before Silas could recover.

"Grady Trafford, 52, is a retired police officer from Boston. No awards on his file, but no black marks either. One corruption charge dismissed through lack of evidence. Peter Stuart, 38, was a security guard for the Private Officer International corporation in Los Angeles for twelve years, before he was discharged as unreliable. Both are now working for Aldous Huxton, and paid by his production company Airtight Films."

That was clever, thought Silas. Huxton could offset the ranch as a loss against the royalties still coming in from his production company. He would claim the salaries of the two guards as part of the ranch expenses.

The problem for Huxton was that the production money was going to run out sooner or later. What would someone like Huxton, used to a large income, do if he wanted to maintain a substantial cash flow? The income from the ranch wasn't going to be anywhere near enough.

"How's Devon doing?" said Tarrant, changing tack.

"Very well, considering his situation," said Silas. "I think he's blocked the court date out of his mind, and he's concentrating on sports and schooling instead."

"They get all that at a youth residence?" said Tarrant, and Silas confirmed it.

"Good thing the coroner found the blow to the head caused Stodge's death," continued Tarrant, "and not the stab wounds. At least the murder charge has been dropped," and Silas agreed.

"How are you coping?" said Tarrant, and that was so unexpected it stopped Silas cold. Tarrant had to prompt him again.

"Not so good," he said, finally. "The rules these people play by have changed, somehow. There's an overseas influence in the mix, and I'm finding local crims who are bolder than I've ever seen before. I wouldn't be surprised if there were more deaths in this unholy mess."

There was silence at the other end of the line for a while.

"Yeah, well, Stodge's death was no accident," said Tarrant eventually, "and you think there might be more?" Silas told him how close it had come to violence when he was up on the plateau with Gummy the day before.

"Put in a report and we'll book the bastards!' said Tarrant. "Both of those idiots would get a stretch inside for that, this isn't a country where the public carry handguns!"

"I don't think that would help," said Silas. "It would just drive the organization further underground. They're very confident about what they're doing right now, and I have to encourage that. I'll wait until they make a major mistake, so I can bring in all the top figures in one go.

"But that's not what's bothering me," he said flatly, and Silas took a while to find the words.

"It could be my family that gets hurt," he said. "It could be friends, and it could be you. That's never been a real possibility before, Dave, and it's hard to deal with. This feels personal."

"Your job is to find out what you can and help us put these ratbags away, Silas," said Tarrant. "We've always known in our job that there could be casualties, but we can't pick and choose who gets hurt.

"Those dear to us, or those dear to someone else, it's all the same. People trying to live normal lives need saving from the greed and stupidity of others. Do you want the cop who could save one of yours to sit on his hands because his friends or family might be in danger?"

No, said Silas, he did not.

"Thanks, Dave," he said quietly. "Sometimes it's hard out here on my own, sometimes I'm not sure who I'm supposed to be."

"You don't stop being a cop when you resign, you idiot," said Tarrant, and Silas had to smile. He thanked Tarrant for digging up the info on the two 'security guards', and rang off. Then he put the cell phone back in his pocket and relayed the conversation to Annabel, who was sitting beside him. They were sipping tea on the couch at her place. When he had finished, she turned to him and echoed Tarrant's words.

"It's a numbers game, Silas," she said. "A few good people suffer so that a lot of bad people get put away. It's the only way we know how to stop the criminal underbelly of our society intruding into the lives of ordinary people."

Silas nodded. That much he could understand.

"Let's get moving," he said. "We should be at Gords' place by now." It was past eight in the evening, and minutes later they were in Silas' Outlander and driving through Hamilton toward Gords' flat.

Gords, and his flatmates Simon and Dianne, were under house arrest. They wore tracking bracelets and were allowed to travel to work or study, and come home again, and visit one designated supermarket on the way. That was it.

"Anything new from Tracey Donovan?" said Silas, when he and Annabel were sitting with Gords at the kitchen table.

"Nothing," said Gords, putting down a cup of tea. "The situation's much the same. She's hopeful the judge will agree with you that the drugs were too poorly hidden, and had to be planted. The fact that none of us in the flat have a previous conviction is a bonus.

"She has to argue the opposite point of view, of course, being the prosecutor, but she can see both sides."

Then Silas told Gords about the trip up onto the plateau, adding what he'd learned about the security guards. He didn't mention Tarrant's involvement, or the fact he appeared to have the unofficial blessing of Flynn. Annabel was the only person who knew that.

Silas had often told Gords about the cases he was working on, at least what he thought the boy could handle as he grew up. But it was the first time he didn't leave any of the unpleasant bits out.

"These people will do whatever they have to do to protect their secrets, won't they?" said Gords, and Silas nodded. His adopted son had nailed it in one. That's what happened when you had an investigative officer as a father for most of your life.

"So you're in real danger now," he added, and Silas nodded again.

"But you have to do this because you're the police," said Gords.

"Ex police," said Silas, "but yes, somehow this one has fallen to me to deal with, and I can't walk away from it."

"And no one else can do it," persisted Gords. Silas confirmed that unfortunately, that was about the truth of it. Gords thought about the situation for a bit, and then he nodded to himself.

"You come back alive," he said, "or Annabel and I will go down to the cemetery every day and spit on your grave!"

Silas didn't know whether to laugh or cry. Annabel knew which was best, and she was crying. "What Gords said," she managed at last, and punched him on the arm, hard.

Chapter 24

Silas got up from taking some notes about the case to stretch his legs, and decided he needed a cup of coffee. He was at the sink, pouring water into the jug, when he heard the growl of a powerful engine. Moments later a car rolled into the courtyard by the back door of his restored villa.

He wandered out onto the porch to see Stephen Foy climbing the steps. Foy had that same cloak and dagger smile Silas hadn't liked when the police car stopped him on the way home from Rotorua.

"Beautiful day, previously Senior Constable Chambers," said Foy, and Silas sensed the same 'off' feeling he had detected about the man on their first meeting.

"What brings you to The Pines?" said Silas, making sure he kept his voice cordial. He had actually named his property 'The Pines' at one stage, but he hadn't replaced the slab of macrocarpa at the start of his drive when it rotted away.

That sort of ostentation was a young man's game. His seventy acres of radiata pine trees still surrounded the house and its grounds though, so it was a fair way to name the place.

"McCabe would like a word with you," said Foy, still smiling like he was doing Silas a favour.

McCabe would know by now that Silas had tricked Huxton's two goons, and Silas figured neither Huxton nor McCabe would be happy about that. Technically, Silas and Gummy had been trespassing, and McCabe would want to make a song and dance about that. He figured it was best to go along with the lawyer's invitation though. He didn't need to make waves about this when his time was better spent on his investigation.

"Be right there," he said, and disappeared back inside.

Foy looked around the courtyard. The far side of it looked like someone was halfway through a building project. It was actually more like an assault course. Silas had started running every morning, and the equipment stretched around his yard was his version of the police physical competency test. But Foy didn't recognize what he was looking at.

"I'll follow you in," said Silas, and Foy waved at the patrol car. "McCabe said to bring you with me," he said.

I'm sure he did, thought Silas. He would want to remind me who has the power around here. A chauffeur could so easily become a jailer.

"I've got some business in Tokoroa," he said. "I'll need my car to bring a few things home."

Foy's face fell, and Silas could see that McCabe had laboured the point with the probationary constable. He could imagine McCabe saying: bring Chambers in the damn patrol car! Show him who's boss!

The interesting question, of course, was why Foy was doing McCabe's bidding. Maybe Flynn had authorized Foy's trip to keep the peace with McCabe, at least until Silas could get more evidence of what McCabe and Huxton were up to. Maybe not.

Fifteen minutes later, both vehicles were parked outside McCabe's legal chambers.

"My client is unhappy, Mr Chambers," said Julian McCabe, once they were both seated. Foy was standing to attention in front of the door to the office, which was a twist Silas had not foreseen.

"Mr Huxton is not at all impressed with your little stunt, and I'm afraid he has asked me to do something about it," continued the lawyer.

"Out of respect for your distinguished past, I have talked him down from pressing charges of impersonating a police officer, and I hope you appreciate that."

Silas' eyebrows rose. Of the times he had impersonated – well, suggested by omission – that he was a police officer, walking the plateau to get a look at Huxton's ranch wasn't one of them.

"I'd like to see you make that stick," he said calmly. "It's two against two and I'd say Huxton's security men aren't reliable witnesses."

A look of annoyance crossed McCabe's features, carefully smoothed over a moment later.

"On top of that, you and your associate were trespassing," he continued, "and I have the trespass notice here." McCabe tapped a neat document, folded in three on his desk, for emphasis.

Silas said nothing. If he and Gummy 'offended' again the maximum penalty was a thousand dollar fine or three months in prison. For a first offence he figured maybe five hundred bucks and that would be it. It wasn't going to deter him.

"Look, Silas," said McCabe, spreading his hands in a gesture of bonhomie. "We all know how this works. People push too hard and things go wrong, maybe there's an unfortunate death or two. Eventually those people get a little shake-up, and they return to more civilized ways.

"What if I could assure you nothing else is going to happen in this area that might concern you? No more deaths, and the hard-working people of Tokoroa and Tawhiti can sleep easily in their beds. Isn't that what you want?"

Silas was intrigued. Had Huxton authorized McCabe to make this offer? Was the lawyer really saying the criminal element had learned their lesson, they would be 'good' now? As long as Silas let them go back to skimming profits off the lives of ordinary people?

It wasn't something Silas would agree to under any conditions, but especially not when he knew that McCabe controlled Assoulin, and Assoulin had killed both Ella Brekken and probably Ernest Graham. He just needed to prove it had been Assoulin, and then the connection to McCabe.

"It would be worth your while to be on board with this," said McCabe smoothly. "Nothing as crass as money, of course, but your way could be made smooth, your voice could be important in this town."

No, thought Silas, nothing as crass as money. When the devil bargained for your soul, he didn't want you to feel cheapened by the deal.

"Nothing doing, McCabe," said Silas. "Your 'client' is up to something a long way outside the law, and I'm going to find out what it is."

McCabe shrugged. "Just remember," he said, "I made you the offer. No more people need to die.

"How are you going to feel if someone else has an accident, and you know you could have prevented that? Maybe even someone close to you."

"Are you threatening me?" said Silas, moving in his chair so he could get his hands around McCabe's throat in a hurry if he needed to."

"Tut, tut, Mr Chambers," said McCabe, noting the movement, "violence is not the answer, particularly not in front of Constable Foy."

"Probationary Constable Foy," said Silas, the policeman in him wanting to get it right.

"Ah, no, Mr Chambers," said Foy's voice from behind him, "my full appointment as an enforcement officer came through last week."

"Fast-tracked, you see," said McCabe with a smile. "The least I could do for my nephew, don't you think? And I can do things for you as well, Silas, just think about it.

"I've got big plans for this town, and you can be for me or against me, it's up to you. Come on, man, why not join the winning side?"

Silas felt sick. McCabe thought he was the centre of the world. He had no emotional connection to anyone else, and he certainly felt nothing for the pain of other human beings. He would, indeed, sell his own grandmother for sixpence.

Silas wondered if Billingham had cut Foy's probationary period short. Flynn had said that McCabe had closed down the Ella Brekken case, not Billingham, but that didn't mean Billingham wasn't bent. It was clear that McCabe wanted Silas to know his power extended everywhere, even into the police force. Silas had a momentary vision of tentacles spreading out in all directions, ripping and tearing.

"I think we're wasting our time here," he said, rising from his chair. "I'll be going now, unless your lap dog wants to try and stop me."

A look of annoyance flickered over Foy's features, but then it was gone. He had learned that from the master, thought Silas. I wonder if pyschopathology has been linked to genetics yet?

"Remember, it was your choice, Silas," said McCabe, and lifted the trespass notice so he could let it fall back onto the desk. "Trespass notice has been served."

Silas left his Outlander outside McCabe's offices and walked into the centre of town. He hadn't had his morning coffee yet, but mostly he just needed to walk off some steam.

It was time to ramp things up. He needed to take the fight to Huxton and his criminal organization, and for that he was going to need Tarrant's help.

Chapter 25

"There was nothing about Stodge's disappearance that the coroner's office thought had any connection to the Huxton place," said Tarrant, "but I kept digging. You taught me how to do that!"

Silas smiled at the recollection of their early days together. Not that Tarrant could see a smile on the other end of a phone call.

"You sure you're leaving no electronic tracks?" he said, concerned that someone might stumble onto the fact that Tarrant was helping him with his inquiries.

"I'm using a Skype account through an ancient computer in my garage, sound only," said Tarrant. "That's the best I can do. I can always say I dumped the computer years ago and don't know where it is now."

Silas nodded to himself. It was enough to protect Tarrant from a police audit, though maybe not from a full investigation.

"In the end I put aside three cases from the last six months," said Tarrant, continuing his report. "The first was a helicopter crash on the lower slopes of the Huxton property. I thought the helicopter might have been bringing in drugs, or people essential to Huxton's operation that he didn't want to be seen entering the property. Then I found a photo of the accident site and the chopper was clearly rigged for spraying.

"The second was the death of a middle-aged man on a property less than a kilometre from Huxton's place, but the coroner's report said he died from some type of early-onset heart disease.

"The last one doesn't seem to be much better. A hunter was mistaken for a deer and shot by another hunter, though the shooter took off and has never been found. The killing took place up on the plateau, but it was several kilometres away from the Huxton place."

"That's the one I want," said Silas, all his senses tingling. "Did the firing team do an analysis of the bullet?"

"Two bullets, actually," said Tarrant, "and both were high-powered 22 calibre."

"Don't you think that's odd?" said Silas, and Tarrant grunted an affirmative.

No one went hunting a large animal like a deer with small calibre bullets. It was much more likely that the person who fired the shots was a weekend sportsman after goats or rabbits. The problem with that scenario was the middle of the plateau was a long way from a public road. It was too far to tramp in unless a hunter expected a deer at the end of it.

"No one questioned the size of the bullets?" said Silas.

"They did," said Tarrant, "but who's got time to check all the 22 rifles within a reasonable travelling distance of the accident, or tramp the top of the plateau looking for evidence?"

Silas was annoyed that the investigative team on the Rotorua side had let it go at that. It would have been difficult to follow up, but if he had been the officer in charge he would have taken the investigation further.

One thing was clear to him though, and it was the fact that Huxton's security guards had made a serious mistake. Bored with their placement in the middle of nowhere, they had brought in a high-powered 22 rifle, probably semi-automatic, definitely fitted with a telescopic sight, to shoot at targets and small game.

When the now deceased hunter had seen something he shouldn't have, it was the only long-distance weapon the guards had to bring him down. Silas wondered how that had played out. The hunter must have realized he was being followed. Was it a game of cat and mouse that the man had lost?

It wouldn't have taken much to move the body to another part of the plateau, using the guards' off-road vehicle.

"The widow said her husband hunted up on the tops all the time," continued Tarrant, "and that day was just another hunting trip. He often went up there alone like that, and he didn't have any enemies that she knew of.

"Oh, and she was insured against his death," he continued. "Something about protecting the future of their two children. She got a good pay out."

"That was what I wanted to hear!" said Silas sharply. "I bet she held back part of the story from the police, because she thinks it might jeopardize her lump sum from the insurance company. I would say she knows a lot more about what really happened.

Tarrant was silent for a while. Then he said he hadn't thought of it like that, and passed over the widow's contact details.

"There's one more thing," he said. "It saddens me to say this, but you were right about Foy. You told me he was working for McCabe on the side, and I couldn't believe he had been bought, body and soul. He looked like one of the better ones we've had join the police lately.

"But he warned me off helping you yesterday. Just bowled up to my desk and came out with it. Didn't mind if other people overheard him.

"He told me you had gone off the rails, that you were obsessed about something or other and didn't have any evidence for it, and you were ringing people looking for sympathy. I told him you hadn't rung me, and he seemed okay about letting it go at that.

"I sent him to you with that message about Assoulin dropping out of sight in Auckland – back when I trusted him – but since then I've had no reason to mention you. I've been covering my tracks when we talk lately, particularly now the situation has got more serious."

Silas was glad of that. It also made him think about the people in his life he might have to protect. He would need to have an escape plan in place for Mereana and Eli, and Annabel and Gords, and anyone else Huxton and McCabe might target. How could he work out a plan that covered them all?

"I've got everything I need from you at the moment, Dave," he said. "I just need to assemble the pieces in the right order, and then shake the trees to see what falls out of them.

"I have really appreciated your help in all this, but it makes sense to keep radio silence from now on."

Tarrant understood. 'Radio silence' was the old wartime signal that the enemy was very close.

"Why don't you write up a report for the police so we can bring some of these characters in?" he said, on impulse. "That would give us a chance to work on them in our own time, and we might get a few to implicate others."

Silas had thought about doing that, but a sweep at this stage would only bring in minor players. Some of them would get jail time, but he was nowhere near those at the top of the organization yet. It was clear that

Assoulin had killed Ella Brekken, and probably Stodge, but Silas didn't know why McCabe was protecting him, or what Huxton had to do with it.

Was the American just a passive investor, while McCabe worked his client's millions through property and second mortgages to make them both rich? Silas figured that was far too slow a way for an ambitious man like McCabe.

"So, what are you going to do now?" asked Tarrant, and Silas brought his mind back to the conversation.

"I'm going to find out what this latest victim saw that got him killed with 22 bullets," he said, "and I'm betting his widow wants to unburden her conscience to someone. As long as I can convince her it won't affect her insurance pay out."

Tarrant laughed. "You were always better at that sort of delicate stuff than I was," he said. "I'm too much of a 'by the book' man. I hope talking to her leads you somewhere useful!"

Tarrant rang off, and Silas sat down at his computer so he could pull up a Google maps image. The widow lived in Rotorua now, and he figured she had moved there soon after her husband was shot. He memorized the route to her house and thought about what he was going to say.

Silas was feeling good about the meeting. He was getting tired of dead ends, and this woman's story might be the breakthrough he needed.

Chapter 26

Leonora Boss opened the door on the second chime, and Silas still had his finger on the doorbell. He smiled at the sturdy farm woman in front of him, and told her his name. She nodded, and invited him inside.

"I'm sorry to bring this up again for you," said Silas, as they settled themselves in the living room.

He had told her the reason for his visit on the phone. He was the investigating officer at the still unsolved murder of Ella Brekken – which Leonora remembered from the newspapers – but was now retired from the police force. What concerned him were the similarities between that earlier case and a recent death in Tawhiti, and now the death of Leonora's husband, Jakob Boss.

He had told her he was acting in an advisory capacity only, under the oversight of Inspector Matthew Flynn at Tokoroa Police Station. McCabe would have a field day with that claim, if he ever found out about it, no matter how Silas spun it. It was a risk, but the retired policeman needed to take some risks at this stage of the investigation.

"I don't know what more I can tell you," she said. "Everything I can remember is in the notes that were kept from my police interview."

Silas assured her that her time in the interview room had been appreciated, and her description of events had been very helpful.

Then he guided the conversation briefly onto family history, and found that Jakob was a second generation Swiss and Leonora had been a Watkins before her marriage. Their daughter was at university, and their boy would one day be able to purchase his first farm with the help of Jakob's life insurance pay out.

Silas knew that a lot of Swiss immigrants had settled in New Zealand, and true to their homeland it had mostly been where there were mountains, or at least decent-sized hills. The Boss family had sold a large dairy farm and moved to a small run-off property the year before Jakob was killed. Now Leonora was in Rotorua, closer to her son.

"There is something that I want you to know," said Silas, choosing his words with care.

It was important Leonora know how sensitive he felt this matter to be, because he was laying a foundation for the conversation that was to come.

"I understand you were with Safeguard Insurance," he continued, and she nodded. "Good," said Silas, "they're a fairly straight-shooting bunch. Some companies will try to claw back a payment if they find a minor clause in the contract that allows them to do so.

"What I'm trying to say," and here he slowed his voice, "is that there is no reason to involve the insurance company in my current investigation. I understand your concern about that, and I can give you a promise there will be nothing in my report of interest to Safeguard, or that might affect their payment to you."

She visibly relaxed at that.

"Thank you," she said, and she meant it. Then she paused.

"Though I'm not sure I can add anything to what was said in the first interview," she continued, "even if it's not going to be reported to the insurance company."

"Don't worry, that's my job," said Silas, with a smile. "If you don't mind me asking a few more questions, that is."

She shrugged. That would be fine, since he was here and all.

"Tea?" she said, and Silas nodded gratefully. That was another part of a successful interview, particularly when there were no clear lines of inquiry. Sharing something as basic as food or drink established a familiarity.

"Tell me the things that would send Jakob up onto the tops after deer," he said, when she got back. "The weather perhaps, or a tip-off from another hunter, or maybe an empty freezer?"

Leonora laughed at the mention of an empty freezer.

"Nothing like that," she said. "It was always a random thing, depending mostly on whether hinds had fawns at that time, whether the roar was on, or whether the last hunt had been successful. Sometimes he went hunting out of wounded pride, I think!"

Silas smiled at the comment. He kept asking about small details, right down to whether Jakob wore the same cap every time he went hunting, and what sort of sandwiches he was likely to take.

"There was one thing," she said, and her brow furrowed in thought. "I didn't think anything of it at the time, but the last three or four hunting trips were always right on the new moon."

She reconsidered. "No, that's not right," she said, "some were a few days after the new moon. Well, they were all on or shortly after the new moon for a while. At least they were until," and her voice caught, grief claiming her again as she realized that he would never be coming home to greet her. "Until he was killed on the tops," she finished bravely.

Silas waited respectfully for her to continue.

"We had a vegetable garden by the house," she said after a while, "and I was experimenting with planting by the phases of the moon. That's how I can remember that."

Silas tucked the information away with a few other snippets Leonora had told him, and they were all things that weren't in the original police file. He didn't know how to use the information yet, but he might after it had rolled around inside his head for a while.

Shortly after the tea was finished he decided to call it a day. Leonora had given him everything she could think of, and she had been able to cast her mind over the events in a relaxed manner. That made it a successful interview, as far as Silas was concerned.

He was in the Outlander, driving home, when he started thinking about Jakob's death. Stodge had been driven to reckless things by the thought of money that would get his niece's face restored, but what had pushed Jakob into dangerous territory?

Silas could imagine how it had happened. Jakob would have been warned off the Huxton property, and that would have incensed him. The older hunters knew the farmers around the edge of the plateau, and they were free to come and go as long as they dropped off a few back steaks, or a leg, to the farmer occasionally.

Jakob would have sworn that no 'foreigner' was going to rob him of his rights, entirely missing the irony of his Swiss ancestry, but in this he was not alone. To the older people at least, New Zealand was a land of equals where no one set themselves above others. Kiwis were unusual in that way. They were the most helpful, and sometimes the most pig-headed, people in the world.

Different points of view would have become arguments, decided Silas, and arguments would have led to push and shove with the security guards. Then Jakob was running for his life in a gun battle he never expected would happen.

Such a thing was unheard of in New Zealand, but the murder rate in the States, along with the low clearance rate, allowed a lot of crimes to pass unnoticed. Messrs Trafford and Stuart were about to find out just how different things were in New Zealand though.

Back in Rotorua, Leonora had cleaned the tea cups and put everything away, but she couldn't put off an unpleasant task any longer. She picked up the telephone, and then put it down again.

She was troubled. Silas had been professional, charming even, and certainly not evil. Not the picture McCabe had painted of him, and shouldn't an important man like a lawyer be right about these things? Julian McCabe had told her how believable men like Silas Chambers were, like any good con man.

But if Leonora couldn't tell if a man was a good person when she spent time with one, did that mean she was no better than a con man herself? She had believed Silas. He was trying to bring a murderer to justice, a murderer who had killed several times and might have had something to do with her husband's death.

On the other hand, a deal was a deal.

Not knowing why she felt so strongly that it was wrong, she phoned the number McCabe had given her. When his secretary answered, she mentioned that McCabe had done her a favour once – as the lawyer had instructed her to do – and the secretary put her straight through. Leonora wondered how often calls like this came into his office.

"Mr Chambers came to see me this afternoon," she said, when McCabe answered. "You said that he might."

McCabe was reassuring. He had been expecting this.

"He kept asking questions," she continued, "but what could I say? The account of events that I gave you, and the police, is the truth. My Jakob went hunting on the plateau about five in the morning. According to the coroner, he was dead by ten am, and the police haven't yet found out who did it, and he didn't have any enemies that I knew of."

She let a small tear slide down her face, and her voice changed to accommodate her grief. "In the end Mr Chambers left."

McCabe gave her time to recover, and then asked a question.

"Oh, he left about half an hour ago," she said.

"I want to thank you again for paying for the funeral," continued Leonora, "and for easing my daughter's way into her course at university. It was a miracle that Massey found an extra place for her.

"No, that's all right," she concluded. "Glad to be of help."

Then the conversation was over.

Leonora sat down, and wondered what she was turning into, now that Jakob was gone. Not all of it was bad, she decided. She had kept faith with Silas Chambers revealing a few inconsequential things that no one else knew, and she had kept faith with McCabe by ringing him as she had promised.

She was turning into a politician, and she hated politicians. Then she smiled. She hoped that the nice Mr Chambers had got whatever it was he wanted from their little talk.

Chapter 27

Later that evening Annabel was ready to agree with Leonora that Silas was nice. In fact she was thinking he was absolutely scrumptious, as she eyed his bare chest with a slowly rekindling interest.

He had told her some time ago about his half-hour run each day, and the activities in his courtyard that were equivalent to the police competency test. Now his muscles were firming up, and she didn't mind that at all – not that the relationship depended on the state of Silas' muscles!

The two of them had been talking about safe places over dinner. What Annabel should do if she became a target for Huxton and his security guards, or Assoulin and his two Devil's Outlaw henchmen, or even some trumped up charge McCabe tried to bring against her.

None of it was likely, and the preparations they were putting in place probably wouldn't be needed, but if Silas slipped the word 'basement' into his conversation – maybe because someone was listening to his phone call and he didn't want to be more specific – she was to pack a bag for a few days and head for Gords' flat. She could go to work from there, and work should remain a safe place.

Gords was a fit young man, and nobody's fool. Simon had a blue belt in something or other, and their flatmate Dianne had thought the arrangement was a good idea. After being falsely accused of dealing drugs, the three of them were growing up fast. Annabel, with her greater age and medical background, would be the brains of the outfit.

Silas had impressed upon them the need to use their problem-solving abilities, rather than going for a weapon. Bullies made stupid mistakes when they thought their prey was defenceless. It was better to use a distraction, and put another door between you and them, than try to battle it out. They had also agreed to call the police at the first sign of anything unusual, and been coached in exactly what to say to get a rapid response.

It had taken a while for Silas to convince Annabel that he shouldn't carry a weapon in his investigations either. Apart from the difficulty of getting hold of a handgun in New Zealand – though Silas knew people who would loan him a shotgun or hunting rifle – carrying a weapon changed the rules of the game. It made people think they could shoot you in cold blood, and Silas would trust his years of experience over firepower any day.

Mereana and Eli would also head for Gords' flat if the situation was bad enough for Annabel to take refuge there, and Gords was in the process of storing supplies for at least a week. Gummy had refused to shift from his house among the pine trees, but he wasn't sleeping inside any longer. He had finally agreed he would only shoot intruders in the leg, to Silas' great relief.

It all seemed like science-fiction, at least it did in New Zealand, but Annabel believed in being prepared. She was also discovering the link between danger and sex. Ever since Silas had got so serious at the start of the evening, and outlined in no uncertain terms the risks he was taking – and that meant those associated with him was taking – she had wanted to bed him.

Now she did so, again.

"Tell me why you can't go to Flynn with the information you've already got," she said, as she rested beside him half an hour later.

"It won't prove who killed Stodge, or Ella Brekken," he said, "and that's the main reason I'm doing this. Besides, Flynn can't act on an unsubstantiated tip-off from a member of the public, and technically that's all I am now. Deciding whether to take action or not gets political at inspector level."

She sighed. "So you have to battle on by yourself," she said, annoyed by the state of affairs.

"No," he said, "I've got you, and Gords, and Mereana, and so many good people with me."

She grunted at that. He assumed it was an affirmative grunt.

"You've faced death, Silas," she said, suddenly. "What do you think a person feels like at the end of their life?"

Silas was surprised by the change of topic.

"Ah, you're the nurse, you tell me," he said.

"It's not the same when people are expecting to die," she said. "Not when there are doctors and nurses around. What about when someone is on their own, and they're up against it, and they might or might not make it?"

Silas thought about that for a while, and then he had to confess he didn't know the answer. "Facing death is one thing," he said, "but knowing you're going to die is another. Police face death often – some things can get out of hand really quickly – but the idea of death doesn't have much weight. I guess, deep down, we all think we'll get out of the situation somehow."

There was a moment's silence while she thought about it.

"Oh," she said, "I see what you mean. We're all hopeful of a miracle. It's just that I would really like to know. If I'm with them, as their nurse, people seem to be okay with their death, but there are many more who die suddenly and alone. I would like to know how they get on."

"Can't help you there," said Silas, "though I think it's okay. I'll let you know if I ever find out. Is that enough?"

"I guess so," she said sleepily.

Silas was silent for a while. He knew he should tell her what he felt about their relationship. Let her know he wanted to be with her through thick and thin, whatever happened in the days ahead.

"Um, Annabel," he began, and she stretched a hand up towards his face, and felt around until she could press a finger against his lips.

"Not now," she said, and Silas almost laughed. Was he that transparent? Then he felt her body relax as she dropped off to sleep, and he was alone with his thoughts.

Most of them were about getting back on the plateau. The next new moon was three days away, and then Gummy had been adamant Silas wasn't going up onto the tops at night by himself.

The old man had been quite indignant about Silas' attempt to get him to stand down. To tell the truth he would be glad of the company. It helped that Gummy was right about one thing too. Silas was very likely to lose his way on the plateau in the dark, since he wouldn't be advertising his presence with lights.

Silas wasn't sure what he felt about the situation as it stood now. It was getting complex, but pushing on with the investigation was something he had to do, and once it was underway his training took over.

He hoped there would be some answers up on the plateau. What was Huxton up to, and why would McCabe take such risks to help him. In the meantime, he had decided, a visit to Huxton's house might bear some fruit.

Chapter 28

The Outlander climbed up the long drive to Aldous and Irena Huxton's double-storied mansion, and Silas was driving through a large paddock that had the look of a lawn about it. It was either mowed regularly with an industrial-sized machine, or managed well with sheep. The building didn't look right among New Zealand's green hills, but it would have fitted right in among the homes of the rich and famous in California.

According to council records, Huxton and his wife had bought the property a little over eighteen months ago. That hadn't given them time to build the mansion from scratch. The man must have shopped online until he found exactly what he wanted.

The second story, with the wide balcony along the front, made Silas nervous. A good sniper could take him out with one shot, even while the Outlander was moving. What kept him relaxed was the fact that Huxton didn't know he was coming.

There was a loop at the end of the road, in front of the house, and some parking on the far side of it. Silas chose the parking. He couldn't see security cameras, which he'd been expecting to see, but it would be prudent to act as if they were there.

"Mr Chambers, to see Mr Huxton," he said, when some sort of housemaid answered the front door. Where did anybody get a fifties maid's outfit like that, and why was she being told to wear it?

The maid hesitated, and Silas dusted off his reason for coming to see Huxton, the one he would use if the direct approach didn't work. But she wasn't hesitating because Huxton wasn't taking callers.

"You're the police officer that looked into the case when my brother died," she said at last. "I could tell straight away that I knew you from somewhere!"

It took Silas another few seconds to recognize the woman as well. He had a good memory for faces but it had been five years, and the maid outfit had distracted him.

"Yes," he said. "He was a Hope, ah, Brydon Hope wasn't it?"

She nodded. "I'm sorry I don't remember your name," Silas added, and she told him to call her Summer.

"We were so pleased when you were able to show us that there was no foul play involved," she said. "That was a turning point for the whole family. We could let Brydon's death go once we knew it was an accident."

Silas smiled. He often brought good news, and sometimes had to deliver bad news, and he was remembered for both. A young man dying in a fall from the upper storage level of a barn had needed a full coroner's report, and Silas had been brought in as the investigative officer.

"Do you want to speak to Mr Huxton, or Mrs Huxton?" said Summer. "Or perhaps both?"

Silas was trying to work out what course of action would be best. It might be good to talk to the Huxtons together, and get Aldous' reactions to the questions when his wife was present, but he didn't get a chance to say that.

Summer leaned forward and whispered, "Except Mrs Huxton is having one of her headaches again. She won't be available if I ask for her. The poor woman seems to suffer from anxiety an awful lot. Either that or depression."

Silas' ears pricked up. It was sometimes the case that a wife didn't approve of her husband's criminal activities, but was too deeply embedded to see a way out. Maybe that was the case here.

"Then just Mr Huxton, if that's okay," he said. "Tell him it's about Mr Graham's death." It was always a good idea to bait the line he was dangling in front of his target.

Summer was back shortly with a very stern looking man. Silas had memorized a recent photograph of Aldous Huxton, and this wasn't him. He also noticed that Summer's attitude had changed. She was an employee now. She stood with eyes downcast, trained not to speak unless spoken too.

"Thomas Creel," said the man, not extending his hand for Silas to shake. "I'm the estate manager. What's this all about?"

His accent had the clipped vowels of the middle part of the east coast of the United States, somewhere near the place one of the security guards had come from.

"An Ernest Graham tried to get money out of Mr Huxton," said Silas, without preamble, "and now he's dead. It's a routine inquiry."

"And you are?" said Creel.

"A retired police officer," said Silas, "working on my own. Ernest was a friend of mine."

"Shouldn't the police be dealing with this?" said Creel, and Silas could see that the estate manager was getting ready to send him packing.

"They could do," said Silas, "but they don't know about the blackmail attempt. We can sort this out now, and Mr Huxton can avoid unwanted attention while Ernest keeps his good name, or I can take what I know to an investigative team at the police station."

He didn't raise his voice, and he didn't threaten. This wasn't a pissing contest, he just needed to get past Creel so he could talk to Huxton, and it didn't take long for the manager to reach a decision.

"Come this way," he said, and Silas followed. He was left waiting in some sort of conservatory off the entrance chamber, and it took a few minutes until he returned with Huxton in tow. There was no sign of the security guards. Maybe they were on their way down from the cottage on the top of the plateau.

Creel stayed in the room, and Silas had been expecting that. There was an ominous silence, and he took the opportunity to sit in one of the chairs by the wall of windows along one side of the room, unasked, and put his cell phone on the table.

"Get comfortable, gentlemen," he said, "we're going to have a little talk. If I don't ring a number in my cell phone in an hour's time, this location will go out to a number of people.

"Some of them are in the police force, and some are not. If I were you, I would worry about the hunters who've lost a good mate and want to know which bastard shot him twice with a 22."

Creel looked at Huxton, and then nodded. Silas was surprised that Huxton didn't give the orders, and filed that away for later examination. When the others had also taken a seat, he continued with a question.

"Mr Graham said that he had seen something on your property, Mr Huxton, and demanded a certain sum to keep quiet about it. Did this matter come to your attention?"

Huxton was looking like he would give anything to be somewhere else right now, and his nervousness was increasing with every word Silas uttered. It wasn't the actions of a crime boss, and certainly not what Silas had been expecting. Then Creel cut in.

"Mr Graham's wild demands for money were directed to me, as the estate manager. Mr Huxton knows nothing about them.

"Mr Graham claimed there were cannabis plants growing inside an animal-proof cage hidden in native forest on Mr Huxton's property. I made agreeable noises in the beginning, so I could find the location or locations of the plants. Once I knew where they were my staff were able to remove the plants and destroy the cages, which has now been done.

"Such plots are so common along the edges of the plateau I didn't bother to contact the police. As to what happened to Mr Graham, I don't read the local papers, and I'm sorry to hear that he has, apparently, been killed. I wondered why he had stopped contacting me."

Smooth, thought Silas. A good cover story. But he was more interested in other things right now. It was clear Huxton wasn't the kingpin in the organization, so who the hell was?

He didn't think it was Creel. The slippery bastard was more like a well-paid accountant, another like McCabe who didn't mind what he had to do as long as he got the right amount of money for doing it.

There was little more to be learned here though, and Silas decided to wrap up the meeting, short though it had been. His ploy with the cell phone should get him out of the house safely, but he didn't want to push his luck. It would be wise to let them think he'd bought Creel's story.

"Your explanation ties in with what Mr Graham's sister told me," he admitted. "Not that she knew the details of his attempt to blackmail you, but she did confide that he was becoming more unsettled, and a lot more foolish, as he got older. Past glories and old men, you know how it can be.

"At least the family will never know the truth about his unfortunate attempt to blackmail you, Mr Huxton," he continued. "Though his death looks like it will remain a mystery.

"His sister lives in Dunedin, and I'm sure she will be happy to let the matter drop now it has been clarified."

"We're glad to hear that," said Creel, as he stood. "Now, if you will excuse us, this is a large estate and there are always matters that need our attention."

Silas was back at his car when Summer emerged from a side door, and beckoned him over. He figured she knew where the security cameras were, and he walked over into what he hoped was a blind spot. He accepted her thanks, once again, for his help when her brother died. Then, on a whim, he asked her a question.

"Are you expecting visitors to the house in a few days time?" and she looked surprised.

"How did you know that? There are always friends of Mr Huxton who drop by every month or so, and they disappear up to the top of the property after dinner. There's an old shearer's quarters up on the plateau. Maybe they go hunting, though I don't know anything about that. Sorry, hunting's not my thing."

It was interesting information, but Silas didn't want to get her into trouble. He shook her hand and said it was nice to meet a member of the Hope family again.

On the way back to Tawhiti he kept trying to fit the new facts he had just learned into the bigger picture, but he always ended up at the same place – who the hell was the big boss if it wasn't Huxton? He had no intention of providing evidence that would allow Flynn to put away minnows. There must be a way to decapitate the organization at the very top.

That left Silas with one last thing to think about. He had just painted a very large target sign on his back, and he needed to stay out of the line of fire for a while. Creel could be talking to the big boss right now, saying that Silas knew too much, and was asking too many questions.

Promising Creel that his investigation would go no further should have helped, but there was no guaranteeing his safety. At the very least, McCabe would now force the police to charge him with trespass. Fortunately, any date for that hearing would be weeks away, and Silas hoped to have cracked the case by then.

Chapter 29

The night of the full moon was two days after Silas visited the Huxton mansion. The evening would be clear with a light breeze, at least it would be according to the weather forecast. That was perfect.

Jakob had been up on the plateau every new moon in the last few months, or a day or two afterwards, according to his widow. Silas figured that meant the weather hadn't always been suitable on the first day of the new moon, or even the second, something Jakob must have figured out as well.

It was an interesting question. What would good weather on the night of a new moon be suitable for, if it was happening on top of the plateau? That could depend on any number of things, but now Silas had a location for the event. He had to be at the broad valley in the middle of the forest, the last piece of Huxton's ranch where it ran along the top of the plateau, on the first night of the new moon.

Two days later, late in the morning, he was getting ready.

"You gonna find it hard sleeping on a dirt floor," grumbled Gummy, as he checked through Silas' pack.

"We'll have to make you a bush bed," decided the old hunter, and headed for the back of his twin cab. Somewhere under the back seat he located a square of tightly woven plastic tarpaulin.

"Light, and waterproof," he told Silas, as he folded it down and stuffed it into the top of Silas' pack. "Better than a regular bed when it's full of mangimangi."

Silas didn't ask. He figured he would find out what mangimangi was when the time came.

"Looks like you got everything else though," said Gummy, and gave Silas the thumbs up.

Silas had been out on search and rescue missions a number of times during his police career, but Gummy had asked him to bring some unusual items for this mission. The old man clearly had everything worked out in his mind, and Silas was happy leaving the planning to him.

It was early afternoon when the twin cab reached the end of Forestry Road Number Three, the starting point of their last tramp across the plateau. An hour later they were closing in on the irregular patch of farmland that was the most isolated part of Huxton's farm.

"Now we take a detour," said Gummy quietly, and turned right, walking directly into a wall of undergrowth. Silas followed him as best as he could, but it was difficult to avoid getting caught up in branches.

Gummy looked at ease in the crowded undergrowth, and he must have done this sort of thing before. He forged ahead while Silas battled to keep up.

"Not far now," said Gummy, when he came back to see where Silas had got to after ten minutes. Another few paces and Gummy stopped in what appeared to be a random part of the forest.

"Trapping line," said Gummy, sounding pleased with himself. Silas looked around. He didn't see any difference in the dense undergrowth in any direction.

"Figured we had to avoid those 'no trespassing' signs, and that electrical jiggery-pokery," he added, and Silas nodded. They had discussed the importance of travelling in to the cottage undetected.

"Possum trappers cover a target area in tracks about 150 meters apart," said Gummy. "Then they place traps every hundred paces or so along the tracks. When the possum numbers get too low, the trappers move on to somewhere else. Maybe they come back to the same place after a few years. Or maybe someone else uses the old tracks. Having good access to set up saves a huge amount of time and energy."

He pointed to his left, and Silas saw what Gummy meant by a possum line. It was barely a track, but there was a daub of spray paint on a trunk further in.

"Bit overgrown," muttered Gummy, and pushed off in a new direction along the possum line. Silas had to admit it was easier than the 'bush bashing' that had got them to the spot, but not by much. An hour later they had moved a fair way south-east down the plateau, and come back north by a more open hunters' trail. Then they started to climb.

"This part of the plateau must have been compacted over time into a harder material than the rest of it," said Gummy, as the climb got steeper. "That's why it's still here, I guess."

Silas could see they were near the top of a low hill, higher than most points around them. A minute later the track ended in a small clearing, and he noticed signs of previous use. There was a ring of stones that had been used as a fire pit and improvised seats.

"This way," said Gummy, and pushed on into the windblown scrub near the top of the hill. Then he stepped left, and disappeared. Silas couldn't see where he'd gone, and it stopped him in his tracks. Then the bushes next to him parted, and Gummy pulled him through a gap in the vegetation. Silas stumbled as he took a step down a slope, and then he was at the entrance to a cave.

"Someone's storehouse," said Gummy. "Never figured out if it was excavated by Maori or early settlers."

He stopped to take a small torch out of his pack, and Silas dug around in his own pack. Once they were underway again, Gummy led him through a tunnel that branched several times. The old hunter never hesitated, and he seemed to have a map of the tunnels in his head. Eventually they arrived at a large underground room, with dappled light coming in through several vertical slits on the far side.

"Go and have a look," said Gummy, and Silas stepped across the room before peering out through the foliage. He was somewhere along the face of a small bluff above Huxton's farm. The cottage lay to their right, close to the edge of the open land, and the old airfield ran from left to right below them. It was a perfect lookout point.

"We set up camp here," said Gummy, "and then we sleep. This could be an all-nighter," and Silas grunted approval.

He had taken most of what he needed out of his pack when Gummy returned, with a large bundle of vegetation under one arm. It turned out to be made up of delicate vines with long leaves that he had rolled tightly into a bale. He dropped it beside the tarpaulin square that Silas had already unpacked.

"Mangimangi," he said. "Bushman's mattress. Fluff it up and wrap the tarp around it."

Silas set to work, and it didn't take him long to prepare his bedding. He looked at the time when he had finished, and it was three thirty in the afternoon. So it was time to take that nap. He settled down on his new mattress, knowing Gummy would wake him when it got dark.

Surprisingly, in the strange surroundings, he did doze off. Later he dreamed of V8 racing cars, something he had never seen, apart from on the sports news.

It seemed like no time at all until Gummy was rousing him. It was well past dusk though, he could tell that much by the darkness.

"Time to see whats we got," said the old hunter, shaking Silas by his shoulder. There was wind soughing through the scrub on the top of the hill, making it unlikely a conversation would be heard down on the farmland below.

"Got your spotter?" said Silas, once he was up. Gummy nodded, and picked up an old night scope, fitting it to his rifle. Silas dug in his pack for his night vision binoculars, borrowed from a friend at the police station who did a lot of surveillance. Without the binoculars, everything was a ghostly grey. With them, it was a much more detailed green.

Silas was ready to lay his eyes on the farmland outside, but first the two of them needed to eat and drink. There might not be time later, depending on what they discovered during the night. The meal consisted of water from a bottle and a filled roll. Using a gas cooker was too much of a risk.

When that was done they each took one of the cave 'windows', leaving the middle one vacant. The openings were like narrow tunnels, about a meter in length and just high enough to take a crouching figure. The two men trimmed away foliage from the outside where they needed to, so they had an unimpeded view of the airfield below. Then they put their scopes to good use.

Silas saw at once why he had dreamed of V8s. The bulldozer was gone, and so was the pile of rotting logs beside it. He found the bulky machine on the far side of the airfield, down in a hollow. The hay barn had disappeared, so that must have been on skids. He couldn't see where that had gone either.

The most surprising change was the disappearance of the three fence lines that had previously run across the air strip. The posts couldn't have been properly buried in the ground if they'd been removed in a few hours. Silas supposed it made sense. If the fences had to be taken out, and re-installed, on a regular basis, then some sort of dummy arrangement would be needed. Something to make the posts look normal at a distance, but easy to remove.

He looked to his right, and saw that the flat paddock beyond the airfield had been joined to the airfield. It added more than fifty percent to the length of the old topdressing strip, and Silas figured that any plane smaller than a civilian airliner could land there, if it wasn't fussy.

He was astounded at the extent of the operation.

"Plane, you reckon?" said Gummy, who had come to stand behind him. Silas agreed. He now had a location, and a method, but he still didn't have answers to a host of other questions.

What was the plane carrying? Where would it come from? How was the load paid for? And most importantly, how did the organization disburse the cargo across the country?

Chapter 30

The steady murmur of the wind through the scrub covered the sound of Silas and Gummy discussing the airfield. Most of the time the two men stayed vigilantly at their posts, but there was little to see or do for the first few hours. The narrow tunnels cramped muscles, while the night wore on with glacial slowness.

The workers' cottage to the right of the airfield remained in darkness, and Silas wondered if this was the night for the delivery after all. The airfield had been prepared that day, but there might have been a last minute change of plans.

It took him a while to work out what the lumps along each side of the runway were. They showed up on his night vision the same shade of green as the grass around them, which wasn't helpful. Then Silas got it. They were signal lights.

Each small cannon-shaped device pointed down the runway to Silas' left. When they were switched on an incoming plane would be able to see them, but only if the pilot was coming in on exactly the right flight path. Silas wasn't sure if the devices generated visible light, or some other part of the spectrum, but they wouldn't be seen by satellites overhead, or other aircraft.

Around ten thirty the sound of vehicles drifted up from Huxton's mansion, and Silas relaxed. Tonight was the right one after all. He and Gummy waited a little longer, until they could see headlights flicker on and off among the trees at the edge of the plateau. Then a small convoy descended the gravel track that led to the workers' cottage.

The vehicles stopped by the cottage, but the headlights stayed on. Two dark figures got out of one vehicle and disappeared into a shed behind the building. The dull growl of a generator started up, and the lights of the cottage came on shortly afterwards. Then the headlights went off.

Silas nodded to himself. The generator would also power the landing lights, but there were other problems too. This was a highly illegal operation, and the aircraft was hardly going to descend onto the runway with its lights on. That meant the pilot was instrument rated. It also meant he had a huge amount of flying experience, and pilots like that didn't come cheap.

Silas recognized most of the people leaving the vehicles as they climbed the steps to the cottage. His gut tightened as he recognized Assoulin, mostly from the way he walked. There were two others with him, and they had to be his Devil's Outlaws juniors. Creel was there, but Huxton seemed to be absent. Trafford and Stuart were last, and they had a swagger about them that annoyed Silas on principle.

Foy was present, and if Silas had any doubts of how deeply McCabe was mired in it all he lost them now. Foy would be keeping an eye on McCabe's 'investment'.

The cottage seemed to have been set up as one large room with a bunk room and bathroom at the far end. A small L-shape to one side of the larger room must be the kitchen, since a cowling-topped metal chimney came out of the roof. It was a typical workers' quarters, not intended for a long stay.

The lights were on in the one large room – several lights judging by the number of shadows each figure was throwing outside – and there were no curtains on the windows.

The figures had grouped themselves in the centre of the room, presumably around a table, and Silas figured a briefing of some sort was taking place. It was hard to figure out what was going on inside the building from the shadows on the grass outside.

"What do we do now?" said Gummy, and Silas realized the old hunter had come across to the slot he was occupying, and was squeezed in behind him.

"We try to get some evidence," he said automatically. His police training told him that a story was nothing without verification.

"How we gonna do that?" said Gummy, and Silas was thinking the same thing. The evidence he needed was on the table in the cottage. Unfortunately, the cottage was full of people who would do anything to stop him taking it, and two of them, at least, were armed. Silas looked at the time again. It was just after eleven.

"I think the drop will be at midnight," he said, and smiled at the cliched nature of the timing. Midnight, the time when all dark deeds were done, when the dead left their graves to walk among the living.

"I think they will turn the lights off in the cottage some time before the delivery," he said, giving his best guess. The generator sounded like a small one, and it would take a lot of power to work the signal lights. The pilot also wouldn't want to be distracted by lights from the cottage when he was limited to flying instruments only.

"So I've got maybe half an hour to get in there, while the lights are still on, and take some photos of whatever's on that table," he said. Then he checked his cell phone, and reassured himself it was fully charged. It was the only timepiece he had with him, and he would need it to take the photos.

As if in confirmation of his reasoning, the group in the middle of the room broke up and the shadows drifted apart. The two security guards came outside, and started to walk the perimeter, keeping to the furthermost reaches of the light from inside. More lights came on in the kitchen, and the bathroom, which reduced the number of people left by the table.

It hadn't reduced it enough, though. It was unlikely all of the occupants would be out of the main room at the same time, but Silas was thinking he should have a closer look at the situation. Maybe he could take photos through the windows, and they could be enlarged later to show something useful. But his big problem now was Gummy.

"I'm going down there," he said, "and I want you to keep an eye on things up here. If I'm discovered, I want you to head back to the twin cab and go straight to Constable Dave Tarrant. His number's in the phone book, and you know where he lives, right?"

Gummy nodded. "Not going to leave you though," he said stoutly, and Silas appreciated the loyalty. Unfortunately, it was misplaced here. Gummy was not a man easily able to understand the tactics involved, and it was ten minutes before Silas convinced him to do as he was asked.

Then Silas began his descent down the bush-covered bluff, the glow from the cottage coming up slowly ahead of him. It painted one side of the tree trunks a ghostly grey, and forced him to look away to preserve his night vision. He found a vantage point among the trees, slightly higher than the back of the building, and looked down into the main room.

Creel and Assoulin were standing at the table, looking at something on a map. The two security guards had settled in outside the front of the cottage, and the rest of the men were in the kitchen or the bunk room. There was a back door to the left of a large double window, and no one had used it yet as far as Silas had seen. He figured he could get up to the double window without the two men spotting him, and put the idea into action.

He moved further down the slope until he came to the edge of the trees, and set up his cell phone so he could point and shoot. He was about to move from the trees to the side of the building, coming in at an angle that was blind to the people inside, when he started getting flashbacks. A procession of still images flickered on and off across his vision, and a background roar built up until he could have sworn he was hearing words in it.

Not now, dammit! he growled under his breath.

Ever since Mereana had explained these strange events to him, he had feared them. But he soon discovered that they were different this time. The images slowed, and the roar in his ears settled to a steady hum. The sensory distractions were replaced by a feeling that he was safe. As long as he stayed exactly where he was, he would not be noticed by anything that wished him harm.

It was a conviction beyond reason, and he found he couldn't shake it off. Forcing himself to carry on with his original plan, he rose to a crouch and angled in toward the window, arriving to one side of it. And the feeling of safety continued, as strong as before.

Silas raised the cell phone toward the corner of the window, ready to take a shot of the interior, and every alarm imaginable went off in his head. He jerked his arm down and stayed where he was, crouching under the window. Cold sweat ran down under his arms. What on God's good earth was happening to him?

Chapter 31

Silas crouched at the corner of the window, trying to overcome the panic in his head. The alarm bells were something entirely new.

The images, and the roar in his ears, had something to do with Stodge, he knew that. Or Ernest if he preferred that name. Silas wondered idly which name the old Tawhiti identity had liked, or still liked. He heard Stodge laugh then, clear as if the old man was crouching beside him.

Then Silas discovered something new, an extension of his senses. He knew that to his left was safe, and in particular the back door was safe. Everywhere else was murky. He decided to follow the feeling of safety, and slid sideways toward the door. Then he began to feel panicky again, and the only safe place was through the door at the top of the steps. But that was madness, and then his brain was screaming at him to move.

Figuring that Gummy would get justice for whatever evil was about to befall him, Silas opened the door and slipped through. There was silence as he shut it quietly behind him, and the shouts of alarm he was expecting never materialized. Looking around, he saw that the room was empty, and the door to the bunk room was just closing behind a pair of heels.

A moment later voices sounded from the other side of the back door. Trafford and Stuart were on one of their perambulations around the cottage, and Silas had just escaped them. With his heart racing, he realized that he had to take advantage of the situation, and do it now. Two quick steps took him to the table, and he quartered the top of it in his mind, taking a quick photo of each section.

Silas had just finished when the alarm bells went off in his head again. It was like a physical blow this time, and it slapped him to the floor. He huddled against one of the wooden chairs beside the table, while one of the men passed from the bunk rooms to the kitchen on the other side. He knew the man was looking down at him, could see the top of his head and the slope of his shoulders, but somehow it wasn't registering in the onlooker's mind. It took him the greatest of efforts to keep still.

Then he was up and at the back door, slipping through and closing it behind him. Moments later several people entered the room and congregated around the table again. Silas heard several high-pitched giggles that sounded like they should have been made by a woman.

It was enough to make his blood run cold. He had only once interviewed Assoulin when his fellow Outlaw members Luke and Terz were present, and the insane nature of the two lackeys had made a mockery of the interview. Silas had closed it down and come back to talk to Assoulin when the man was alone.

It was the giggle that had haunted him. There was something psychopathic about it. Both Luke and Terz did it, and they wielded it like a weapon, a cultivated madness that broke any human link that might exist between them and others.

Silas shook his mind free of the memory, and realized it was time to move away from the cottage. He decided to test his strange new abilities, and visualized himself moving from the back door into the trees. Something told him the short dash would be fine, and he hurried across to hide in the undergrowth. A minute later he was climbing above the cottage again, hidden from anyone below.

Once he knew he couldn't be seen, he sat down on the slope, surrounded by undergrowth, for a long time. What was happening to him? He wished Mereana was there to explain it, but she wasn't.

In the end he forced himself to get up and make a circuit of the hill, a better choice than scaling straight up the bluff. It meant that he came into the cave system from the back, the way he and Gummy had first entered it. There were no lights inside the cave, but his night vision was at its best now, and the pumice seemed to reflect whatever starlight was coming in through the 'windows'.

"What the hell happened down there?" whispered Gummy, as Silas appeared inside the main cave. "You tol' me you weren't going inside, an' then you did! I damn near shit meself right then.

"Hey, boy," he continued, "you all right? You look like you seen a ghost."

I wish I had seen a ghost, thought Silas. He figured that was better than having heard a ghost, felt a ghost right next to him, and then was possessed by a ghost.

"Yeah," he said slowly, "some strange things happened down there, Gummy, and I'll tell you about it one day, but it won't be tonight. I'm thinking that plane can't be far off."

He looked at the time, and it was ten minutes to midnight. It took him a moment to resume his lookout post, and then confirm that the airfield still looked the same through his night binoculars. This time, though, the cottage was dark. While he had been walking back through the trees, around the hill, the lights in the cottage had gone out. Silas presumed that the airfield landing lights had gone on shortly after, though he couldn't see them.

His nerves steadied over the next ten minutes, and he was almost feeling human when a shape blotted out the northern stars. There was a crosswind, but it didn't seem to affect the aircraft that was coming in. It sounded like a jet, but much quieter, and it didn't have any running lights. Silas figured the engines must have been modified.

The aircraft took all of the available runway to land, and then it took the full width of the last paddock to turn around. It came to a stop opposite the cottage, and two of the vehicles assembled beside the building turned their headlights on, marking a corridor between the aircraft and the front of the cottage.

It was a twin-engined jet, one engine either side of the rear fuselage, and Silas took several photos of it. The aircraft type and manufacturer should be easy enough to identify. He noticed six passenger windows on his side, and presumed there were the same number on the other. That meant it had long-range capabilities, well beyond New Zealand if need be. That was something he would have to look into as well.

The side door unfolded, and became a set of steps that reached almost to the ground. Someone in a white uniform came out first, and Silas presumed it was the captain. Once the white figure was standing on the ground beside the steps, two men with gun belts and holsters appeared, one of them carrying a short machine gun.

Creel went across to meet the arrivals at the foot of the steps. There was some discussion, and Creel waved a 4WD farm bike over from the cottage.

One of the security guards was on it, Trafford as far as Silas could see. The guard handed something to Creel, who handed it to the pilot. Once the item had been checked, the two armed men from the plane hauled a large plastic bin down the steps, taking an end each.

The way they moved suggested it was heavy, and the bin went onto the carry frame behind the 4WD bike. Then Trafford drove his new cargo back to the cottage, where he disappeared behind it to stow the cargo. There was a longer conversation between Creel and the pilot now, and it seemed friendly enough to Silas. It told him that the two groups had been through these transactions before. Often enough for some sort of trust to become established.

Then the pilot and guards mounted the steps, and Creel walked back toward the cottage. It took a while for the plane to roll to the far end of the runway and turn to line up the runway for its departure, but then it began to accelerate across the grass. As it lifted into the sky it wasn't as silent as it had been during its descent, but the remote location kept the chances of discovery to a minimum.

It wasn't long before the jet was climbing out of sight, and Silas watched it travel north until he could no longer see it. Then he turned his mind to the plastic bin. He figured it contained meth. Called ice if it was in the pure form.

The way the guards had worked to lift an end each, he guessed the weight at somewhere around 80 kilos. He did some rough calculations in his head. That amount had a street value of 120 million in New Zealand, but Creel and company would only get the wholesale value, selling a kilo at a time to the gangs.

Still, that would net them 12 million. It seemed a lot of meth for New Zealand to absorb on a regular basis, and Silas wondered if that much came every month, and whether some of it was moved on into Australia.

But the discovery cast everything in a new light. When this much money was at stake, Silas could guarantee that some heavy hitters were involved. It certainly explained why Huxton and McCabe were taking such risks. Their cut from handling the drugs on the way through must be hundreds of thousands of dollars, and the shipments had to be coming in on a regular basis.

The lights in the cottage went out after a while, and the occupants settled down to sleep. That was when Gummy asked Silas what their plan was.

"We get some sleep as well, my friend," he answered, with a yawn. Tomorrow was going to be a big day, and it involved talking to Flynn. He wanted to be ready for it.

Silas' bushman's mattress had done a fine job of supporting him during the afternoon, and he was looking forward to it doing a fine job again.

Chapter 32

Silas was busy back at Tawhiti the following morning. He was compiling an investigative report so he would be ready for a meeting with Inspector Flynn in the afternoon.

"And you're sure this hunter you mention, the man who accompanied you to the airfield, can't add anything to your story?" said Flynn, when Silas was seated in his office. Tarrant had been called in as well, and nodded a greeting.

Silas shook his head. It had taken years to earn Gummy's trust, and putting the old hunter through endless questions at an interview would make him clam up entirely – and lose all faith in Silas.

"The aircraft we saw at the airfield that night was a Cessna Citation SII twin-engined jet," said Silas, moving swiftly on. "It can carry a maximum of eight passengers for 3680 km, and cruise at 750 kph."

Flynn nodded, and Tarrant came to look at the photos of the plane Silas had taken at the airfield. There wasn't much detail outside the areas lit up by the vehicle headlights, but it had been enough to identify the jet. Tarrant was the only person at the briefing apart from Flynn. That had been one of the conditions Silas had requested for the meeting.

"It's an older aircraft design," continued Silas, "produced from 1983 to 1997, but there are plenty of them still in service. It's a simple aircraft to operate, and a popular choice if there's just one pilot."

"Which ties in with the single pilot you saw at Huxton's farm," said Flynn. Silas nodded. Flynn and Tarrant had already been sent a brief rundown of the surveillance.

"Now it gets interesting," said Silas, bringing up a map of the Pacific Ocean and its attendant land masses on his laptop.

"I don't believe the flight originated in New Zealand," he said. "It would be a complicated way of moving a high-value product around the country, when a van and a couple of minders would do the job just as well.

"There's also no single source in New Zealand that could produce that much meth on a regular basis.

"No," he continued, "that plane came from overseas, but there's a problem with that idea too. It didn't refuel here, so its range is at best half of the 3680 km fuel tank capacity, or 1840 km.

"That would take it to a few hundred kilometres off the coast of Hobart, or Sydney. Apart from the fact it doesn't have the range, what's the point of moving drugs around Australia and New Zealand so extravagantly? Again, there are much easier ways.

"No, this is an attempt to bypass New Zealand and Australian border controls, which are more or less seen as one unit by criminal organizations overseas.

"It may surprise you to know," he finished, "that the closest overseas point to Rotorua, excluding Norfolk Island, is New Caledonia."

The others looked up in surprise.

"From Rotorua to the capital of New Caledonia, Noumea, is 1996km in a straight line," he said quietly, "and from Rotorua to Newcastle, the closest Australian city, the distance is 2293 km.

"Then we have to remember that New Caledonia is on a direct route from Rotorua to Papua New Guinea, one of the new places for large-scale meth labs in the Pacific. It's a country that is almost impossible to police."

He tabled a paper he had printed off the internet. *An Overview of Organized Crime in the South Pacific*, by Schveld and Pearson, Victoria University.

"So a small addition to the fuel tanks would do it," said Tarrant thoughtfully.

"To give the aircraft an extra 160 km range, plus an hour or two of spare flying time," added Flynn.

"And it's all that would be needed to make the round trip to New Zealand in one go," said Silas, "with one pilot."

It was an ingenious plan.

"Did you learn anything from the photos you took inside the cottage?" said Tarrant, and Silas was pleased to see his former pupil's investigative skills at work.

"Not as much as I had hoped," he said. "There were a couple of names on a list that had been jotted down, and one of them was the Devil's Outlaws financial adviser, in other words the man who launders money for the gang.

"It ties this operation to the Devil's Outlaws, but we expected that. They're the biggest dealers in meth and ice in New Zealand.

"There was a map of our part of the Pacific though. Several flight paths had been pencilled in to different parts of New Zealand, so the organization must have been considering a number of landing sites originally. But the one from Rotorua to New Caledonia had been drawn in permanently. I think that confirms my guess as to where the aircraft came from."

"Let me put a team on it," said Flynn. "I'm sure we can turn up more information if we systematically work through what you've turned up so far."

"No," said Silas. That had been the other part of the deal with the inspector. The investigation had to stay in Silas' hands. Flynn would try to do things by the book, and that wasn't going to work in this case. Silas hadn't told the inspector everything, which made it harder for him to understand why Silas wanted to keep the investigation in his own hands, but he wasn't going to change his mind.

"What's the advantage of doing it your way?" said Flynn. "The downside, as you know, is that I can't protect you if you run into trouble. I can't provide back up, and McCabe will be able to prosecute you on behalf of the people he wants to protect among the drug traffickers. He'll be able to insist that the police level criminal charges."

Silas had thought this through a hundred times, and he always came to the same conclusion. Right or wrong, he couldn't live with himself if he let the investigation close out too early.

"I think I know who killed Ella Brekken, Ernest Graham, and later Jacob Boss," he said, "but I can't prove it yet. Solving those cases is my first priority. It may not be yours, but it is mine."

Flynn thought about that for a while, and he clearly didn't like it. "Be reasonable, Silas," he said. "There are eighty kilograms of methamphetamine out there, heading for markets in New Zealand and possibly Australia. It will cause irreparable social harm, and we have to do something about that before it disappears."

"And we will," said Silas sharply. "Foy will already be back at work after last night's drop. The only other individuals at the cottage responsible enough to make the run to Auckland, where the Devil's Outlaws can distribute the meth to their outlets, are Creel and the two guards. I can identify which is Creel's vehicle from the photos I took at the cottage, and the Organized Crime division in Auckland can pick it up as it enters the city.

"You get on with rolling up the distribution network around the country, and I'll get on with solving the murder cases."

Flynn looked doubtful.

"I just need a couple more days, inspector," said Silas, trying hard not to beg. "Surely you can give me that much."

Flynn looked at Tarrant, who shrugged. He would back Silas, but it wasn't his head that would roll if the meth disappeared while it was in transit. Questions would be asked of the inspector.

"The sooner I get you back in uniform, Mr Chambers, the sooner I can bring you into the chain of command," said Flynn grimly.

"You have two days," he conceded, "and I will contact the Auckland drug squad so they can start tracing the shipment once it arrives up north. They'll have to follow the trail on to other cities as well if they can't pick up the shipment immediately. I can't hold them back for long, but they won't start raids on the outlets they identify for two days, I can guarantee that for you.

"That's more than I should be doing," he growled. "Don't let me down!"

"No, sir!" said Silas firmly, though it sounded like an empty promise even as he said it. He had bought himself two more days, but he had no idea whether he could wrap up the murders in that time.

At least it was better than the alternative. If the police took in all the suspects he had unearthed right now, those individuals would clam up tight. Then the real story would never be told, and the heads of the organization would never be caught.

But the drug trafficking was a sideshow for Silas. If the police brought in everybody Silas had identified in the organization, he wouldn't have enough evidence to convict Assoulin and his side kicks of the first two murders, or the security guards for the third one.

That meant Ella and Stodge would never get justice, and Silas wouldn't be able to show how Devon and Gords had been set up. On top of that, Leonora deserved to know exactly how Jakob had died.

Chapter 33

———————

Then the investigation started to heat up. The drug traffickers had no idea Silas knew about their regular shipments, but he had done more than enough to annoy them about Stodge's disappearance. Now someone had decided to put a stop to his interference.

McCabe hadn't managed to buy him off either, and despite Foy's attempts to influence Tarrant, Silas had kept asking questions. Then he had turned up knocking on Huxton's door, and the organization might possibly know he had been to see Leonora by now. That was a lot of attention to draw to himself.

His cell phone rang early in the morning, just after breakfast at his restored villa among the pines.

"You want to know how the old man died?" said a gruff voice, undoubtedly male, and Silas figured the caller was disguising his voice.

The old man he was referring to had to be Stodge. Only he and Jakob Boss had noticed something strange at Huxton's topdressing strip, and Jakob's body had turned up with two bullets in it. This was about Stodge.

"I'm listening," said Silas, keeping his voice steady.

"Be at the end of Perimeter Road in half an hour," said the voice. "Big, open space, you know it?"

Silas knew it.

"Half an hour, only chance you'll get, one on one. Be there," said the voice, and it was gone.

The end of Perimeter Road had recently been felled by a forestry crew. It was, indeed, an open space, and that meant there was no cover for an ambush. All the same, Silas took his time thinking about the offer. Even when something promised to reveal this much information he wouldn't go to a place where the odds weren't in his favour.

The problem for him was that he was running out of time, and he desperately needed more leads. It was a tough decision. In the end he loaded a short rod of heavy tropical hardwood into an inside pocket of his jacket, and drove to the end of Perimeter Road.

He had always been good with a police baton, and he had trained hard with one in his early years. The length of hardwood was the closest thing to a police baton he had. Except it was heavier, and harder. Silas was taking it with him for reassurance more than defence.

He was still on the tar seal when a black saloon car came up behind him. There was one man in it, someone Silas didn't recognize as he looked in his rear view mirror. The car stayed behind him as they climbed a long rise on double yellow lines.

Then they were over the top, and the car surged past Silas' Outlander. Near the bottom of the following dip it slewed sideways, coming to a stop in the middle of the road. Silas had the barest of moments to react.

Part of him noted the car had four people in it, and he figured three of them had been flat on the seats as they went past. He also saw the marshy ground to the left of the road, and the wooded slope to his right, but he didn't make a logical decision.

The black car had stopped in a way that blocked a little more of the left lane than the right, and Silas spun the wheel toward the woods. He went over the bank in a long, squealing slide, and hit a fence post square on.

The momentum behind the rapidly descending Outlander snapped the post off at the base and knocked it down. The car hurtled past the wires, and then Silas was trying to avoid the more substantial of the trees as they rushed at him.

He had a minimal amount of steering on the damp litter of the forest floor, and then debris began to pile up under the front axle. The Outlander went oblique to its path, and the right front crumpled as it hit a tree far too solid to think about moving.

The side of the car facing the road reared up and stayed at 45 degrees, pushing Silas toward the door on his side. He had been wearing his seat belt, and he was thankful for that now. Then he was working hard to get free.

He didn't think much time had passed, but all of a sudden he could hear voices, and they were perilously close. A childish giggle echoed among the trees, ending in a long squeal of delight. Moments later the windows along the side of the car disintegrated as a stream of bullets tore them apart, and a scattering of holes appeared in the thin metal of the car's roof.

It didn't take much to work out it was Luke and Terz doing the shooting. Assoulin would be with them, and there was one other. If Silas' guess was good it would be an Outlaws heavyweight.

The window next to him was open, though he didn't remember driving with it down. Maybe he had touched the button accidentally during his mad descent. He finally pushed the seat belt over his shoulder, with some difficulty, and went to crawl out the opening.

His foot delivered a jolt of pain, and he realized it was caught under the brake pedal. He wrenched the foot sideways, ignoring the pain, and toppled out the window. There was a short drop to the ground, and he dragged himself away from the car and toward the nearest patch of dense undergrowth. It was a blessing he was on the opposite side of the Outlander to the shooters, and couldn't be seen.

The rifle chattered its odd cadence again, and Silas figured the target was now the petrol tank. The bullets were small calibre, had to be 22s, and someone had modified a semi-automatic.

Automatic weapons were hard to come by in New Zealand, but a back yard mechanic had rigged a re-engagement mechanism and extended the magazine of the weapon. It was slow, but it sounded like it was firing three shots a second for a good five seconds each time.

Another high-pitched giggle floated through the trees, and more bullets thudded into the underneath of the car. Unless a stream of petrol hit the hot exhaust, they were wasting their time, and the tank was lower than the exhaust in its present position.

Real life wasn't like the movies, but it gave Silas an idea. He crawled back to the car, and looked for signs the petrol tank was leaking. He could smell petrol easily enough, and figured any flame near the rear of the car would be rewarded.

He reached in through the open window and extended his hand for the glove box. At first it wasn't enough, and he had to wriggle his upper torso through the window. He tried not to think about the front of the car coming free of the tree trunk and the whole thing rolling on him. Then he had what he needed.

He carried a small survival kit in the glove box, and once he opened it he had a fire starter. A few deft strikes later and a patch of petrol-soaked moss by the rear door was on fire. It would be enough, he figured, and headed for the same section of dense undergrowth.

He was still short of it when the car went up. He looked back, and the brightness of the flames seemed strangely out of place among the dark browns and greens of the forest. He hurried into cover, and listened for a reaction from the other side of the car.

What he heard made him slip the short length of hardwood into his hand. He twisted his fingers around it to make sure he had a good grip.

"That should make our annoying friend nice and crispy," said one of the gang members.

"I do like them bits of chicken skin when they're extra crispy," said the other, and Luke and Terz dissolved into high-pitched squeals again.

"I was looking forward to having a bit of fun with him," said one of the voices, "before he was pumped full of embalming fluid and had that far away look in his eye." There seemed to be a high five over that comment.

"Nothing like a grown policeman begging for me to take the pain away," said the other. "I never miss a chance to show the bastards who's the real power in this country. Think they're so hot!"

"Check out the car," said a new voice. It was cold, and had a lifelessness about it. Silas knew that voice. It was Assoulin.

He watched from his hiding place as one of the junior gang members came around the boot and stood looking at the car from Silas' side. He was so close Silas could have risen from the undergrowth and knocked him unconscious in a heartbeat, but he didn't. It might have been Luke or Terz, it was hard to tell.

The fire had taken hold, and the large amount of working gear that Silas had stored in the car was now burning fiercely, giving off a thick, black smoke. The gang member backed off, and made his way around the boot, choking on the smoke he'd inhaled.

"Was he there?" said Assoulin. "You got eyes on him or what?"

"He sure was," said the gang member. "It's the breath of hell in there, and he hasn't got any face left!"

Assoulin seemed to take the man at his word, and Silas smiled. Some of his gear from the back seat must have fallen forward and landed behind the steering wheel, and the way psychopaths and con men habitually lied to make things easier for themselves had just worked in Silas' favour. It was a very acceptable result for the retired policeman.

Silas waited ten minutes for the men to clamber back up the slope, and even then he was cautious. It was difficult to hear anything over the roar of the flames.

When he came out of hiding he checked carefully where the shooters were, and they weren't anywhere close. As he climbed back up the slope and neared the road, he saw that the black car was gone.

Chapter 34

The blue hatchback slowed, and turned back onto the other side of the road. It advanced cautiously until it stopped at a farm gate, not far from where a wooded slope joined a close-cropped field dappled with sheep.

A figure emerged from the trees and climbed the fence. When it could see there were no cars on the road, and no one working nearby, it limped quickly to the car and slid into the back seat. Silas stretched himself out along the fabric so he was hidden from view.

"What on earth is this all about?" said Annabel, speaking from the driver's seat.

"Nice disguise," said Silas. "Still knew it was you though. Too sexy to hide it."

Annabel gave an exasperated laugh.

"Start driving and I'll fill you in," said Silas, and she pulled out onto the tar seal and picked up speed. She had on an overlarge floppy hat, which she never wore, and had brushed forward a fringe that partially obscured her face. The car was borrowed.

Silas recounted the events that had led up to him being forced off the road and shot at. Annabel's lips pressed together in a thin line, and her knuckles went white on the steering wheel.

"You could have been killed!" she said, turning to look down at him grimly, before turning back to watch the road again.

"I think that was their idea," said Silas, still feeling his heart pumping faster than normal. Then he saw how upset she was. Maybe flippant remarks weren't the best approach.

"Okay," he said, "I knew it was a high-risk call, and maybe I wanted to get some leads on these murder cases more than I should have. It's just that, well," and he didn't know. What was his 'just that' reason exactly?

"The Ella Brekken case got away on me once," he said at last, "and that should never have happened. It's not going to get away on me a second time!"

"So this is about professional pride, is it?" she snapped.

"No," said Silas slowly, though he wasn't so sure when she put it like that. "Its about Ella, and Stodge, and Jakob, and making sure good people can rest easy knowing I've put on the uniform and I mean to uphold it. Even though Flynn says he'll back me out of uniform at the moment."

She snorted, but she didn't say anything.

"So the Outlander's a write off?" she said, more gently.

He agreed that it was. The loss of the Outlander hadn't really hit home yet. Not to mention all the stuff in it. He had always been prepared for a change of plans, and knew he could count on the gear in the back of the Outlander if he arrived in his own vehicle. The car felt like part of him.

Had felt like part of him, he corrected. It was gone now.

"I'm glad you got to me first," he said. "Someone would have phoned in the flames, and I didn't want to face the fire and police departments. I'll drop by the police station later and make a statement.

"The car was insured against fire," he said, "but I'll miss it, you know?" She reached back and patted him on the arm. She knew.

"How did we get from you and Gummy being chased off Huxton's ranch to you being shot at today?" said Annabel. Silas closed his eyes at that. Now he was in real trouble. The tension-filled clash with the two security guards had been the last part of the story he had confided in her, and he hadn't been keeping her up to date as promised.

So he told her about the airfield and the jet, and the secret meeting with Flynn and Tarrant. Then he told her about the deal. The police would follow the meth shipment to Auckland, and Silas would have two more days to work on the murder cases.

"You didn't tell me any of this!" she exclaimed angrily, as soon as he had finished the story.

"I couldn't demand that Flynn and Tarrant be the only ones at the meeting, and swear them to secrecy, and then tell you!" he protested weakly.

"Silas Chambers," she warned, her voice dangerously low, "I am either your other half or I'm a quick bounce on a bed. Now you're going to have to choose which. In fact, don't choose. I'm so angry right now that you choosing either one will just remind me that a mind-numbingly stupid choice had to be made in the first place!

"You went out into a high risk situation, where you could have been killed at any moment, without telling me first! I am so angry I could kick you out of the car right now, and make you walk to your place."

She actually touched the brakes, in some sort of subconscious reflex, and Silas could see that she was seriously considering it.

One part of Silas' mind wondered if nurses got some 'good nurse, bad nurse' training, like police in interview rooms were supposed to get – if you believed the movies.

Then he realized he was thinking like that to avoid dealing with his emotions. It was almost painful how much he wanted to be her 'other half' as she called it, and that was only the beginning. He wanted to be her other half in the 'all in, no compromises, share everything' way that she obviously had in mind.

He decided he might be guilty of professional pride, but he was damned if he was going to let personal pride get in the way of his future happiness.

"It won't happen again," he said quietly, "and you know I've never broken a promise to you."

She looked down at him briefly when he said that. She didn't look convinced.

"Okay," he said, "I've not told you things I should have told you, but that's different."

He raised his right arm, which was difficult when lying in the back seat of a moving car. It gave him something of a Nazi salute look.

"I, Silas Chambers," he said, "being of sound mind," – and she snorted very loudly at that, – "do hereby swear under all provisions of church and state that I will never withhold information from Annabel Kirsk again, so help me God!"

She appeared sightly mollified by the declaration.

"Where are we going?" he said, after a minute's silence.

"Where do you think?" she answered curtly.

"Your place," he said quietly.

"Almost correct," she said, and swung in to the side of the road.

They were coming up on Tokoroa at this stage, and the first suburban houses were appearing. Annabel walked away from the car, and talked for a long time on her cell phone. Then she came back and slid behind the steering wheel again.

"That call was part of a few things that I've been organizing lately," she said. "I've had to put them in place because of the increasing gravity of the situation, and it would have helped a lot if you had told me more, earlier!

"Now, I'm not obliged to tell you anything about them. But because I'm not you, thoughtless as well as stupid, I might let you in on what's been happening in your absence!"

Silas accepted the rebuke. She had the high moral ground at the moment, and it would take a while for her annoyance with him to wear off. Then she opened the back door of the car and looked down at the foot he had limped over to the car on.

"After I've taken a look at your leg," she said.

So while Silas complained that this was hardly staying out of sight, stuck on the side of the road on the outskirts of Tokoroa, Annabel knelt to take Silas' shoe off. She dug around in the various tendons that ran through and over the ankle bones until Silas yelped as she struck the damaged area. She ignored him, and continued her examination.

"You'll live," she said, tying his shoe tightly back into place. "At least you can practice resting and elevating your leg while I drive us to Hamilton. We don't have any ice to put on it."

"Can I get back on it tomorrow?" he said anxiously, and she laughed.

"That ankle is going to swell up overnight and you'll have trouble even putting your shoe on tomorrow. You can walk on it if I strap it tightly, but I wouldn't recommend it."

Silas stayed silent. He would have to get by on painkillers and a strapped ankle. He was running out of time, and he didn't have any other choice. Once they were back on the road again, Annabel gave him the silent treatment. At first he thought she was still angry with him, but then he caught the smirk at the sides of her mouth.

She was up to something, he knew that look. She was proud of something she'd done, and was about to surprise him. It was hard to get one over on an investigative officer like Silas Chambers, and Annabel liked to remind him that he wasn't the only one able to work out a plan.

He decided he would accept whatever she had arranged, and with good grace. A little humility on his part would be good for the relationship. He tried a few tentative questions about their destination, but they were quickly turned aside.

Silas dug out his cell phone, and finally found the cartoon image he wanted. It was of a forlorn young man in tattered clothes following a beautiful woman around. It was clear she was oblivious to him. His head was down and he looked crestfallen, and little hearts radiated off him.

Annabel's cell phone chimed, and she took a quick look at it. Seeing it was a text from Silas she put it aside until she could give it her full attention later. Silas didn't mind. It was a start, and he was determined to win back her confidence in him.

Then there was nothing to do but concentrate on resting his ankle, and work the murder cases in his mind. He spent the time looking for anything he might have missed, but twenty minutes later he still hadn't found anything, and the kilometres kept rolling by.

Chapter 35

The blue hatchback pulled into a nondescript motel on the south side of Hamilton. It slowed outside an end wing containing three units, and followed a service lane round to the back of the middle unit.

"In you go," said Annabel, once she had unlocked the back door of the unit and opened the car door for Silas. She was standing so she blocked any view of the short distance between the car and the building. He scrambled awkwardly across, keeping the weight off his leg.

Some of Annabel's things were already inside the unit, and Silas noticed she had brought all of his stuff that had been at her place. He was pleased to see his laptop. It contained all his notes on the murder cases.

"What's this all about?" he said, lying on the sofa with his foot elevated on the armrest at the end while he waved an arm at the unit. Annabel stacked cushions under his calf muscles to make his ankle more comfortable, before she answered.

"Rap on the wall," she said. "Three short knocks only."

Silas did as he was told, and three short knocks came back after a second or so.

"That's Mereana and Eli, and Gords has got Simon and Di, his flatmates, on the other side of us," she said. "For the moment all apprenticeships and studies are being done from home. Devon should be safe at the youth residence, Mereana's put her housecleaning business on hold, and I've taken some leave without pay."

It was a total lockdown. Gummy was sleeping rough somewhere on his land, and Emily was back in Dunedin, and no one should know that Tarrant had been helping Silas earlier. That covered everyone Silas was concerned about. The fact he was now 'dead' should help. The organization would have no interest in getting leverage over him through his friends and family.

Silas was stunned by Annabel's ruthless efficiency. But wasn't it a bit over the top? She perched beside him on the sofa, and took his hand.

"I can't let you know what's happening here when you don't let me know where you are and what you're doing," she said quietly.

"Mereana had some idiots squealing tires outside her house three nights in a row. Then someone threw a petrol bomb that landed mostly in her metal carport, and she was able to hose it down before it did any real damage.

"The police couldn't keep a patrol car outside her house indefinitely, so I brought her here."

"Why didn't you ring me?" said Silas.

"I did," came the reply, "but you didn't answer."

Silas wondered when that had been, possibly during his meeting with Flynn and Tarrant yesterday, when he had turned his cell phone off.

"I was also wondering what sort of technology this criminal organization of yours has," she said. "Could they listen in on telephone conversations? You said they had an inside man in the police force."

Silas conceded the point.

"There's something else," said Annabel. This time she looked even more worried, if that was possible.

"One of the juvenile offenders living in the youth justice residence with Devon attacked him in the sports gym they have there. Devon's a fit young man after all that rugby, and he managed to hold his attacker off until the guards arrived. The attacker was trying to stab him with some home-made implement.

"Don't worry," she continued, "in the end it was more scrapes and bruises than anything else."

"But you think it's a consequence of my investigation," finished Silas. She nodded.

"The offender has a long history of gang association. All he would say to the police is that Devon deserved it, whatever that means, and people need to learn to keep their noses out of business that isn't theirs."

That had to be aimed at Silas, the same way harassing Mereana was meant to get to him. He felt his stomach sour at the thought. Other people had been taking punishment that was meant for him.

"Hey," said Annabel, shaking him roughly, "we talked about this, remember? We all know that we have to stand up to bullies. You just carry on with your investigation, and put these criminals away where they can't harm innocent people!"

Silas nodded slowly. His friends and family could think for themselves, he realised, and he had to accept their decision. At least the pressure should come off them now he was presumed dead – as long as he wasn't recognized anywhere.

"Who's paying for the motel?" he said, thinking he could foot that bill at least.

"It's not costing us anything," said Annabel, waving the idea away with her hand. "You can thank Tracey Donovan when she gets here after work."

Silas tried to sit up, and got a stab of pain from his ankle for his trouble. "Donovan?" he said. "What's she got to do with this?"

He was now operating so far outside the law that the thought of the senior police prosecutor in Hamilton knowing anything about his activities was rather alarming.

"Relax," said Annabel, "we girls have been discussing your activities for a long time now."

At that, Silas did manage to sit up, and he swung his legs to the floor, grimacing as he did so.

"This is not a game, Annabel," he said sharply. "What I've been discussing with you shouldn't have gone any further. If the wrong people discover how much of their organization I've uncovered already, there could be . . ." and he tailed off.

He was going to say 'deaths on my hands', but it felt like there had been too many deaths already. Annabel looked at him calmly.

"Tracey is a senior police prosecutor, Silas. If anyone asked her a question she didn't want to answer, she would lie with an absolutely straight face. Nothing I say to her goes any further.

"On top of that, you had better get used to the idea that Tracey already knows everything you've told Inspector Flynn."

Silas sat open-mouthed, and then clamped his jaw shut. He had suspected as much for some time.

"What is it with those two?" he said, and Annabel smiled.

"Maybe you'll get the opportunity to ask them one day," she said, and dug out her cell phone to check her calls.

She tried not to smile when she saw Silas' cartoon text. A moment later she changed the topic.

"The best cure for a sprained ankle is to have lunch, and then take all your clothes off," she said.

"You're sure about that?" he said, a smile slowly growing across his face. He was short of time to work on the murder cases, but a break from them would certainly settle him down nicely. He was still twitchy after the attempt on his life

"Absolutely," she said. "Extensive research has proved it."

"Well in that case," said Silas, "perhaps the lunch part could be omitted?"

She made a show of thinking about it, then nodded.

Some time later, Silas was working on his notes at the small table in the kitchen of the motel unit. It was late in the afternoon. He was wondering where he might scrape up more leads for Jakob's death when there was a tap on the back door, and Annabel let Tracey Donovan in.

"And what has the prodigal son been up to now?" said Donovan, taking a seat on the sofa Silas had vacated earlier. He raised an eyebrow, but declined to comment. The morning was still too recent, and too raw, for him to summarize it easily. Annabel gave Donovan the short version of what had happened.

She described how he had been run off the road, shot at, and had to set his car on fire to cover his escape. Donovan's eyes grew wider with each passing detail.

"Are these murder cases that important to you?" she said at last. He nodded, and then went back to his notes. His answer was not open for discussion.

"Talk to me, Silas," she said, and he knew he wasn't going to get away that easily. "We didn't like you being hung out there like bait," she continued, "and if there was another way, we would have taken it.

"The problem is, we believe you. You can find out who's behind these murders where we can't, and that matters as much to us as stopping the meth shipment getting onto the streets."

Silas relaxed a little. It was good to hear the truth spoken so openly. "By us, you mean you and Flynn," he said quietly. She nodded, while Annabel reached over and hit him on the arm.

"Don't I count?" she said, "and what about Mereana, and Tarrant, and a lot of others! We don't like hanging you out as bait either, but it seems the only way to get results, and we think you're the best bet to find answers."

Silas bowed his head. Their trust was almost too much of an emotional burden to bear. He just wanted to get on with his job, which was a much easier task. Annabel must have sensed this, and broke in on the conversation to get some tea and biscuits underway.

"Who's paying for the motel?" said Silas, glad of the change of topic. He would pay his own way if he could.

"It's your lucky day," said Donovan.

"No, really," said Silas, looking directly at her.

She frowned back at him, and sighed.

"I own half of this motel," she said, "a fact which is not generally known, and I would like to keep it that way. It has been a bolthole for a number of people who needed a safe place over the years. Nothing tracks this place back to me, and you'll be fine here as long as you make sure you're not seen coming and going."

Silas nodded, and she went on.

"It's also my retirement plan. What's yours?"

"Ah, pine trees," said Silas. She wasn't that much older than he was, and yet she was planning for her retirement. He was impressed. It would take a mind as sharp as hers to hold down a senior prosecutor's job.

Silas had inherited his land from many generations of Chambers before him, and he couldn't think of anything to do with it except grow pines on it. Then he realized she was still looking at him.

"Ah, thanks for your help, Tracey," he said quietly. "I really appreciate it. We all do."

And she accepted his thanks with a gracious nod.

Chapter 36

By the next morning, Silas was getting desperate. He needed to make some headway and make it fast. He had one more day before Flynn started pulling in all the suspects for the murders, and he would start by charging them with drug trafficking. Silas didn't have any new leads to work on, and he was wondering where he might apply some pressure to get some results.

Everyone from the motel units on either side had come to see him the previous evening, and it had been a good time. When it came time to turn the lights out the motel bed had been surprisingly comfortable, and sleeping with Annabel in unfamiliar surroundings had been like a holiday.

Silas made a firm resolution, as he finished his breakfast, to host more social occasions like last night at his villa outside Tawhiti, or at Annabel's house in Hamilton. But that was the future. Right now he had to make the most of the time he had left to move the murder cases forward.

"You've decided, haven't you," said Annabel. "I know that look."

She was checking her phone messages and emails while he worked on his laptop. While no one knew where she was now, she wanted to keep an eye on things at work, as long as it didn't give away her location.

Silas nodded. "Some combination of the maid at Huxton's mansion – Summer, remember her – and Irena, the anxious wife, is my best bet. I could track down Devon's supposed friend Barnsey, but I don't think he's involved with the Outlaws at a high enough level. He's unlikely to know anything important."

"Nothing from your personal hot line?" she said.

Silas shook his head. He had AA members in Tokoroa and Tawhiti on the lookout for suspicious activity, but none of them had reported back to him. He couldn't tell them exactly what he was after at this stage, and that didn't help.

The location of the industrial freezer where Stodge's body had been kept would be useful, or a sighting of a human-sized package that had been moved around during the last two weeks.

"Still not carrying a weapon?" she asked, worried that he might be run off the road again, or worse. He shook his head.

"Not carrying a weapon gives me more options," he said, "strange as it may sound. I've been practising with a police baton when I have the time, it used to be my favourite enforcer when things got out of hand."

He went over to his jacket and slid out the length of strangely white tropical hardwood.

"That's not a baton," said Annabel, though she could see the similarity.

"No, it's better," said Silas, and handed it to her. She whistled when she felt the weight of it.

"But it's something I would only use if I could see a clear advantage, and a definite avenue of escape," he said. "It's not something to wave around in the face of trigger-happy thugs."

She looked worried all over again, and came to put her arms around him. He buried his face in her hair.

"I wish you didn't have to do this," she said.

"So do I," said Silas, "but there's no one else." Then he paused. "It has to be done if Ella and Ernest are to rest easy in their graves, and Jakob as well, and the people left behind are to believe there is justice in this life."

"But you won't have time to ring me today," she said, and he nodded. He needed all his wits about him when he was on the job. If he was constantly reminded that Annabel didn't want him putting himself in danger, he might start second-guessing his actions.

She accepted his decision without another word, and then sat him on the sofa while she strapped his ankle again. She seemed impressed that the swelling had almost gone.

Once that was done, Silas borrowed Simon's car, which was the least recognizable of those available to him. Not long after that he pulled over under some trees just out of Hamilton. He sent a chatty text about coffee and doughnuts, and waited for Tarrant to ring him back on his old garage Skype line. It was a code, of sorts.

It didn't take long to get a reply. Tarrant must have been out in Tokoroa following up an investigation.

"How's it going?" said Tarrant, and Silas filled him in on his narrow escape the day before.

"Hell's teeth, Silas!" exclaimed Tarrant. "This is getting out of hand. Leave the murder cases alone until we've got the suspects inside on drug charges, and then you'll have some leverage over them. You know we can eventually turn one of them against the rest!"

Silas didn't know that. McCabe would be watching everything the police did, and he would protect Assoulin, and Huxton and Creel. There was too much money involved in this operation, and somehow, money always bought immunity. Look at the way the original Ella Brekken murder case had been squashed.

"Can't do it," said Silas. "Sorry Dave."

He carried on before Tarrant could attempt to convince him.

"Got some information for you though," he said. "Gordon and his two flatmates have disappeared. Very hush-hush. Just a precaution, but you can understand why."

"Damn it, Silas, that will bring a ton of heat down on them," said Tarrant. "Possession is one thing, but there was enough evidence found at the flat to convict them of dealing! Not that I believe that, but the police have to take dealing very seriously."

"Stop panicking," said Silas, with a laugh. "The bracelets are still at the flat, and they're still working. By the time someone wonders why the occupants never leave the flat, this whole thing will be over."

"What did you do?" said Tarrant.

"Come on Dave," said Silas. "They were the old PT3s, and I still have a locking key. You boys want to update your equipment more often."

Dave was silent for a moment, then he came back with news Silas didn't want to hear.

"The meth raids will take place at dawn tomorrow, Auckland and elsewhere," he said. "The tracking operation has gone better than we thought it would. There are more than fifty addresses to be visited by police and Armed Offender Squads tomorrow.

"Flynn's making sure Foy knows nothing about it."

"Good for you," said Silas. "I'm really pleased. I wish I could say I was that far ahead in my own work."

There was nothing else that Tarrant could add, and Silas rang off.

Next he called Mrs Hope, and got Summer's cell phone number. She told him she ran errands in Rotorua occasionally, and he arranged to meet her there in an hour and a half. Once he was back on the road it was a long drive through intermittent showers.

"Thanks for getting here so quickly," he said, as he and Summer sat in a back corner of a cafe that was largely deserted this early in the morning. He asked how Irena Huxton was, and Summer had a lot to say about that.

"It was the strangest thing," she began, "and I only heard part of the conversation. From what I could make out, Mr Huxton wants to send his wife back to his family in California.

"I was cleaning windows in that big entrance hall. The manager was in the side room with him, and some guy I think is the lawyer for the estate."

"Julian McCabe," said Silas, but Summer just shrugged. She didn't know the name.

"Then Mr Huxton said something that frightened me," she continued. "He said, 'let her go, you've got me'. It sounded like he was begging. They talked some more, which I didn't hear, and then people started getting up from their chairs.

"The whole thing sounded weird, so I hurried away to clean windows on the other side of the house."

"Did Mrs Huxton go back to California?" said Silas, and Summer leaned forward at that.

"That's the thing," she said. "Mrs Huxton has now disappeared. She wasn't there last night at dinner, or at breakfast today, and I'm wondering if this is more than just one of her headaches."

The organization knows something is up, but they don't know what it is, mused Silas. They think I'm dead after the hired muscle ran me off the road, and they're expecting a huge police response to the death of an ex senior constable.

He decided that Irena was probably half way across the Pacific Ocean by now. Huxton's words also confirmed what Silas already knew. The man was a pawn in the operation, somehow caught up in this by accident. He wasn't one of the crime bosses.

"I think you should pick up your mother and go somewhere off the beaten track," he said, "where no one can find you," and she sat up in alarm.

"The next few days are going to be very difficult for Mr Huxton," he said quietly, "and you don't want to get caught up in the middle. You had the option of staying on and protesting that you've said nothing, but I've just taken that away from you. Now you'll be trying to hide the fact you heard something from me.

"It's also complicated because the people that have power over Mr Huxton think I'm dead, so you can't say you saw me here today."

Summer looked completely floored by this.

"So I think it's best that you leave right now," said Silas. "Throw away your cell phone so you won't be tempted to answer calls, and it will also stop you being tracked."

Summer was gamely trying to get her head around this.

"You can't tell me anything more?" she said hesitantly, and Silas shook his head. Then he got up from the table.

"You've been very helpful, Summer," he said, "and you will know everything soon enough, when it's in the newspapers. Please pick up your mother and go somewhere safe."

She nodded, and Silas left the cafe.

Chapter 37

The rest of the day saw Silas working his contacts. By nightfall he had the name of a coolstore owner in Tokoroa who might, or might not, owe the Devil's Outlaws a favour. The lead came from one of the AA members who did work for the man in the busy kiwifruit season, and had seen gang members talking to the boss.

It wasn't much, but Silas would pass it on to Tarrant. He doubted the owner was involved in the distribution or sale of drugs, so Flynn could execute a warrant to look for evidence at his leisure. It helped that the DNA in blood stains wouldn't deteriorate in a coolstore.

But that was it. His two days were up. Some time before midday tomorrow the suspects in his murder cases would be in custody for drug trafficking. It would effectively stonewall him, and he felt like a failure.

Silas headed for Hamilton, and the motel unit. He was about to be the key witness in a huge police operation that would put most of the meth distribution network in New Zealand behind bars. In fact he was the only witness. At least the organization thought he was dead.

He was determined to keep Gummy out of the courtroom, and that meant Flynn and Tarrant had to conveniently forget Silas had ever mentioned he had a guide on the plateau. A police trial of this magnitude would be a nightmare for Gummy, and there was nothing he had seen that Silas hadn't seen.

What was troubling Silas the most was his staying at the motel with the others. It was a small chance, but someone could recognize him and follow him back there. They could pass that information on to the 'Mr Big' who was financing it, and the Devil's Outlaws gang. Huxton just provided a place to bring in drugs, so Silas was wondering who else was financing and organising everything.

Flynn would offer to find him somewhere to go to ground if he was worried about leading trouble back to the motel, but then he wouldn't be close by if anything happened to Annabel and the others. Tonight would be the last night he had with his people, the extended family he hadn't quite realized he possessed until now. Tomorrow he would have to find a hideout, he decided.

The outskirts of Hamilton appeared before him, and he made his way by back streets to the motel. Then he parked Simon's car outside the motel containing Gords and his two flatmates.

Annabel was pleased to see him, but she was not at all impressed by the fact he was going to stay somewhere else from the start of the next day.

"Well, I'm going with you then!" she declared stoutly, and he had to smile at that, which only infuriated her more.

"I'm going to be living rough," he told her, "and I'm going to eat fern roots and get very smelly."

"Nice try, buster," she said, putting her arms around him, "but it's not going to work!"

"Let's not fight on an empty stomach," he said into her hair. She went to push him away, and he pulled her back toward him.

She didn't say anything, and he kissed her neck gently and held her for a while longer. Then he turned away towards the tiny kitchen. He wondered what they could find in there that could be turned into an evening meal, and she came to help him. Cooking was something they enjoyed doing together.

In the end he left the motel in the morning while it was still dark and she was sleeping. He hadn't had time to ask Simon if he could borrow his car again, and hoped the young man would understand. It turned out to be a pleasant early morning run to Tawhiti, and he enjoyed the peace and quiet.

The sun rose as he stepped onto Gummy's land, and walked past the house with his hands held high. He didn't get far before Gummy stepped out from a cleverly-constructed hide, with his rifle cradled in his arms. The hide gave him a view of the several ways in.

"Would've shot you in the leg, like I promised," he offered, and Silas smiled.

"Save your bullets, you might need them," said Silas, and they settled down inside the hide. Gummy had done a good job building it, and the place looked weather tight and comfortable.

Silas was aware that the dawn raids, being carried out as they spoke, would stir up a hornet's nest by mid-morning. Smaller players on the drug scene would be ducking for cover, and criminal heads would be trying to minimize losses. Anyone remotely linked to the case would be at risk of intimidation, or worse, and he explained all this to Gummy.

"So we form a defensive perimeter and wait for anyone that comes," said Gummy. "No one knows the tracks and hiding places around here better'n me. I take it you're a fair shot?"

The offer was tempting. It would be self-defence, and that was allowed under the law. Silas, though, was just here to warn Gummy to stay low for a while. Someone might have seen them together on the way to or from the plateau, and Huxton's security guards would be able to give a fair description of the old hunter.

"You want me to move off my land?" said Gummy, and Silas nodded.

"First place they'll look, if they figure you've been helping me," he said. Gummy took it surprisingly well.

"Aint nothing of value in the house, and the place is insured. Got a fren' down south would be good to catch up with."

He thought for a moment. "Sure," he said, "why not?"

Silas left an hour later, behind Gummy's twin cab. The vehicles went separate ways at the end of the street.

Silas was on his way to Cambridge. He knew the owner of a camping ground overlooking the Karapiro hydro dam near there, and the owner was a man who knew how to keep his mouth shut. Silas would hole up in a cabin there until he saw what the fallout from the dawn raids was going to be, and he would be twenty minutes from Annabel if he was needed.

Which reminded him. He had ignored two calls from her when she realized he had left the motel while it was still dark. Now she was obeying his rule of radio silence during a job. He texted her briefly. Explanations would get too involved. He settled for 'love you, will make it right,' and got on with his driving.

Silas hadn't wanted to make any noise when he left, so all he had with him was the clothes he stood up in. That meant he would have to shop in Cambridge at some stage. He was contemplating a disguise for the excursion when he pulled into the camping ground in Simon's car.

Bob Simmons nodded when Silas explained what he wanted.

"Will always back you, you know that," said Bob, and tossed him a key to number four. Silas had been called to some serious police business at the camping ground in the past, and Bob was grateful.

"Don't say anything to anyone when you see today's papers," said Silas, and Bob looked pained. "I'm not stupid, Silas," he said with a grunt, and the retired policeman smiled. He put his hand up in a gesture of appreciation before he walked away.

The cabin was small and utilitarian, but clean, and stocked with tea and coffee, and tea towels and bath towels of a reasonable quality. Silas put the jug on for coffee. He would have to go back to Bob's little shop to get the makings of a late breakfast.

He was just finishing the coffee when he got a text. It was from Tarrant, and it said: 'Computer not working. Random phone. Meet at my place half an hour.'

Silas sent an affirmative, and then realized he wouldn't have time to eat. He would have to hurry, he still had 40 km to cover.

He was back on the road in a few minutes, and wondered what this was about. Tarrant would want to update him on the dawn raids, and that was good, but in person? Flynn must have given him a message to pass on. The two of them had to be worried about security to want Tarrant to meet him in person.

Tarrant's place was a red brick family home off Baberton Street in Tokoroa. Tarrant had stayed on after the kids left home, and his ex wife had moved to Matamata. A police car was parked outside, which reassured Silas that the man was still here. He had hit some heavy traffic on the way over and was now five minutes late. Silas knocked on the back door, and got a subdued, "come in."

First he walked through a large laundry and storage area, with a toilet cubicle in one corner. Then he crossed a passageway and stuck his head into the lounge. Tarrant was seated on the sofa, and there was a large, hard-looking man Silas didn't know next to him. What Silas did know was the man had prison tats at the corner of his eyes, and a scar on his chin.

Silas backed up fast, reaching for the hardwood rod in his jacket. Something hard jabbed into his back, and he stopped moving. Turning slowly, he saw a sawn-off shotgun, wielded by Assoulin. Another jab reinforced the idea it would be foolish to resist.

"I'll take that," said the coffee-colored man of Syrian extraction, lifting the hardwood baton out of Silas fingers. Then he pushed his captive into the room with the end of the shotgun barrel, and told him to sit in one of the chairs. There was no surprise on Assoulin's face, and that meant he knew Silas hadn't died in the car fire. And that was why they had tried to get to him through Tarrant. They had certainly succeeded in that.

But how did they know he was still alive? It had to be Summer. Either she hadn't fled as he had told her to at the cafe, or they had tracked her down when she didn't return to Huxton's mansion. That was another loose end Silas had to tidy up.

He said a brief prayer that she was all right. Everything was slipping out of his control, and he was going to need all the help he could get, supernatural or not.

"I didn't send the text," said Tarrant, and the tattooed man next to him hit the side of Tarrant's head with an elbow, snapping his head to the side.

Silas understood. Tarrant hadn't gone along with the deception willingly. Now that he was closer to the sofa, he could see how much of a beating Tarrant had endured.

Well that little play was quick, thought Silas. Now we know what the organization's response is going to be. They want to play hard ball.

Chapter 38

Assoulin seemed to be in charge.

"Turei," he said, "bag that sack of shit. It's time to show him what happens to his ex wife if he squeals. I'll call in your ride now." When Turei nodded his understanding, Assoulin pulled out a cell phone. This had to be the Outlaws heavyweight that Silas had seen in the back of the car that forced him off the road.

Then he watched as Tarrant was hauled to his feet, and something like a long farmer's wool sack was dropped over his head. Tie downs strapped his arms against his sides, and his legs together. They were ratcheted up until they had to be cutting into flesh, and Tarrant started swearing that he couldn't breathe.

The one that Assoulin had called Turei dropped a shoulder and bent Tarrant double as he picked him up. Silas heard a vehicle cruise down the drive and move round the back of the house. It must have been waiting round the corner.

Then he was blindfolded with a dirty rag – he could smell oil and scorched metal on it – and guided through the laundry and out the back door. He was patted down and his cell phone removed. Then he was forced to lie face down in the back seat foot well of the car, which was too short for anyone to be comfortable.

He heard Tarrant being loaded into the trunk of the car, and the lid being slammed. Assoulin rested the soles of his shoes on Silas' back as he sat in the back seat.

"How does it feel, policeman?" he said, with a snarl of personal satisfaction. "About time we got your boots off our necks."

Silas wondered why the man was talking in slogans. It was the behaviour of people who had been radicalized by extremists, and fed tales of colonial and current injustices. Such things had a grain of truth in them, but were distorted to serve other purposes.

Silas couldn't see anything outside the vehicle, but he visualized the path it was travelling. Each left and right turn built up a picture of where they were going, but the long straights were harder to gauge. Had they just passed two side streets or three?

By the time the car stopped he knew he was still in Tokoroa, and somewhere in the industrial area. Then he was hauled out of the back seat and taken inside a building. He noticed the darkness as the sunlight was cut off by the roof, and the echoes of footsteps once they were inside.

Silas was pulled to a halt while something rumbled open in front of him. If it was a door, it was extremely thick and heavy. Then he was thrown forward, and instinctively put up his hands to protect himself.

The chill of frigid air hit him immediately, and a moment later he lay sprawled on the floor. He pulled his hands away from the icy surface before his skin froze to it, and that was when the first boot thudded into his side.

It was a brutal assault, and his ribs were on fire by the time his attackers had finished. He rolled onto his side, gasping for breath as his lungs tried desperately to inflate themselves again.

"What are you, completely stupid?" hissed Assoulin's voice from a point above his head. "You were given enough warnings, but you couldn't stay away, could you. Even a car crash didn't get through your thick head. You've got a death wish, asshole, and we can oblige you on that one!"

"Dumb fuck brought it on hisself," said a high-pitched voice, and then there were two of them, giggling and squealing with laughter.

A few minutes after the door had rumbled closed, Silas dragged himself onto his knees, and then gradually to his feet. Lying on the floor was going to lose him too much precious body heat. At least he still had his jacket, but that wasn't going to be enough if he was in here for any length of time.

He couldn't hear anyone nearby, so he dragged the blindfold off his face. There were traces of light coming in around the door, and through the blades of a large fan at the other end of his prison. After a while his eyes adjusted, and he could see he was in a concrete room. It had been white once, but the paint was now grey and peeling.

There were a number of stains on the floor, and one of them looked fresh. He figured that was where Stodge's body had lain while the Outlaws were figuring out what to do with him.

The room wasn't large, about three paces by four, and the fan was set into the wall at one end. There were rails overhead to carry carcasses, and the place had to be a blast chiller. It was designed to drop the temperature of animal bodies quickly. If his captors decided to turn the blast fan on, he would be dead in minutes.

Trying to adjust, Silas set himself a routine. Each circuit of his concrete cell was a dozen paces, and he gave himself a target of five circuits every minute. He would lose heat from his body if he was stationary, and that would happen long before he ran out of energy reserves to fuel movement.

The theory was good, but when he stepped out on the first circuit of his cell the pain in his ribs flared again. Gritting his teeth, Silas forced himself to continue.

After a while the pain receded, and he could think. His first thoughts were ones of regret. He had been given the address of a suspicious coolstore only a day ago, but he hadn't passed it on to Tarrant or Flynn. It had to be the one he was now a prisoner in, and the tip-off from his AA helpers had been wasted.

For a while he wondered why Stodge's presence hadn't warned him about the trap at Tarrant's house. It took a while before he got a reply, and then it was a gradual realization that it was better this way. His role at the moment was to take the part of a prisoner.

When he asked himself why that was, he couldn't really grasp the answer. Part of it was that good could not act directly in this world, only indirectly, and part of it was the human need to be tempered with suffering to grow into a greater understanding. He snorted in disbelief. When had he become a philosopher?

After a while he wished he had something to mark his circuits on the wall with, and lost count of them after two hundred. It was hard to judge the passing of time, but he thought most of the day had gone when he heard voices approaching the freezer door.

Silas dropped down into a corner, and prepared to act as though he was freezing to death. It might be the only chance to escape he got.

He was hauled roughly to his feet, and dragged out of the freezer to a loading dock. Everything seemed hot and humid after the freezer, and the light hurt his eyes. Then his vision adjusted, and he saw that the tattooed thug was there, along with the others from Tarrant's house.

Silas didn't know how bad things had been for Tarrant, but he forced himself to push his fear aside. He had to stay focused. He was surprised they had kidnapped a policeman though. It suggested the organization felt it was invincible in Tokoroa.

"McCabe wants to see you," said Assoulin. "Don't know why he would bother. The sooner he gives the word the sooner you're going to be one less problem. I'd crap myself if I was you, boy!"

The trick with interrogation was to stop your captors from getting inside your mind, so Silas stayed calm, and noted as many details as he could. One small observation might save his life later.

Then Assoulin hit Silas hard in the ribs, driving him to his knees, and fresh agony swept through him. His back felt like an unresponsive log of wood, and he hoped it was just muscles going into spasm. Assoulin's two monkeys jeered and giggled.

Eventually Luke and Terz got him upright again, and led him to the back of a nondescript van. There were bench seats down the sides, and the windows were painted over. The one called Turei sat on one side with Silas, while Luke and Terz sat on the other, and Assoulin did the driving.

It was the first time Silas had been able to study Luke and Terz in detail. It confirmed his first impressions. They were not related, but they affected the same mannerisms. The only difference was that Terz dressed and looked more like a woman.

Silas wondered if they were so cut off from normal human interaction that they were forced to find all social needs in each other. A psychologist would have had a field day with them, but what they were to him right now was obstacles. Obstacles to his freedom, and obstacles to solving the murder cases that drew him on.

A few minutes later the van drove into a modern three-bay garage attached to the back of an older building. Once the vehicle was away from public scrutiny, Silas' captors took him out through the back doors of the van and up some steps into a room inside the building. Once he could see the interior, Silas recognized the substantial old brick building McCabe had set up as his law offices.

He was given a wooden chair to sit in, and Assoulin left the room while the others stood guard. Silas figured McCabe wouldn't be long.

Chapter 39

"And what, exactly, did you think you were going to do with this?" said McCabe, hefting the length of tropical hardwood Assoulin had taken off Silas.

"It's a police baton," said Silas, shrugging his shoulders at the question. Part of him wanted to say 'hand it here and I'll show you what a well-trained policeman can do against thugs like you', but it wasn't the time to listen to that part of himself.

"Not exactly regulation issue, is it?" said McCabe.

He didn't wait for an answer, but handed it back to Assoulin.

"I don't know how you did it, Silas," he said, pulling another of the wooden chairs over and sitting in front of his prisoner, "but I'm impressed. Losing that shipment is going to set us back months. Not to mention having to replace half the distribution network."

Yes, thought Silas, until your bosses find another airfield and more mugs to peddle your poison, and you can start raking in your massive cut again.

"As you will see, we've escaped most of the raids here in Tokoroa," said McCabe. "I was tipped off, as I expected to be, and it didn't take much to keep my boys here away from the Outlaws base while it was being searched. They'll have to lie low for a while, but I'll find a way of getting them off any police charges.

"Creel's being questioned, along with Huxton, and that's all part of the plan. Huxton will have to be sacrificed, of course, but he's no use to us now the airfield has been compromised.

"His security guards will get well paid for a short stint in prison, and I'll argue they were just following orders. I'll get Creel off as knowing nothing about Huxton's activities, and he's got a clean record. That clean record cost me big, Silas."

McCabe was smiling broadly. He was enjoying this, and only someone like an investigative officer could appreciate how clever he had been.

"I've been 'borrowing' Foy for 'community work' over the last few months," he continued, "part of his training as a community constable. It was all a back-up plan for a situation like this. I'll have no trouble spinning it that he heard something about the Huxton place and was doing some undercover investigation.

"Foolish of course, but an overzealous young cop who's just been made a full constable, well, it can be expected, can't it?"

Then McCabe's voice changed.

"Who told you about the airfield?" he said, with a new sharpness. The lawyer must be thinking there was someone in the organization who had rolled over and given the airfield up.

No one had rolled over, and Silas wasn't going to mention Gummy, even in his minor role as a guide, or Leonora. McCabe waited, and when there was no response he sighed.

"I made you a very fair offer not that long ago, Silas," he said. "You can be someone special in this town, and you can have the deep pockets that go along with that.

"Be reasonable. There will always be people wanting drugs, and there will always be a distribution network to get it to them. When you lock a supplier up, someone else will step forward to take their place.

"You're being dishonest. All the police are doing is farming criminals. They skim some of them off the top every so often – which is instantly replaced – and charge a huge amount in taxpayer money to do so. If the police let the system regulate itself, yours and my taxes would be halved!"

It was a tidy argument. Silas could see why McCabe was a lawyer. But there were two problems with it. Firstly, if the criminal underground were left to regulate itself, it would take more and more from society to meet its insatiable greed, and it wouldn't be long before there were armed gangs fighting each other in suburban streets.

The second problem was something McCabe would never grasp. What you were depended on where you stood. Even if he could never fully win, being on the side of protecting others defined Silas, and that allowed him to sleep soundly at nights.

"You need to think hard now," said McCabe, patting Silas familiarly on the knee. "You could be a great part of this organization. We could use a flexible sergeant-at-arms, a firm but fair disciplinarian, and your years of training wouldn't be wasted."

Silas didn't respond, so McCabe got up and turned to Assoulin. "I'll be back in ten," he said. "If Mr Chambers doesn't make the right choice, well, you know what to do with him."

Assoulin nodded briskly. He would have no trouble with that.

Silas used his ten minutes to try and make sense of McCabe's behaviour. The man obviously wanted to be liked, one of the most basic of human needs, and it seemed Silas had earned McCabe's respect. Probably because of his dogged perseverance with the case. Getting the approval of someone he respected would give the lawyer some sort of validity, at least in his own mind.

Silas remembered his textbook readings in criminology. Most of the people like McCabe just wanted a sense of belonging, but it was an attempt that was always met with derision and scorn, because of their behaviour. It was like inviting someone to a party and them being faced with dismay when they wanted to pull the wings off flies.

All the people on one side of a certain fence knew such behaviour was wrong, but the ones on the other side did not. Silas remembered reading somewhere that the damage was done in the first few years of life, when basic emotional needs weren't met.

When he heard McCabe returning, Silas took a deep breath. You better be right about this, Stodge me old mate, he said to himself. He still wasn't comfortable with the idea that it was his role to be a prisoner, to endure until the situation became clearer. But he steeled himself for what was to come.

Silas was surprised when Foy walked in with McCabe. Maybe the lawyer thought the presence of Foy would have an influence on Silas. Here was a police officer who understood how reasonable McCabe's offer was. Maybe Foy's presence was meant to intimidate, to show how extensive the organization's reach was in this town.

"Well, Silas?" said McCabe. "I'm sure you're ready to make the right decision."

McCabe didn't even see the irony in saying the morally wrong decision was the right one. But Silas was not here to argue semantics, and he just shook his head.

McCabe's voice dropped almost to a whisper. "I am really sorry to hear that, Silas," he said, "but this is a free country, and you are free to make that decision."

There was no choice involved when a decision was made under duress, but again there would be no advantage in pointing out McCabe's puzzling use of words to the man.

"See he doesn't suffer," said McCabe, looking at Assoulin. The coffee-coloured man nodded, but McCabe must not have been reassured. He turned to Foy.

"Go with them," he said, "and make sure my orders are carried out."

Foy checked something on an electronic tablet.

"Sure thing," he said. "I'm due for a stint on traffic patrol today. A trip out with the boys will fit in nicely."

Then McCabe was gone, and Silas was led back to the van. There was no attempt to blindfold him this time, and why should there be? Whatever he saw was going to the grave with him.

The journey was much longer this time, and near the end Silas heard the van's wheels crunch onto a gravel road. He hadn't seen much with the windows in the back painted over, and his location now was a mystery to him.

When the van stopped, a fitful wind was gusting outside. Then Silas heard another vehicle pull up behind them. The back doors of the van popped open, and he was pushed roughly out. He saw Foy's patrol car first, and then he looked around. He understood where he was immediately, though he had never been to the place before.

It was an old quarry, one that had probably been a source of road gravel in the early days of the province. It was surrounded by regenerating forest now, and Assoulin must have driven in off a forestry road. Looking back, Silas could see weeds growing up between the gravel tracks.

The vehicles were on the upper side of a giant hole that had been dug into the side of a hill, and they were parked on a rocky outcrop. Judging by the floor of the quarry, part of which Silas could see, there was a ten meter drop off the edge. If he was lucky, he would land in a lake where gravel had been dug out, but it wouldn't matter either way. He had the feeling he would be dead by then.

For a moment he wondered why he wasn't feeling anything. He understood the mechanics of shock, but it didn't feel like that was the case right now. It felt like he was playing a part, and any moment now he could step off the stage and take up his normal life.

Except part of him knew that wasn't going to be the case.

Chapter 40

Foy came up beside him, and Silas asked a question.

"Humour me," he said. "Consider it a last request.

"Who do McCabe and Creel answer to? Who organizes the flights in from New Caledonia? And who's the intermediary with the gangs?"

Foy looked stunned when Silas mentioned New Caledonia, and he figured that bit of information was known to very few people. Silas was also surprised that McCabe had told his nephew. Then Foy roared his head off.

"You hear this dumb shit, Turei?" he said. "He hasn't figured any of it out yet. We're doing the police a favour getting rid of him."

Turei chuckled, but Assoulin just looked sour. Luke and Terz didn't seem to know much about anything. They looked on as if this was some form of entertainment.

Foy stepped right up in Silas' face. "McCabe runs everything," he hissed. "Man's a genius, and no one suspects anything."

Silas tried to process that, but it didn't make any sense. He didn't have time to ask another question though, because Assoulin was getting bored with the two of them talking.

"Time to weigh this asshole down," he said, and dragged chains out of a cavity under one of the bench seats. Luke went to help, while Terz perched delicately on a rock to one side. But Foy hadn't finished taunting Silas.

"You ever wonder where McCabe was before he turned up here?" he demanded, and Silas thought about it. He remembered his own attempts to find out something about McCabe's early life. There had been suspiciously little information.

"He was clawing his way out of the gutter, man!" spat Foy. "I was ten when I used to stand lookout while he ransacked homes for loan sharks, and cut the clients up a bit if he couldn't find enough to clear the debt. Then my mother overdosed, and McCabe was all I had."

Silas hung his head. The poor little bastard, he'd never had a chance at a normal life.

"One day McCabe realized he was working damn hard and taking big risks, for bugger all money, and he looked around to see who had all the control in this world. It was lawyers. So he went and became a lawyer, and he specialized in criminal law so he would meet the people he needed to build his empire.

"Can you believe what it takes to do that?

"As soon as I was old enough, he sent me to Outward Bound and every assault course he could find, and got tutors for me, so I would pass the police entry test. Once I made it into the force he helped me through the probationary stage. Then someone who owed him a favour fast-tracked me to a full constable."

There was a long pause.

"So I hope you die happy, mister policeman, with all those questions answered for you."

Foy stepped back, and Turei kicked Silas' legs out before slamming him to the ground. He was held down while Assoulin and Luke wrapped a length of heavy chain around his middle, and secured it in place with wire. Then they tied his arms behind him with rope.

That was when Silas lost his calm feeling. His body came to life of its own accord when he realized there wasn't a way out of this. But he made a supreme effort to stop himself from struggling. It would accomplish nothing.

"Not so funny now, is it Chambers," said Assoulin, dragging Silas to his feet. "You'll piss yourself before you bounce off the rocks on the way down, but you'll still be alive when you hit the water!"

"We're not going to kill him first?" said Turei. "Foy's got a pistol in the boot of his car."

"Not this one," hissed Assoulin. "He pushed hard after Brekken died on me, and that forced me back to Auckland. It was only after McCabe buried the investigation that I got any peace. I want to see him suffer."

"You should have come forward and said it was an accident," said Silas, and Assoulin's eyes narrowed. "How you know that, Mr Detective Asshole? If you knew it was an accident, why did you come after me?"

Silas didn't try to explain that it was still manslaughter. If a bunch of idiots hang out at a car park looking to steal stuff, and something goes horribly wrong, it is not an accident. If only people would take some effing responsibility for their actions, he thought.

Silas doubted that he would ever be able to explain that Ella's ghost had told Mereana what had happened to her.

Doubt replaced anger in Assoulin's eyes, and then a trace of fear.

"This fucker got to die right now," he said roughly, and pushed Silas toward the edge.

"Hamstring him! Hamstring him!" chorused Luke and Terz, giggling wildly. "Make him crawl to the edge!"

Silas looked at Foy, and saw him look sick. That was why McCabe had sent his nephew along, to toughen him up. There would be more killings over the years to come, and McCabe needed to know he could rely on Foy.

"We get the job done quick and clean," said Foy, stepping up beside Silas.

"You two," he said, pointing to Assoulin and Turei, "grab an end each. We'll toss him, and I want this done properly."

Silas figured Foy didn't want to pull the trigger on the handgun, and the thought of Silas drowning slowly in the lake below bothered him less.

That was when Silas heard Stodge's voice. The words were clearer each time he felt the old man's presence, but they still weren't making sense. The day seemed brighter, somehow, and his eyes hurt, but there wasn't the flickering passage of images he'd experienced in the past.

The sense of safety and danger came back though, stronger than before. Every path away from him was a dead end, even assuming he could get away from his captors with his hands tied behind him and weighted down by chains. Every path except the one to the cliff edge.

That way beckoned him like a shining path, a way to freedom, a definite salvation. But that was suicide. Then he had to make a choice. Assoulin grabbed his shoulders and Turei bent to pick up his feet.

Silas kicked Turei in the face, hard, and dropped a shoulder as he twisted the upper part of his body. It was a judo move he remembered from his police training, one he had used before. His shoulders tore free of Assoulin's grasp.

Powering across the few meters to the cliff edge, he was thankful for his morning runs now. He picked up speed quickly, and kept his fear of drowning at bay with the thought he had to clear the rocks Assoulin had talked about. He jumped at the edge, pushing himself out into space.

Then he was falling, and bending his knees to absorb the shock of the impact. He hit the water far enough out and got a clean entry. There was a noisy deceleration, and then silence

He was under the water when Stodge's message got through to him. Not in words, not as an explanation, but in memories. He had been here before.

It was hard to tell what was Stodge and what was himself, but he saw what he had to do. The bottom of the lake came up fast, and he landed on his feet in the sludge. He turned and faced the cliff face. Leaning forward, he started up the slope, thankful for the heavy chains that gave him purchase against the lake bottom.

Up ahead a wall of shadow showed where the lake undercut the cliff, the result of the quarry men chasing a big layer of rhyolite. Silas didn't know the word for that type of rock, and figured Stodge's memories were doing the thinking for him. He remembered that it was a something that fetched a premium price from the roading contractors of the day.

Silas almost laughed out loud at the information buzzing around inside his head. He didn't give a damn what rhyolite was. He had just thought that he was a dead man, and then he was given a way out, maybe. And now his air was running out fast.

Chapter 41

Silas kept lifting his feet and putting them down, and leaning forward, so he could climb the underwater slope. He passed into the shadow cast by the bottom of the cliff, knowing somehow there was a cave ahead. If he could just make it up the slope he would rise out of the water inside it, reborn. The thought focused his mind, and he held his breath with a grim determination. Then he saw the rocks blocking his path.

He tried to focus in the murk. Stodge's memories said that the way was clear, but Silas' eyes said the way was blocked by rocks. For a moment he thought of swimming out to the base of the cliff and taking a breath before continuing, but then he remembered the chains weighing him down. He thought of going sideways along the slope until he could climb out of the lake, but that wouldn't be any better. Any sign of him surfacing would bring Assoulin and Turei down to finish the job.

It was an all or nothing realization, and it drove him desperately on. As he got closer to the rockfall he could see that it consisted mostly of one large boulder, and there was a gap to the side of it. He aimed for that.

Halfway through the gap he felt the walls on either side scraping against his shoulders, and then he was stuck fast. There was little he could do, with his hands tied behind his back. He twisted his shoulders in the same judo move he had used to free himself from Assoulin, and hoped for the best.

His shoulders scraped across the rocky surface, and came free. Then he was through. But there was still water above him, and he was at his absolute limit. He pushed himself forward with his feet, in one last effort, and then there was only movement and blackness.

When he came to he was lying on a sandy shore in darkness, his face just out of the water. He took a while to orient himself, and then he saw the faint glow in the water from the entrance to the cave. He was already shivering with the cold, and the way his arms and legs hurt told him he had accumulated a number of scrapes and bruises.

His left knee was on fire, but that appeared to be the worst of his injuries. He flexed the joint experimentally, and discovered it still worked. He wouldn't be putting much weight on it for a while though.

The sense of calm he had experienced on the way to the quarry returned. He didn't feel like moving, but he hauled himself further out of the water to stop the cold sapping his body heat. Then he rested, staring up into the darkness. He wondered how Stodge had known about this place, and the answer came at once.

Stodge had been here as a child. He had been a hunter and adventurer from his earliest years. The quarry was still in operation back then, and the big machines added to the attraction for the boy. It was a small matter for him to scale the mesh fences during the weekends.

Then it dawned on Silas that there was another way out of the cave. He didn't know how he knew that, but it was further in, towards the back of the shelf he was lying on. If he could just move himself away from the water, he would be moving in the right direction.

Groaning softly, Silas rolled his body over. He managed a meter or two by shuffling forward on his knees, with his hands still tied behind his back. Then he stopped for a breather. When he lifted his head and looked up, he could see a narrow chimney, angling away to his left. There was sunlight at the end of it.

It took a while to orientate himself to the cave and the lake, but in the end he decided the chimney would come out on the easterly slope of the rocky outcrop above the cave.

His eyes were getting used to the dark now, and he could see shapes to one side of the rocky shelf. It looked like Stodge had dragged some mementos in here, and started his own collection of quarry memorabilia. That made Silas cough up a weak laugh. It looked like the old hoarder had started collecting almost as soon as he was born.

Stodge's collection gave Silas an idea, and he shuffled over to examine it more closely. It didn't take him long to find what he was looking for. An old biscuit box had a jagged edge where something had torn it open. It was rusty, but the metal was thin, and it should be sharp enough.

Silas backed up to the box, and started sawing away at the ties around his wrists. He had to stop several times to rest, but at last his hands were free. Once he had removed the rope from his wrists he undid the heavy chain around his middle. He felt unbearably light when he'd finished the task.

He was exhausted now, and decided it would be wise to rest for a while. He needed to recoup some energy, and it would also be wise to wait until the van and the police car were gone. He made a nest in a sandy area, and that was all he remembered for a long time.

The first thing he did when he woke up was to crawl across the floor of the cave, not yet trusting his damaged knee, to look at the chimney. The blush of a sunset met his gaze as he looked up through the opening.

Unless he was going to spend the night here, he would have to attempt the climb now. His clothes hadn't dried off yet after his immersion in the lake, and he was still shivering. At least there was no wind down here to make his condition worse, but a night in the cave would not be a good idea.

The climb up the chimney took a long time. Silas had to hold himself in place with his elbows and hands while his good leg found a place to push off from, and he rested often. The chimney stayed narrow all the way up, and that helped.

It was getting dark when he finally reached up and grabbed hold of the bushes that had grown around the entrance to haul himself out. He emerged into a cool evening with a steady breeze from further up the slope. Lights were just starting to come on in isolated houses across the farmland beyond the forestry plantations, and that was where he needed to go.

It was a very surprised farmer who opened his back door an hour later to a filthy man who had clearly been hobbling along with the aid of a home-made crutch. The man looked in too poor a condition to be much of a threat, but the farmer glanced across at the steel box of a free-standing fireplace, where a stout iron rod hung.

"Sorry to bother you," said Silas, "but I've run into a bit of bother. Could you phone Inspector Matthew Flynn of the Tokoroa Police at his home number, and tell him that one of his agents from Tawhiti needs a ride?

"I can wait out here while you do that if you like. I understand people need to be careful with strangers these days."

"Maree," said the farmer, turning his head to bellow into the living room, "come and take a look at this sorry-looking geezer, will you? He looks familiar, but your memory for faces is better than mine."

"Oh!" exclaimed Maree, when she got to the door. "Constable Chambers, you must come in! No, wait there for a moment while I organize a shower, and get you a change of clothes.

"Freddie, grab that warm jacket our Tommy wears in winter. Can't you see the poor man is freezing?"

And that was what it was all about. McCabe wanted to destroy communities – and that was what drugs did – because it made people easier to control. Silas wanted to build up communities, because people who banded together were so much stronger.

Chapter 42

Silas was sitting at the dining table when Flynn arrived, making sandwiches for himself. His hair was tousled from a shower, and Freddie was carving the last of the meat off that night's roast for him to put on the bread. There was a hastily constructed pudding waiting on the sideboard.

Dressed in the hard-wearing and warm farmers' clothing that had been handed to him, all browns and greens, Silas looked a lot like a thinner version of Freddie. When he had made the introductions, Silas gestured at the table.

"Can you wait a while, Inspector?" he said. "I haven't eaten all day."

Flynn could see Maree's first aid work on Silas' hands and elbows, and one leg sat straight out to the side with a compression bandage on his knee. The inspector didn't doubt it had been one hell of a day for the ex senior constable.

"Actually," he said, pulling up a chair opposite Silas, "I think we should debrief here – if that's all right with you, Mr Taufmann."

Freddie looked at his wife, and she gave a curt nod.

"There's just the two of us home at the moment, Inspector Flynn," she said. "We're happy to help, if it's important."

Flynn nodded his head. "It is," he said, adding, "Thank you," quietly.

Silas told the inspector the full story as he ate, carefully avoiding any mention of Stodge's presence. He said he had been 'lucky' to see the cave through the murk, and some quick thinking had done the rest. The Taufmanns listened incredulously. At the mention of the quarry, they glanced briefly at each other. Silas could see they knew the place.

He wasn't worried about them knowing too much. He would need to swear them to secrecy anyway – he was supposed to be dead, for example – and it was always best to tell people exactly why they should keep a secret.

Inspector Flynn had heard and seen a lot in his many years in the police force, but Silas caught little indications of surprise flickering across his face from time to time. When Silas had finished eating, he pushed the empty pudding plate away.

"Keep it simple, keep it fresh, always the best, isn't that so, Maree?"

She smiled with pleasure. The best start in life she had given her children was to feed them right.

"Could we set up a table somewhere?" said Flynn, and picked up the slim briefcase he had brought in with him. "Somewhere we can work?"

"Right here will be fine," said Maree, "if you can wait for me to clear the plates away."

Once she had done that, Flynn set up a workplace. He had a laptop, and Silas got an electronic tablet to take notes on. There was a sheaf of paper, a map of the area, and a collection of pens.

"I'm not sure if we will need it, Mr Taufmann," said the inspector, "but could you password us into your internet connection. Assuming you have the internet of course."

"Freddie, please," said Freddie, and spelled out the password for the inspector.

"So, what do we know?" said Flynn, once he and Silas were settled. The Taufmanns had gone through to the lounge and shut the door behind them. Flynn appreciated that. This was now official police business, and he and Silas would work faster not having to worry about client privilege and confidentiality when it got to the legal stages.

"McCabe is fairly certain I discovered Huxton's airfield during my investigation," said Silas, "and probably assumed I passed the information on to the police.

"He doesn't know if I went there myself, or just heard something. He asked me if someone in his organization had rolled over and coughed up the information, so he doesn't know where the leak is."

Flynn nodded. McCabe wasn't sure how the airfield had been compromised, but the lawyer had assumed the worst and gone to full damage control. Part of that had been to order Silas' murder. It was an attempt to stop the ex senior constable from disclosing any more information, or acting as a police witness.

"I still can't believe he's the crime boss behind this whole operation," said Flynn. "Though he's intelligent enough to pull it off, but there's definitely something wrong with his thinking. I can imagine him being insanely driven by power or greed to feed his inner demons, but it's a multi-million dollar operation, and we're a sleepy little town!"

"I know," said Silas. "We didn't see it coming. It's a matter of professional pride. It feels like we've been caught napping on the job."

Silas suddenly remembered Annabel using the same words, professional pride, and he realized she was right. There was nothing wrong with wanting to know if you were good at your job, but he had let it control his life.

Flynn smiled ruefully. "I think you're right," he said quietly.

"Fortunately," he continued, "the collapse of the Devil's Outlaws' distribution system means there's very little help the gang can give McCabe at the moment. They've been severely weakened by the members we've taken off the streets, and other gangs will be trying to muscle in. They'll have their hands full."

Silas remembered the man Assoulin had called Turei. He would be an Outlaws enforcer, sent south to beef up the operation in Tokoroa when things started to fall apart. Assoulin, Luke and Terz were the only full members of the fledgling local branch.

"McCabe is having to rely on gang prospects for some of his work," said Flynn. "There has been some surveillance of the Tokoroa police station over the last few days, and I wouldn't be surprised to learn that extends to your place, Silas, and Tarrant's as well."

Flynn laughed. "They were amateurs. I spotted them immediately, and put telephoto images up against the data base. There are three I've seen so far, two locals with minor charges against their names and the one you already know from Devon Findlay's case, Joseph Barnes."

Silas nodded. Prospects were people who wanted to be members of a gang but had not yet 'proved' themselves by committing a serious criminal act. Most of them were burned off when the gang wanted someone to take the fall for gang activities.

"And what do we know about Tarrant?" he asked. For Silas, this was the first order of business. Once Tarrant was back in action they could start on the long list of things that needed to be done next.

"The two of you disappeared about the same time," said Flynn. "When Tarrant didn't put in a work plan for today it came straight to my attention.

You've now explained what happened this morning, and the first priority has to be locating him and finding out if his ex wife is safe.

"I wondered whether he might be at her place, but the patrol car I sent to Matamata found no one there. There were a lot of clothes strewn around the bedroom, and it looked like she had packed a bag in a hurry."

"Helen," said Silas. "Her name is Helen. She was a good copper's wife too, bit prickly, but loyal. I never understood why they split up when the kids left home."

Flynn looked at him. This was the local knowledge he needed from Silas.

"She's a tidy person," said Silas, steepling his hands together, as he assembled a number of possibilities in his mind, "so a messy bedroom suggests she's been abducted. The kids have left home so her absence wouldn't normally be noticed for a while. Abducting her would be the only way for McCabe to guarantee Tarrant's silence.

"It's only a short term solution for keeping Tarrant quiet though," he continued, "so McCabe must have another plan in place for when he has to release her. Let's hope it doesn't involve murder. He has shown an ability to go down that road if it suits him."

Then Silas was struggling with something that didn't make sense to him, and Flynn waited patiently while he sorted it out.

"I was wrong," he said at last. "I thought Mrs Huxton had gone back to her family in California. Some of the things Summer said supported that idea, but I don't think she has.

"McCabe needs her nearby and under his control, so he can keep Huxton quiet about McCabe's role as the mastermind of the operation. It's the same M.O. he's using with Helen, it's the way he operates."

Silas looked across at Flynn. "We'll find the two women together," he said finally. "Now we just have to find McCabe's safe house, and I know the group of people who can help us do that.

"I won't use your cell phone, Inspector," he continued. "I'm not sure how much control Foy has over the police communications system yet, and I don't know if he can trace individual calls. I'll use Freddie's landline. That will be safest."

The Taufmanns readily handed over their cordless phone. Silas smiled as he took it, and said, "I bet there's been too much excitement in your lives for one day already. Something you can tell your grand-kids when it's all over."

"Blow that!" said Freddie, "we'll be dining out on this story for months! Er, when you tell us it's safe to talk about it, of course."

Flynn looked on. It was clear that Silas knew his people. He seemed to move effortlessly through the community he inhabited, liked and respected as he went. The group of people who would look for McCabe's safe house were probably the members of the local AA groups Silas worked with.

Flynn shook his head. It was local knowledge at a level that had never been described in police manuals. It was what he'd been looking for as a foundation stone at the Tokoroa Station.

That was when Flynn decided that Silas would do. He had been waiting for a long time to find a police officer like Silas Chambers, and he would put him into a senior position when he finally managed to encourage him back into the force.

Silas put the phone to his ear, and spent the next hour organizing his troops.

Chapter 43

"Motel coming up now," said Suzanne, and Silas shifted his position under the blanket on her back seat. Suzanne might have been a pretty blonde once, but years of alcohol and drug abuse had aged her badly. Smoking hadn't helped.

She was clean now though, and Silas had decided to boost her confidence by trusting her with an assignment. She had also been sworn to secrecy.

Simon's car was still outside Tarrant's house, and Silas figured asking one of his AA crew to pick it up might make McCabe's underlings suspicious. He wanted to leave that particular hornet's nest alone, for a while anyway.

Suzanne was a Tawhiti member of the AA, and she would visit her daughter on the far side of Hamilton after she dropped Silas off. It was mid morning, and there was fine weather. Silas had stayed at the farmhouse overnight and slept in – by farming standards – after the hardships of the previous day. Flynn had headed home around ten thirty the previous night.

"Stopping by the back door of the middle unit," said Suzanne, and got out of the car a moment later. She knocked on the door, using the code Silas had provided, and a surprised Annabel looked at her uncomprehendingly.

"Package for Annabel Kirsk," she said, and Annabel nodded. Suzanne opened the back door of the car, hiding Silas' passage into the unit, much as Annabel had done after Silas' car was forced off the road. Silas scrambled though to the unit in an undignified crouch. He paid for that as his knee flared with pain.

Annabel wrapped her arms around him at once, and buried her face in his shoulder. She only released him when he put a hand on her shoulder to make a little space, and turned to thank Suzanne for her help.

"You seem to be in very good hands," said Suzanne, with an amused smile. She accepted his thanks with a fluttery wave of her fingers, and pulled the door closed as she stepped out to her car.

"You didn't ring!" said Annabel accusingly. "I can accept that you're preoccupied during the day, when you're working, but you told me you would ring as soon as you had some time each evening!"

Silas looked past Annabel to Mereana, who was sitting at the small motel table. Mereana frowned and shook her head. This was serious.

Silas felt a pang of guilt. He had brought Flynn up to date as soon as he arrived at the Taufmann farmhouse, but he hadn't even thought of Annabel.

He decided it was a guy thing. Someone had tried to kill him, and the only way to get on top of that was to marshal his troops and get a counter strike underway as soon as possible. Thinking about the people he was trying to protect would only distract him. Unfortunately, he doubted that Annabel would see it that way.

"You talked to Tarrant first, didn't you!" she said, when his silence dragged on. "What happened to sharing our lives, equal in all things?"

She drew back her hand and made a fist, as if she was going to belt him on the arm, and then lowered her hand as she looked in his eyes. His face had betrayed him as soon as she mentioned Dave.

"What happened to Tarrant?" she said. Mereana got up from the table and eyed him intently. Her husband had died in the line of duty. She knew how easily Tarrant might go the same way.

"Sit down, both of you," said Silas, "and I'll tell you what's been happening."

It took a while to get all the details across, and by the end of it Annabel was waving her finger in his face. He had an irrational urge to bite her finger, something like a dog instinctively chasing a ball, but he knew this was no time for games.

"You've almost died twice now, Silas Chambers!" she said, and her voice was shaking. "Even you can't be stupid enough to try your luck for a third time!"

Silas took her hand, and shook his head contritely.

The truth was something different. He didn't know what he might have to do to close the murder cases and get the perpetrators behind bars. For that matter, McCabe was still out there, and still untouchable. But at the same time, he would do anything for Annabel. They were contradictory statements, but sometimes love was like that.

"I could stand the risks involved in ordinary policing," she finished loudly, "but this current madness is getting out of hand!"

He nodded his agreement. An international, multi-million dollar criminal operation in the area was a once in a lifetime occurrence for Tokoroa. More likely once in several lifetimes.

The two women were instantly concerned when they heard that Helen Findlay and Irena Huxton were missing. Silas outlined the plan he had worked out with Flynn to deal with the situation. Unfortunately that mostly meant waiting for his AA helpers to get back to him.

The two men had decided against using police contacts. Anything official could get to Foy, or could spook McCabe. Assoulin had taken Silas' cell phone, so he had borrowed one from among his AA contacts and made some adjustments to his phone tree.

"We also have to disable everyone's cell phones for a while," he said, and Mereana and Annabel looked at him in surprise.

"Assoulin has got my cell phone," he explained, "so we have to assume Foy has it by now. There's a remote chance he could use the GPS feature on the phones to track any one of us. Your numbers are all on my phone.

"The only way this can be done in New Zealand is through the SIS, with a court order, but I don't want to underestimate the tricks Foy has learned. He went through police training with the intent of using everything he was taught to help McCabe."

They shrugged, and handed their cell phones over. It took a bit longer to get the mobiles from the others. Silas popped the SIM cards out, and taped each one to its phone.

"How's everyone coping?" he asked the two women, once this was done. It was the morning of the third day since Annabel had rounded up everyone McCabe might attempt to harm or coerce, and set them up at this motel – with Tracey Donovan's help.

"Gords and his flatmates are getting a bit stir crazy," said Annabel, "but they have Eli with them, and there are a lot of things that four people can do, from card games to long discussions about what's going on. I don't think Simon will worry too much about his car, as long as he gets it back in one piece.

"Mereana and I can handle a bit of waiting," she went on. "Donovan goes to the front desk once a day, to check up on how the motel's running – very 'hands on' that lady – and she drops off books for us, which the manager brings down.

"Did you know Flynn owns the other half of the motel?" she added.

Silas shook his head. "What is it with those two?" he said, and Annabel shrugged. "You already asked me that," she said, "and I didn't know a lot then either."

"Well they're pretty close-mouthed about it," said Silas, his investigator's instincts starting to worry away at the question. Mereana distracted him with a question of her own.

"Have you felt Ella's or Ernest's presence since the last time we talked about it?" she said.

That put him on the spot. "Yes, well, I have," he began, "but it's a long story."

Mereana patted the other side of the table. He limped over to tell her what had been going on, wondering how he could put his experiences into rational sentences.

Annabel noticed his limp straight away. He got a five minute reprieve while she fussed around his knee.

"Your ankle looks fine," she said in surprise, as she looked at that too. "It can't have been as bad as I thought."

"What about my superhuman powers of recovery?" he said, and she lifted an eyebrow. "I wouldn't put too much faith in those if I were you," she said archly.

She replaced Maree's tight bandaging around the knee with some heavy duty strapping, and then surveyed her handiwork.

"You still need to stay off it," she warned, and he nodded dutifully. Whether that would be possible was another matter.

Then he hobbled across to the table, and sat opposite Mereana.

"You shared Ernest's memories?" she said a few minutes later, looking dumbfounded. "I didn't know that was possible."

"It was probably because I couldn't hear what he was trying to tell me," said Silas hesitantly. She thought about that, but didn't seem convinced.

"You shared the memories of a kehua, a ghost?" she repeated, and he nodded.

"And you felt it was Ernest making some directions feel 'safe' and some 'unsafe'," she added, "when you were in dangerous situations?"

Silas nodded. Yup, he thought, it sounded weird to him as well.

There was a long silence.

"Well, you're not a matakite then," she said. Fine, thought Silas. So he wasn't a seer.

"You're a tohunga kehua, possibly," she added, which seemed to Silas to be worse. It meant he was some sort of medicine man who specialized in ghosts.

The ability to know what was safe for him had saved his life twice now, and that was a big plus. But the experiences had been getting stronger. They had been taking him over, and he was uncertain where that might end.

Chapter 44

Silas took a call on his borrowed cell phone that evening. It was one he had been expecting, though it had arrived surprisingly soon. Every one of his AA contacts must have been out and about, keeping their eyes open.

Suzanne was currently head of the telephone tree, and she was reporting in with some very useful information.

Silas' eyes and ears knew by now that the drug-related busts up and down the country were due to the work of the Tokoroa police, and that must have been a motivating factor. They would also know that Silas was in the thick of it, somewhere, and they understood their role as his information gatherers. They drew a simple conclusion – duty called.

"Tarrant's back in his house," said Silas, as soon as he got off the phone to Suzanne. Annabel left to get Mereana, and then the others. Silas soon had a circle of upturned faces watching him closely as he paced back and forth between the motel sitting room and kitchen. These people had already been through a lot because of him, and they were his family and friends. That meant they had a right to know what he was thinking.

Annabel and Mereana had seen Silas in full investigative mode before, but the younger members of the group were struggling to keep up with the flow of information, conjecture and conclusion.

"Tarrant will have made no attempt to contact Inspector Flynn," said Silas. "He will play McCabe's game for the moment. He also knows that Assoulin has my cell phone, so he won't try to contact me on that.

"I'm thinking Tarrant will have called in sick at the police station for a day or two. McCabe's orders will be to keep silent about my disappearance, and about the abduction of his ex wife. If he's been beaten by McCabe's enforcers it won't be in places that are visible, but he will need time for the bruises to heal so he can move normally.

"Tarrant knows that Flynn has been brought up to speed about the airfield, and McCabe's shipments. That makes me think he will go along with

McCabe's instructions until we contact him. His main concern will be his ex wife, but she's only useful to McCabe while she's still alive, and that will give Tarrant strength.

"I've now been told about three possible locations in Tokoroa for McCabe's safe house," he continued, "the place where we think he's keeping Helen and Irena. One of them is opposite Tarrant's house in Maraeti Road, though it's three houses along. That's where I think the safe house will be. It allows McCabe's henchmen to keep an eye on Tarrant, and it reduces the number of locations that have to be manned around the clock."

Silas paused in his thinking, and Gords gave a small chuckle, part amusement and part awe.

"Is he always like this when he's working a case?" he said, and Mereana nodded.

"He has shielded you from this when you were growing up," she said quietly. "He didn't want you to find out how sick our society can be, not until you were older."

There were a lot of very adult concepts in those words, and Gords lapsed into silence while he tried to find places for them in his understanding.

"The problem now is the airfield," said Silas, stopping to drum his fingers against his lower lip. "We have to hit the safe house and the airfield at the same time, so the women are freed before McCabe knows what's going on at the airfield, and can order the women to be moved. And I don't see any point in waiting for the next shipment at the next full moon. It probably won't happen, now that McCabe suspects that too many people know about it.

"He could get the jet over so he can leave the country though," said Silas, "and that would be my best bet. It's another reason to hit the airfield before he has a chance to get away, and he may be trying to organise that right now.

"McCabe would need to call Noumea at least two hours and forty minutes before he wanted the jet to arrive here. That's the distance divided by the speed of the jet. He would need to allow extra time for fuelling at the New Caledonia end as well, and for the pilot to draw up a flight plan.

"Then there's the matter of the jet arriving at night. I wonder if McCabe would try a daytime landing? The aircraft would probably be seen on its final approach and reported, but if he never came back to New Zealand that might not matter."

"Don't we have extradition treaties with just about every country now?" said Mereana, who knew something about this from her time as a constable's wife.

"That's what's so clever," said Silas. "New Caledonia is essentially a self-governing part of France. If McCabe has prepared an emergency plan in advance – and I'm betting he has – then he will already have French citizenship, probably paid for through a corrupt official in New Caledonia.

"The original French constitution guarantees its citizens certain freedoms that would make McCabe untouchable if he was living in France. Fortunately, the European Union has passed laws that member states are required to uphold. Under those, McCabe could be extradited.

"But there's a problem for us. With the amount of money he has already made importing illegal drugs through the airfield, he could pay constitutional lawyers to hold up the courts for years. By then he would have disappeared into eastern Europe, and be untraceable."

"How much money has he made?" said Simon, suddenly looking interested.

"At a rough guess," said Silas, "if the gangs took half and McCabe took half, and some of it had to go on providing the jet, and assuming he's put through a few shipments by now, it could be $10-15 million in our dollars."

The massive tally stopped the conversation cold.

"So crime does pay," said Gord's flatmate Dianne, and then immediately wished she hadn't.

"Not if I have anything to say about it!" said Silas grimly. He could see her discomfort, so he hurried on. "The problem now is getting our forces into position before McCabe manages to leave the country.

"Somehow I have to talk to Flynn, and he has to prepare an Armed Offender's Squad for when it's needed at the safe house, and they'll probably need to take out all three houses I've been informed about, just to be sure. I saw gang members with enough weapons when they thought they had me captive, so the AOS will have to go in hard."

"What about the airfield?" said Annabel, and deep down she already knew the answer.

"That shouldn't be a problem," he said. "We'll bypass Huxton's house and come in over the tops to take over the cottage, which we can then sweep for evidence. A police team should be okay for that, although it will be issued with sidearms and rifles.

"I hope we do trigger some of those sensors they've got up there, and Huxton's two 'security guards' come racing up the farm track ready to bully people again. We can do them for carrying sidearms, and I'm sure they'll dig themselves into deeper holes as well."

"And you will have to lead them in, I suppose," said Annabel, and Silas could see where this was going. She didn't want him out there in harm's way, not again.

"Yes," he said, "Gummy and I will be needed as guides. But we'll be no more than civilian observers, and we won't be carrying weapons."

He paused to marshal his thoughts, and noticed that Annabel still didn't look happy.

"Gummy and I have information the ground team will need," he said quietly, "and if we don't do our part it puts their lives at risk. Good men, and women, have done the same thing to protect me over the years, and you can't expect me to let them down now."

Annabel hesitated, but she finally accepted that. She didn't like it, but he saw a look of grudging consent as she acknowledged the underlying principle. Law enforcement personnel needed to look out for each other.

"So," said Silas, thinking aloud, "how do I contact Flynn?"

"At his house, straight after work," said Gords excitedly. "That gives him time to set up a dawn raid on McCabe's safe houses tomorrow, and time for you to get your police squad together. Then you can be at the airfield at the same time as the raid hits the safe houses."

Mereana smiled at Gords' enthusiasm, and Annabel rolled her eyes. "You've been hanging around Silas too long," she said.

"Honestly, I tried to give him a normal life!" said Silas, and Gords chuckled.

"You did," he said, "and I appreciate it. You also taught me logical thinking, and how to look at all the possibilities."

It was something Silas would never forget. At that moment he was a proud parent, and all the trouble bringing Gords up had been worthwhile. But there was one thing he had to do that had been impossible for the last few days.

"Where on earth did you get to?" said Penny, as she checked in at the usual time and found Silas' Skype call waiting. "It's been almost a week!" which was a long time when he was supposed to check in every evening.

"You won't believe what's been happening," he answered, and then proceeded to give her the short version of recent events.

"So I think we've got it all covered down here," he said, "though I want to say how helpful you've been! I don't operate well without someone to bounce strategy off, and having you and later Flynn to check over my decisions has given me confidence that I wouldn't otherwise have had."

"Well, it looks like you've got everything covered," said Penny, as she reviewed the notes she had taken as he spoke. "But Maric and I are both intrigued by this little town of yours, and we must arrange a visit some time."

"You're always welcome!" said Silas, and a short time later they ended the call.

"I still think they're out of their depth," said Maric, when she called him in later that evening to hear what Silas had been up to.

"Any number of things could go wrong with someone like McCabe involved," he continued, "and the Outlaws are likely to turn nasty when they see there's no way out." There was a long moment of silence while Penny let him turn over the new parts of the case in his mind.

"Let's hope the next few days will see the end of this criminal enterprise," he said at last, and she nodded. She fervently hoped so too.

Chapter 45

Silas was sitting with Inspector Flynn in the kitchen of the inspector's house, in darkness. The lack of light was another layer of security. Flynn hadn't noticed any surveillance of his property over the preceding days, but Silas had been lying on the back seat of Gords car all the way from Hamilton as a precaution. He was getting used to travelling that way lately. Then Gords had dropped him off in Tokoroa and he figured Flynn should be home from work soon.

Silas had found the house behind Flynn's unoccupied, and came over the fence to wait by Flynn's back door. He was discovering that he much preferred an up front style of policing though. Too much cloak and dagger stuff wasn't for him. He waited until Flynn had driven into his garage and gone in the side door of the house before he knocked.

"You want a small police team, issued with sidearms and rifles, ready for tomorrow morning?" said Flynn, and Silas nodded.

"A Tawhiti local will drop me off at the end of Forestry Road Number Three at 5am tomorrow morning," he said, "and Gummy will come up from a friend's place down south to meet me there. How much preparation time will the Armed Offenders Squad need to take out the safe houses?"

"You're asking a lot, Silas," said the inspector slowly, and Silas nodded. He was.

"Am I right about this, though," he countered. "Can you think of a better way to proceed? One that covers all our bases? We definitely have to hit both places at the same time, and I'm certain that McCabe will be getting ready to flee the country."

Flynn thought about it for a moment, then shook his head. He couldn't think of a better way to proceed, and he reached for the landline nearby. "I guess I better get things moving," he said.

"Use this," said Silas, handing over a cell phone. "It's untraceable. Probably not necessary, but I don't want McCabe to get wind of what we're doing."

The inspector looked surprised, but then he accepted the phone and dialled the number he needed.

It was a small group that met at the end of Forestry Road Number Three at 5am the next morning. There was Silas, Gummy, and two armed police constables. Silas would have liked more, but it should be enough. It was unlikely that there would be anyone at the airfield.

There was a quick round of introductions, and then it was time to move out. There was a half moon, and their eyes would adjust shortly. It helped that the track was easy to follow for the first half an hour.

"You gents ready?" said Gummy, and everyone nodded.

"Operational matter, Mr Chambers," said one of the constables, a young man Silas hadn't met before, "we don't normally have armed civilians as part of a police team."

The constable had a point. Gummy had a high-powered rifle with a scope attached slung over his pack, and this wasn't a civilian matter any more.

"Sorry Gummy," he said. "Those are the rules. I should have warned you. We have to leave it up to the police now."

Gummy didn't seem fazed. "I'll lock it out of sight under the back seat in the twin cab then," he said. "You know the way up onto the plateau, Silas. Head off and I'll be right behind you."

A few minutes later Silas heard the steady tramp of Gummy's boots join the tail end of the little column. Half an hour later they stopped at the top of the long incline for a breather. Silas had taken a heavy dose of painkillers for his knee, and Annabel's strapping was holding up well.

Then he spotted Gummy's rifle, still slung over his pack, and broke into a smile. It took him a moment to stifle it.

"I thought you were going to leave the rifle behind, Gummy," he said, speaking seriously, as the constables turned to see what was going on.

"You need me," said Gummy defensively. "On the off chance things get out of hand. An extra weapon could be very useful, and I'm your guide, I know this area best."

"I'm sorry, Mr Watkins," said the lead constable, "you'll have to return the rifle to your vehicle."

But Silas had already done the sums. If they waited for Gummy to return the rifle to his truck it would put them too far behind schedule. On the other hand, Gummy couldn't be expected to abandon expensive equipment behind a bush until they picked it up on the way back.

Most importantly, the team had to be at the airfield early, so they could set up before the raids in Tokoroa began. Anyone working for Huxton who was at the cottage next to the airfield was bound to get a call as soon as things went sour at the safe house. That would cause one hell of a reaction, and the four members of Silas' team needed to be in place to stop anyone present from fleeing the airfield.

"Let him bring it," said Silas, after he had explained his reasoning. "You know I answer to the inspector, and Gummy can answer to me. I can deputize him if you want."

He doubted any 'deputizing' he did would be legal in any sense, but the idea seemed to satisfy the two constables. After a few moments there was a curt nod from the one who had questioned it.

"Let's move out then," said Silas, and the party headed off across the plateau. It wasn't long before it was time to slide sideways through the trees toward the possum lines. There was some swearing from the constables, and Silas smiled to himself. He remembered the difficulties he'd put up with the first time Gummy led him off the path like this.

Then it was a straight run south-east along the plateau and back toward Huxton's spread. Gummy led the way up the last slope until the small team was at the back entrance to the cave. Dawn had begun to make its presence felt as a grey band along the eastern horizon.

"Once we're inside the cave," said Silas, as they stopped for a breather, "we can't afford any noise, especially metal on metal. Sound carries at night, so we'll have to be careful as we set up.

"It's just before six thirty, so we've got plenty of time. The raid on McCabe's safe house will launch at seven, and the sun will be up by then."

Flynn had agreed to hit all three houses Silas' AA contacts had flagged after he reviewed the information they had provided. One of the buildings was almost certain to be McCabe's safe house, and the other two were worth investigating on suspicion of illegal activities alone.

Silas waggled his borrowed cell phone toward the others. "We'll get updates as the raids progress," he added.

The two constables nodded. Silas was in charge at the moment, and they would follow his lead until they saw what they were up against on the airfield. Then police protocol would take over.

Gummy led the way expertly through the knot of passages that took the team to the main cave. The constables were as impressed with the layout of the place as Silas had been.

His first look out one of the cave openings onto the airfield brought Silas up short. The same twin-engined jet was standing on the grass runway, by the cottage, and there was a lot of activity going on around it. It was being unloaded, and that meant it wouldn't be long before it took off again.

He brought the others over, so they could see the same thing he was seeing.

"Goddammit, we've hit the jackpot," he whispered, "just what we didn't want!"

Then he looked to his right, and saw the line of vehicles on the far side of the cottage. Something was going on here that involved a lot more people than last time.

The constables set up their rifles in two of the slotted windows that looked out over the airfield, while Silas made a quick trip out the back entrance to call the Armed offenders Squad. A vigorous discussion ensued on his borrowed cell phone.

When Silas returned to the cave he had bad news.

"The quickest any backup can get here is a little over an hour," he said quietly to the others. "It turns out it will be easier to wait for the squad in Tokoroa to finish their raids, and then catch a helicopter up to the plateau, than call in a fresh squad from anywhere else.

"A helicopter will be airborne from Hamilton in less than half an hour," he added, "and it will collect the squad when they've finished at Tokoroa.

"The problem for us," he said slowly, "is that someone in that cottage is going to get a call from Tokoroa as soon as McCabe's safe house is raided.

That means we have to keep the jet here until backup arrives around seven forty. That's a big forty minute hole we have to fill."

There was a moment's silence, and then the others nodded.

Chapter 46

There wasn't much to do for the next fifteen minutes, except try and figure out what was happening with the meth shipment. The same 4WD farm bike from last time was moving something into the shed behind the cottage, so maybe the shipment had already been unloaded from the jet.

It looked to Silas like the jet had made an emergency trip. A last attempt to ship out all the meth the organization had back in New Caledonia before the police closed down the New Zealand end of the operation.

Once the aircraft had left, the shipment would be hidden away until the heat died down. It would help the Devil's Outlaws gang get established again as they re-built their distribution network, and it would give McCabe one last payout.

The New Zealand police would be notifying the police in Noumea soon, and life would get equally hot for members of the drug cartel over there. The fact that McCabe would go for one last payout, more than anything else, convinced Silas that he was planning to make a run for Noumea. The risks involved for the extra money were too high – unless McCabe intended to be a long way away shortly afterwards.

Silas counted a dozen figures in the lights from the cottage. He grimaced as he saw Foy and Creel among them. McCabe had taunted him with the elaborate background story he had prepared for these two if they were ever arrested. The lawyer believed he could keep the kingpins in his organization from prosecution.

But that wasn't going to be the case if the Armed Offenders Squad caught them at the airfield. Nothing McCabe could do would stop him, or any of his followers, going down for a long prison stretch.

McCabe disappeared into the cottage, along with Huxton's security team of Trafford and Stuart, though Huxton wasn't there. Assoulin and the gang members working with him were probably tied up doing shifts at the safe house in Tokoroa. The same crew of one pilot and two armed men were guarding the jet, and that left four newcomers Silas didn't recognize.

He knew the type immediately though. They were long-standing gang members, from Auckland most likely. They would have been sent at the last minute to look after the Devil's Outlaws interest in this final shipment.

Silas did the math. Twelve of them against his four in the cave wasn't good odds, but only the guards with the plane had military style weapons. Silas counted two shotguns with the gang members, and a 22 with Huxton's man Trafford. Foy might have a sidearm, but he assumed that was the only one.

Pistols were only permitted for target shooting in New Zealand, but the criminal element seemed able to get their hands on prohibited armaments occasionally.

When McCabe came back out of the cottage, there were still ten minutes to go until the Tokoroa raids at 7am. Some of the vehicle headlights were still on, though the sky was brightening, and the lawyer and pilot worked through the details of the payment for the shipment. McCabe might be travelling back with the jet this time, but the pilot wanted to see the cash first. It made sense. He was protecting his boss' in New Caledonia.

Then the vehicle headlights went out, and the jet engines began to power up. Silas had minutes to put a plan into place.

"Can we shoot out the engines on the jet?" he asked, and none of the others knew the answer to that. There were two of them, one on either side of the tail, and disabling the jet that way wouldn't harm the pilot – and Silas had been thinking of shooting out the front windows.

Gummy was the only one present with a powerful scope and a long barrel on his rifle. The Bushmasters weren't a sniper rifle, and the constables weren't trained to use them like that.

"Leave it to me," said Gummy with a smile, and fished around in the bottom of his pack. He came up with a small, worn and stained cardboard box. It contained ammunition cartridges that looked longer than usual.

"Armour-piercing," said Gummy. "Got 'em at a hunting meet years ago. Don't know which war they came from. Always knew they would come in handy though, and I've always wanted to try 'em out.

"This rifle will take the bigger bullets okay, but those ones won't," he added, pointing at one of the Bushmasters.

Silas turned toward the more senior of the constables. "If we're going to keep that jet here, we're going to need Gummy's help to do it. It's his rifle, and he knows how to use it, and the engines are small targets from way up here."

The constable didn't like it, but he eventually nodded. It looked like this wasn't going to be a purely police action.

"What's the plan?" he asked, and Silas waved his hand for silence as he tried to think. Dealing with a situation like this wasn't going to be easy. If Silas had still been in the police force he would have sat tight and waited for backup, but he was contemplating much more active solutions than that this time round. It made him realize just how wild and woolly he was getting away from the discipline of the police force.

He decided the team should give the assembled members of McCabe's organization a chance to surrender. It was pointless, but it was the one 'by the book' tactic he felt he should adhere to. From then on things were going to get very Wild West indeed.

A few minutes later the jet started to roll across the grass in front of the cottage, and it was time to act. Once it had retraced its steps to the far end of the runway it would be able to turn, and begin its take-off. Gummy was already eyes on his target, and the boom of the armour-piercing bullet cut through the whine of the engines, but the first shot had little effect.

"Dammit," he muttered, "that was dead on too. I'll try shooting out the fans," and Silas knew he meant the impellers at the front of the engine.

The reaction at the cottage to the shot, though, was immediate. Trafford started yelling, and let loose into the trees with a stream of high-powered 22 bullets from his modified rifle. That was stupid, thought Silas. The man had no idea where the shot had come from.

Gummy's second bullet produced an odd knocking from the nearest engine, and Silas could see the big smile on Gummy's face. Two more bullets did the trick, and the engines started to power down as the electronics read that something wasn't right.

Then Gummy turned his attention to the parking space beside the cottage. He was targeting the engines of the vehicles from his elevated position, and holes started to appear in the bonnets. Silas reckoned that

Gummy might even be able to crack the engine blocks with bullets like that, but enough shrapnel flying around under the bonnet would disable them just as effectively.

It wasn't long before the sharp impact of the armour-piercing bullets stopped, and Silas looked across to see Gummy loading his five-shot magazine with more deer-hunting ammunition.

The next phase of Silas' plan began when he and the two constables had climbed down the bluff and taken up positions in the tree-covered slope below. He started by shooting out a window at the back of the cottage, and the lights inside went out as someone hit the switches. It made little difference, as the dawn was now far enough advanced to give reasonable visibility, and then the constables took out a couple of windows each.

Once they had stopped shooting, Silas called on the occupants of the cottage to surrender. He was safe behind cover, and the shotgun blasts that tried to locate him weren't unexpected. It did look like the drug traffickers had no intention of coming quietly though.

Silas made his way to a new position on the left side of the cottage, right on the treeline. Then he opened up on the side windows, which was the sign for the constables to shoot out the remaining windows along the back. All Silas had was a Glock from one of the constables, and two spare clips of ammunition, but he took care to hit a window with every shot. He figured his team should give the occupants a show of force.

Gummy put a couple of bullets through the kitchen attached to the right side of the cottage to help out, but there was nothing coming back from inside. Silas figured the occupants were pressed against whatever cover they could find, waiting for the barrage to end.

The two jet engines had finally fallen silent, and Silas looked at the time. It was two minutes past seven. His team had to keep this up for another thirty-eight minutes, and they were seriously short of the ammunition they would need for a protracted stand-off.

At least Tarrant would soon be reunited with his ex wife, and Irena Huxton would be free, if the raids in the safe houses in Tokoroa had gone as expected. Silas hoped Huxton would be okay through all this, wherever McCabe had stashed him. He had always thought the movie producer had been foolish, rather than someone who was actively in league with McCabe.

Silas figured retirement hadn't suited Huxton, and the money had started to run out, and it hadn't taken long for the man to be drawn into the lawyer's web. Then McCabe had taken over the ranch for his own purposes, and now he was threatening Huxton's wife to keep the man in line.

Gummy had stayed in the cave, and now he saw movement at the jet. He put a couple of shots into the side door to encourage the pilot and the two armed guards that had come with the drug shipment to stay out of the fight.

It seemed to work for a while, until the door opened from the top and became a set of steps reaching down to the grass. Gummy put a couple more shots across the top step, and Silas heard the deflections hit somewhere inside the aircraft.

Moments later the two guards exited the fuselage going left and right, and Silas was impressed. They took the fall to the grass smoothly, one rolling across his shoulder and the other flexing his knees as he landed. Then they headed for the cottage at a run.

The engagement was fast getting past the point of being a skirmish. Someone was going to get seriously hurt, concluded Silas, but that was the price that had to be paid for ideals like justice, and his old promise as a policeman to protect communities. Then he heard the dull booms of a shotgun, aimed at the constables on the slopes above him, and Silas hoped they weren't getting hit by the occasional pellet. Then Foy's police sidearm opened up, which was foolish at that sort of range. Maybe he just hoped he would get lucky.

The gang members were wasting ammunition – or was it Creel, and where was McCabe, he thought idly – but it continued to show that they weren't going to surrender. The two guards from the jet seemed to share that view as well and a burst of submachine gun fire followed, before a chatter of smaller 22 bullets reminded Silas that Trafford and Stuart were still busy.

At the aggressive response from the cottage Gummy's rifle fell silent, and Silas edged back into the trees. The constables had good cover on a steep slope, and the most ammunition for their rifles out of the four of them. The plan now was to let the shooters in the cottage break themselves on that solid defence for as long as possible.

Chapter 47

Ten minutes later, several of the shooters from the cottage made a run for the trees, during cover fire from the cottage, and began working their way up the slope toward the position of the two constables. It was a situation that Silas had planned for. When they couldn't keep the attackers at bay any longer, the constables would retreat to either side of the hill.

One would join Silas, who would fall back to the agreed position, and the other would join Gummy, who would come out of the cave the back way and move to the other side of the hill. It would give the team a cross-fire position relative to the ascending shooters and the cottage.

From there it would be a matter of disappearing into the forest when threatened, and returning to harass the cottage when they could. They had to keep the people from the cottage occupied until the helicopter arrived, and Silas' plan was a form of guerrilla tactics that he thought might do the job.

He figured it was only a matter of time before some of the defenders made a run for it though. He wasn't sure how he could stop them doing that, once they managed to get a vehicle to work, and backup was still twenty minutes away. As if in answer to his question he felt Stodge's presence again, and grimaced. The strange sensation in his body and mind always unsettled him, and this time was no different.

The flickering images from previous encounters had ceased, but the strange impression of someone trying to talk to him had grown stronger, until it was the dull roar of a crowd in the distance.

Silas couldn't hear individual words, but suddenly he understood what was happening. There was more than one presence around him, and they all had business with McCabe. It was interesting that the man was known by different names to some of his accusers.

The unsettling feeling that some directions were safe, while others were not, returned. Silas took a deep breath, and then another, but it still felt like he was being compelled to act by something outside his control.

Perhaps it was just wanting to have control over his own life that upset him. If he knew where a lethal threat lay, he would normally take strenuous action to avoid it, wouldn't he? He sighed. Stodge and company were trying to be helpful, but it still felt like someone was taking over his nervous system.

Then he was being urged in a new direction.

Silas gave up his plan to move higher and rendezvous with one of the constables. He moved as quietly as he could across the open ground to the side of the cottage. He had to trust that this feeling of safety was right, and no one could see him while he felt it was so. The sensation continued as he turned the far corner of the wall and slid in alongside the front door.

Then all his alarm bells went off. Everywhere was dangerous, including where he was standing. He knew he had to go through that door, and he knew he would be seen. McCabe was in there, and hesitating would only make matters worse. He didn't want to advertise his presence with the sound of a shot, so he slipped the Glock into a side pocket. Then he pushed the door open and stepped sharply through.

One of the guards from the jet had his hand out, reaching for the door knob, and his eyes sprang open in surprise. Silas hit him hard on one side, under his ribs, with a well-timed punch. The guard visibly wobbled on his feet, and Silas stepped past and turned to strike hard where the guard's neck met the back of his head. The man dropped like a sack of potatoes. It wasn't an approved police manoeuvre, but Silas had been in his share of street fights.

McCabe had been collecting something from the table in the middle of the room. There was glass from the windows over the floor and across the documents on the table. Now he backed up against the edge of the table, looking stunned. His reaction wasn't surprising, since he thought that this man was dead.

Silas wondered where the other guard was, but he couldn't feel a sense of danger coming from the bunk room, or the bathroom next door. Most of McCabe's cronies must be up on the hill trying to dislodge the two constables. The one he had knocked out would have been the one giving covering fire.

"Time to talk, McCabe," he said, stepping toward the man, and his voice thickened and coarsened.

"Time to acknowledge what you have done!" rasped the words, feeling like they were sticking in his throat. Then he felt his features changing, his skin flowing like water.

"You murdered me!" said the shrill voice of a very old woman. Silas could have sworn his mouth didn't move, but he knew her story.

McCabe had been turning over a house for his loan shark masters when he was still young. The owner's elderly mother had arrived unexpectedly, and begun berating him. McCabe had pushed her aside as he left, and she had fallen awkwardly and cracked her head. Then Silas felt himself change again.

"I would kill you in exchange for him, if I could," growled an old man's voice, and Silas knew the story.

Like most of the criminally insane, McCabe could sense the weaknesses of others. He had detected a growing romance between one of his lecturers at law school and one of his fellow students. Then he used the fact they were both male to extort money from the lecturer and destroy the career of the student.

The student was devastated. He dropped out of law school and never recovered. Now he lived on benefits, and occasional part-time jobs. It was his recently deceased father who was talking.

"You let your toady do these things," said a female voice, and Silas knew it was Ella Brekken. "I find you guilty of murder," she said with loathing.

McCabe had recruited Assoulin early on, and he could have kept the man on a short leash. But he liked to hear how Assoulin made others suffer, and how he covered up for the cruelty. He knew that letting Assoulin and the other two go out stealing had to end in tragedy.

"You struck me from behind, you coward," said Stodge's voice, and Silas was surprised to see in his mind that McCabe had committed this murder himself.

The lawyer had wanted to know what it felt like to take a life, and he had murdered Stodge in front of Huxton, at the man's mansion, so it would terrify him. From then on Huxton had done everything McCabe wanted.

"You might as well have shot me yourself," said the voice of Jakob Boss, and Silas knew the story. The two security guards on Huxton's ranch had been told to do whatever it took to keep the airfield a secret. McCabe had told them he would take care of any problems, and there would be bonuses too. In a way, he had paid the guards to kill.

McCabe sat down abruptly in a chair by the table.

"What are you?" he croaked.

"Call me an avenging angel if you like," growled Silas. The crooked smile on his face showed how close he was to ripping McCabe apart with his hands. The man was a monster, and McCabe slumped further into the chair, trying to get away from him.

"I can make it right," he protested feebly. "I can pay out the families, tell them what happened. I can say I'm sorry."

Silas dropped his head and sighed. It was clear McCabe didn't feel any of the pain of those he had killed, or ordered to be killed – or their families. If he truly understood the suffering his actions had caused, his insides would be tearing him apart right now. But the only thing he understood was a threat to himself.

The world would be a lot better off without him, but Silas couldn't bring himself to shoot the heinous bastard in cold blood.

"I know you have money hidden away," he said at last, "and I know you've promised your followers that you'll help them start again if they go to prison. It's a simple trade. If they do their time without rolling over and giving evidence, you will pay them well and set them up when they get out.

"I want you to call your people back here, and talk them into taking the fall," he continued. "None of you have a choice. The police will be here soon, and I'm sure you've already figured that out. I make it fifteen minutes from now.

"Or I could say you just got caught in the crossfire," he said, drawing the Glock out of his pocket.

McCabe scrambled out of the chair, and waved his arms at Silas in a gesture of agreement.

"No, no! That will be fine," said McCabe hastily. "That was the way I was going to play it anyway! If things got bad enough."

Silas doubted that, but he just wanted to get this whole sorry mess wound up. McCabe headed for the back of the room, and started shouting through the broken window panes, and after a while there were some hesitant replies.

In the end, Silas got part of his wish. McCabe managed to talk Foy, Creel, Trafford and Stuart into surrendering, and a little later the trio from the jet. But then Silas heard the sound of one of the vehicles outside turning over. It didn't start, and a little later there was the sound of another being tried.

The four gang members from the Outlaws were going to make a run for it, and Silas racked his brains for some way to stop them.

Chapter 48

Gummy bought Silas some time to think of a solution. The old hunter was running out of ammunition, but he still managed to discourage activity around the vehicles. A howl of anguish told Silas that Gummy was sticking to his promise – he was waiting for opportunities to shoot them in the leg.

Then one of the pickup trucks came to life, and a large toolbox on the tray, hard against the back window, left Gummy blind to what was happening inside the cab. By the time the truck was out on the gravel track, heading for Huxton's mansion, it was moving too fast for him to hit the tires. Silas heard several more shots as the old hunter tried to bring the vehicle to a halt, but it continued to pick up speed.

It wasn't long before Gummy joined Silas in the cottage, and two constables weren't far behind once Silas called them in. It didn't take long to pat down the prisoners, and stack the assortment of weapons on the table in the centre of the room. Silas' Glock kept the peace from then on.

Foy was the only one to share McCabe's stunned reaction to Silas' appearance. Foy had been there when Silas went into the lake at the quarry, hands tied behind his back and a heavy chain wrapped around his middle.

The corrupt police officer looked very nervous. It had been his call to leave Silas to a slow death by drowning, and now his victim had the upper hand – though Silas ignored Foy for the moment. This wasn't over yet, and McCabe's nephew would have the charge of attempted murder added to his sheet, among many others.

Then Silas caught a lucky break. His borrowed cell phone chirped, and he was talking to the head of the Armed Offenders Squad.

"This is squad leader Quentin Smitt," said the voice at the other end. "I'm told I need to talk to Silas Chambers."

A big grin spread across Silas' face. Quentin had been an investigative officer in Rotorua when Silas was doing the same thing in Tokoroa. They had always respected each other's talents.

"Since when did you start going all AOS on us, Quentin?" he said jovially.

"Easy, big fella," said Quentin. "It's just part time. Most of the day I'm elbow deep in paperwork from ordinary cases. You know how it is.

"Now, what's the situation at your end?" he asked.

Quentin was all business, as he should be. Silas got an ETA for the helicopter, and it was very good news. The AOS team was going to arrive at the cottage earlier than he had expected.

"You should be almost over us now," said Silas. "Large, irregular patch of farmland cut out of regenerating forest. Long airfield and cottage to one side. Do you see it?"

Quentin confirmed that the airfield was coming up ahead in the early morning light.

"The situation has stabilized here at the cottage," said Silas. "I suggest you prioritize white pickup truck heading away from you on farm track, large toolbox hard against the cab.

"Suspects have fired on police officers, repeat have used shotguns and automatic 22s against police officers. Proceed with caution."

Quentin acknowledged the information, and the steadily growing beat of the blades rose to a crescendo over the cottage and then diminished again.

The fact the occupants had fired on officers changed the rules, legally and personally. They weren't going to get a chance to do damage to the members of his team as far as Quentin was concerned. He spoke to the pilot through a head mike, and then made a number of hand signals to the others, and they rigged for aerial engagement.

The pickup truck came up fast, and it looked like there were two gang members in the cab and two on the back. The pilot dropped the helicopter down to eighty meters above the ground before swinging round to face the vehicle.

Bright flashes erupted from the windows on either side of the cab, and what could have been a handgun barked from the tray. The pilot whirled the helicopter away, climbing higher as spent shotgun pellets rattled against the underneath of it.

The sun was just over the horizon now, and visibility was good. Quentin made a hand signal to the man opposite him, and the two of them began to target the hood of the pickup.

The front of the pickup truck took increasing punishment, and the driver of the truck swerved the vehicle off the farm track to avoid the AOS efforts. Then it was too late for the driver to do anything to save the truck.

Quentin called a ceasefire as flames began to lick out from around the hood, and the truck began to fishtail in the dewy grass off the track. There was nothing his crew could do as the pickup climbed a low rise, the motor roaring, and hit a log on the ground not far from a forested gully. Then it got airborne, and hung in the air for long, long moments. A moment later it was in among the trees.

The AOS team couldn't see anything for a moment, but then a fireball burst above the treetops. Black smoke followed.

"Ouch," said Quentin, reflexively. The gang members deserved every second of their painful demise, but it was still a hard way to go.

"I think Search and Rescue should be the ones to body bag that lot, and haul them off to forensics," said one of his team, and there was general agreement from the rest. On Quentin's command, the helicopter turned back toward the cottage.

Silas was itching to get everything wound up as soon as the AOS landed nearby, but it was Quentin's show now, and he would take as long as he considered necessary. Before that it had, technically, been the two constables' show. Silas figured there was going to be a lot that he left out of his report.

Quentin called in a convoy of patrol cars from Rotorua for his use, and his team started processing the prisoners. Silas pointed some of the AOS members to the shed out the back of the cottage, and they found close to 40kg of methamphetamine, which was half the size of the normal shipments. It confirmed Silas' belief that the New Caledonian end of the organization had simply sent whatever they had on hand.

The problem now was that Silas wasn't anywhere near finished with his investigation. McCabe's drug trafficking organization had been stopped, and a lot of the people involved were about to be put away for a long time, but Silas still had three murder cases on his hands.

Ella Brekken was a cold case, and Stodge, as Silas had predicted, had been overlooked by the police for lack of evidence. It was up to Silas now. He was the only hope they had of something being done to solve their murders.

Jakob Boss wasn't directly his responsibility, but Silas hoped to get the man's killers convicted somewhere along the path to solving the other two cases. He had a plan to get justice for Ella and Ernest, but he would need Inspector Flynn's help to carry it out. After a moment's thought, he decided it would be best if he acted quickly.

Silas could move about openly – once Quentin was finished with him – now that he was no longer 'dead', and he intended to make full use of that fact. Flynn wouldn't be in his office yet, not this early in the morning, but Silas would make contact with the man as soon as he was.

Chapter 49

Silas sat in with two detectives from the organized crime department in Auckland, as each of McCabe's underlings went through their first interview. He didn't say anything, but he missed nothing.

The investigation was being held at the Tokoroa station, and that meant Flynn had the final say on procedural matters. Silas hoped it stayed that way. Flynn had backed Silas' current plan to shake loose some information.

The appearance of the ex senior constable unsettled most of the prisoners. They had either heard about his murder or been involved in it. Yet here he was, raised from the dead.

The only thing the detectives did, apart from taking a statement, was to grill the prisoners about a small bronze pendant that the police were looking for. The suspects were told that information leading to the recovery of the pendant would substantially reduce their prison sentence. Then they were led back to the cells.

Tokoroa was overcrowded with the influx of eight new prisoners, including McCabe. However it gave Flynn a chance to put them together in the station's main block, two to a cell, where the inmates had a chance to talk among themselves. Silas wanted rumour and doubt to spread quickly.

McCabe was beside himself when a junior partner from his law firm had a request for home detention denied. The Judge was privy to what Silas and Flynn hoped to achieve, but McCabe was not. He was forced to accept the fact that legal privilege wasn't going to be extended to him this time. Silas hoped it taught the man a lesson about what the system felt like for people who were on the other side of it.

Once the trap had been laid, it was time to start closing it. Statements had been taken on the second day since McCabe and his outfit had been apprehended, and all the initial interviews were now concluded.

The organized crime department had taken a while to get up to speed in Tokoroa, and that had given Flynn a legitimate reason to hold the prisoners longer than normally allowed. He had not yet released the known facts to the defence lawyers, and there had been no provisional charges.

The Devil's Outlaws base in Tokoroa had been searched again, and McCabe's house and offices had been turned over as well. McCabe's legal secretary, and his two junior partners in Tokoroa, had protested vehemently. They had promised the police department that it would be sued to the full extent of the law.

Perhaps they believed McCabe was a good man. Silas had found the criminally insane were often very good at cultivating saintly airs. But the employees at McCabe's office all knew Silas, and when he told them it was time to start looking for another job, the outrage diminished to a few unsettled mutterings.

McCabe's trophy wife had been coached in what to say if the police turned up at her door, but a stern warning from the senior constable that she would be taken in for obstructing officers in the course of their duty had the desired effect.

There were two attempts to burn down the Devil's Outlaws base on Baird Street, and Silas was glad Flynn had posted a guard on it. One of the firebugs was caught on the second attempt, and he was added to the tally already in the cells. Silas figured his actions were designed to remove evidence.

Creel was released first. He was told the detectives believed his story, that he didn't know about the drug shipments and was only keeping an eye on Huxton's property as his manager. But he would have a tail from the moment he left the station, and Flynn hoped he would lead them to Huxton.

Two hours later Luke Matto was released. The time between the releases was allowed to slowly increase, to keep the inmates in a state of tension, wondering when it might be their turn. All their questions were met with stony silence, and on one occasion the officer in charge threatened to hose down the cells for civil disobedience. Silas wanted the inmates wound up tight.

Luke left the police station and went to an address on Campbell Street, a few short blocks away. He left five minutes later in a boy racer car driven by an older man with distinctive tattoos on the side of his face. They drove directly to the Outlaws house on Baird Street.

Flynn had pulled the police guard off the house, but the two men still took some time scoping out the property before they moved onto it. Once there they went straight to the garage at the back of the section.

There was no lock on the side door, and no vehicle inside the garage. Sheets of chipboard had been laid over the crosspieces of the roof trusses, and a number of unwanted items had been stored there by previous tenants.

A concrete block wall had been built as a firewall between the garage and the neighbouring garage on the next section. Luke lifted the internal guttering where the roof ran down to the higher block wall, and felt along the top plate of the wall with his fingers. It was an ingenious hiding place. He lifted down a thin wad of hundred dollar notes, and a slim-handled knife that looked like it had been made as one unit out of expensive alloy.

Lastly he slid out a flat bronze pendant, with one end slightly cupped where a stirrup bracket would have lodged, and two holes at the other end to take an attachment to a saddle. It was part of an eleventh or twelfth century stirrup from Norway, and it had once belonged to Ella Brekken.

Silas dropped from his hiding place among the rafters, bending his knees to take the impact as he landed by the side door. There was no other way out of the garage.

"Very kind of you to lead me to that, Luke," he said quietly. "I'm sure you can understand how much it means to my investigation – and to the murder of a Norwegian tourist.

"I'll take that now."

Luke had slid the knife into some sort of sheath inside his clothing, which concealed it. Now he brought it out again, and slashed left and right with it.

"You get in our way, asshole, you die," he said, and started to move forward. The older man closed his fists and came forward on Luke's right, weaving his upper body and jabbing experimentally at the air.

Silas slid out a white baton made of extremely dense tropical hardwood. That, at least, had been returned to him after the dawn raids and the shoot out at the airfield.

He took a long step to his right, so he was facing the boxer, and stepped in between him and the wall. The move crowded the man, and he drove a straight right at Silas' head. The tall man had time to snap his head back, and think that personally he would have stuck with a left jab, when the baton blurred upward and shattered the man's wrist as it reached full extension. An agonized scream died to a whimper as the man folded to the ground, clutching his arm to his chest.

Then Silas flicked the baton out to the full reach of his arm, knowing Luke would be coming in fast to catch him off guard. The gang member pulled up short, the end of the baton right in his face.

"I'll be taking that item we talked about," said Silas evenly, "and that's not a request."

Luke backed up, but then the knife stabbed out for Silas' stomach before slicing up toward his face, and the tall man moved back. Luke still intended to make a fight of it.

Silas dropped the baton to his side.

"Thing is, Luke," he said, "you and all your gangland mates are going inside for a long stretch. The inspector set you up back at the station, and you led me straight to the pendant. There's no going back from here. You can see that, right?"

There was a long pause.

"McCabe won't be able to save you," said Silas. "We know he's the kingpin behind the organization, and he's moved enough meth into the country to get himself put away forever."

Silas let this slowly register. Then his voice took on a more conciliatory tone.

"The problem for you is you've been caught with Ella Brekken's pendant. That means you and Terz will take the blame for her death."

Luke's face twisted at the mention of Terz' name, as Silas had guessed it would. "But it was Assoulin's operation, wasn't it? You were new to Tokoroa, and Assoulin was the boss here. He called the shots."

"You could be an accessory, and not a murderer," he said, "if you gave testimony that Assoulin was the ringleader."

He let that sink in, before finishing with his strongest argument.

"I think you're tough enough to survive a long stretch in prison, to be honest, but I don't think Terz would. What do you think?"

Luke let the knife fall to the floor of the garage. Silas had been right. Whatever twisted relationship the two shared, it was one thing they cared about in a world they didn't understand, a world that didn't care about them.

Silas called in his support. A patrol car was waiting around the corner, and one of the officers inside it called for an ambulance.

Chapter 50

Luke was spirited away to Hamilton for further interviews, with the understanding that Terz would join him once homicide had the evidence they needed. A new team would then move in to re-open the Ella Brekken case.

Silas had ticked off a number of things on his self-imposed list in the last 48 hours, but he felt guilty. He had moved swiftly to get his hands on Ella's pendant, and maybe an extra day on that had been justified, but he was neglecting his friends and family woefully.

He searched among the cartoon emoji he had on his cell phone, and then went online to find exactly what he needed. Silas sent Annabel a cartoon image of a man working frantically at his desk, fingers a blur on the keyboard and sweat flying from his brow, as he looked at the clock on the wall. It said ten minutes to five. On his desk was an impressively large picture of a woman and some kids, the things that were dearest to him. Silas hoped the message was clear.

"Have you been briefed on everything?" he said to Tarrant, ten minutes later when he had tracked his friend down. It was a tired voice that answered.

"I think so," said Tarrant. "At least as far as you leading the police to McCabe's safe house, so they could free Helen. I . . . owe you big on that one, buddy."

Tarrant's voice cracked, and Silas understood just how hard it had been for him, having to sit and do nothing while his ex wife had been kidnapped. Silas couldn't imagine feeling so helpless.

"Is she okay?" he asked, and Tarrant confirmed the fact his ex wife was unharmed.

"Mentally?" said Silas, and Dave took a while answering. "She sounds real strong at the moment," he said, "but the psychologist says she'll have nightmares for a while, and she won't feel comfortable around dark places for a few months.

"A full recovery will take a lot of time and effort, but hey, we were married for 23 years. If she needs me to drop by regularly then I'm okay with that. If she needs me to sleep on the couch for a while I'll do that too!"

"Good to hear it," said Silas. "I'm betting that Mereana will visit Helen soon, knowing her, and Annabel and I will be by as soon as I've finished with these murder cases."

"Someone said you made a major breakthrough on the Ella Brekken case," said Tarrant, his voice firming up, "but it's all hush-hush I'm told."

Silas filled him in on how helpful Luke Matto had been.

"I haven't collared McCabe for Stodge's murder yet," he said, "and that's eating at me. Isn't there something about 'no rest for the wicked'?"

Tarrant laughed.

"You keep going, Silas," he said. "Bring that bastard down for murder as well as drug trafficking. He deserves everything he gets!"

"My thoughts exactly," said Silas, and ended the call.

The tail that Flynn had put on Creel lost him out by Lake Rotoma in the Rotorua Lakes district, but that gave Silas something new to work on. Huxton had to be out that way somewhere.

He rang Flynn to authorize a data search and got put through to 'the dungeon', where some hard-working IT people kept the police filing system on course. They had other skills as well, and it was those skills Silas now needed.

"Any properties in the Lakes area owned by Aldous Huxton or Irena Huxton?" he asked, and got a negative reply after a few minutes.

"Widen the search to include the names of family members back in California," he said. "Failing that, look for beneficiaries in any trust that Julian McCabe administers that have the surname Huxton."

IT said they would ring him back, and Silas resigned himself to the wait. His next task was to check on Irena Huxton, and he was told he would have to hold his horses there as well. She was still being debriefed after a long, sedated, midday sleep. Her kidnapping and confinement had affected her badly.

"She doesn't want our help, and we don't really want to hold her any longer than necessary," said one of the detectives from organized crime.

"She's a bundle of nerves. We could easily tip her over the edge, and for what? We don't think she was directly involved in McCabe's organization."

Silas understood the detective's reasoning. He asked when she was likely to be released, and what sort of car she drove, and took himself to a lay-by on State Highway One heading south. He had picked up Tarrant's car for this one, after the police took Luke Matto and his accomplice away. It had been a short walk to Tarrant's place.

While he was waiting, he thought about his now deceased Outlander. That had been a really good car, he mused, and he missed it. The damn thing had been built solid, and the storage capacity had been great. He wondered if the newer versions of the model had as good a reputation among mechanics. Maybe he would start looking for one when this was all over.

Then he had second thoughts. Should he get Annabel's opinion on the matter? Though really, even if they moved in together, they would still need a car each, wouldn't they? And if they didn't, same deal, right?

His mind was all over the place when the blue Toyota he was looking for buzzed passed the lay-by. He had to hurry to pull out onto the tar seal and follow the vehicle, keeping close enough so he wouldn't lose sight of it.

Then he got his call back from IT at Tokoroa.

"Huxton's been married twice," said the officer. "He has a daughter by his first wife, name of Sophia Huxton. There's a property at Lake Rotoma in her name."

Silas smiled to himself. That was what he was looking for. He got the address and closed the call.

It was an hour's drive, and Silas tried to keep a car between himself and the Toyota all the way, but that wasn't always possible. Not on a weekday in the South Waikato. He doubted he would be spotted though, since Irena Huxton wasn't expecting to be tailed.

Silas lost the Toyota at a roundabout where traffic had backed up, but he knew which of the three exits to take. He caught up with her again well before number 458 State Highway 30, just off the Lake Rotoma foreshore, but he drove past and pulled into a viewing spot looking out over the lake.

He gave Irena and Aldous half an hour to catch up with what had been happening, and get settled, and then he tapped on the front door of the little lakeside home. When it opened, he introduced himself, though he knew it would not be necessary.

Huxton pulled back in alarm. He remembered the man who had asked awkward questions at his house. He also remembered how Creel and McCabe had become increasingly hostile as Silas' investigation bit deeper and deeper.

"How did you find me?" he quavered, and Silas smiled amiably.

"Finding people used to be my job, Mr Huxton," he said gently, "but I'm not here on behalf of the police. Can we have a few minutes to talk about some things?"

Huxton might have declined, but Irena came to the door behind him.

"I know that name," she said. "You're the officer who found out where I was being held."

Silas demurred that he was an ex officer. Irena turned to her husband and asked him to agree to a brief conversation. "Without Mr Chambers's help I might still be at that place," she said earnestly.

Huxton relented, and let Silas in to the house.

"I'm sorry, Mr Huxton," said Silas, once they were seated in the small living room, "but the police will want a statement from you about McCabe and his drug dealings, and the worst case scenario is that you might lose your land for allowing it to be involved."

Both of them looked strained, but said nothing. Silas could see that they already knew that.

"On the other hand," he continued, "I have seen evidence during my unofficial investigation that you were under duress for at least the latter part of the operation, and the kidnapping of your wife strongly supports that idea. So, please do have some hope."

They smiled gratefully.

"As I said, I'm not here about that," said Silas. "What I want to talk to you about is the death of Ernest Graham. He was the hunter your guards found on your land. He kept coming back, even when he was given repeated warnings.

"I believe he discovered the airfield and tried to blackmail you."

Huxton looked very uncomfortable.

"That was all handled by my estate manager, Mr Creel," he said evasively.

Silas looked him straight in the eye. "I'm sorry, but that's not true, is it? I know Ernest Graham was killed in front of you, to ensure your silence. Now, I think we should start this conversation again."

Huxton was clearly startled by Silas' words. How did Silas know that? Had Creel turned on McCabe? No one else knew about the killing.

"What's he saying?" said Irena anxiously, as she clutched at her husband's arm. Huxton sat with his head bowed. Silas understood at once that it was something he had kept from her.

"There's no half way house with this, Mr Huxton," said Silas. "I believe you came to New Zealand to start a new life, and I think that's still possible.

"I want you to tell Irena everything, and then I want you to help the police make McCabe pay for Ernest's death.

"Do it together. Make a fresh start, Mr Huxton, and an honest one. Make your new country proud."

Then Silas got up and let himself out.

Chapter 51

———————

Annabel sat beside Silas on the sofa. They were watching a film that could best be described as something about human relationships, and it was the sort of film men watched to keep their partners happy. Though in this case she had sold the plot line to him rather well, and Silas was beginning to enjoy himself.

Annabel also had him firmly by the arm. Since life had returned to normal she seemed to need some sort of contact if they were in the same room. Silas rather liked the new development. Then she abruptly paused the film.

"Oy!" he said. "Englebert there was about to tell his ex girlfriend's new bloke that they were half-brothers. I was looking forward to that."

"Englebert?" she said, eyebrows climbing across her forehead.

"The lead character," he said, with a mischievous smile. "Englebert's as good a name as any."

"His name is Samuel," she said, "and it must be time for a break. You up for a cup of tea?"

Silas nodded. When she came back with the cups, though, she wanted to talk rather than restart the movie, and it looked like she had been going over recent events in her mind. Silas was okay with that. People processed changes in different ways.

A lot of it she already knew. Annabel knew that Assoulin would be convicted of the murder of Ella Brekken at his trial, and Silas was able to bring her up to date on Jakob Boss.

One of the Auckland detectives was close to getting the security guards to admit to the murder. There were too many other people in McCabe's organization that knew about it, and any one of them could volunteer the information to get leverage. A voluntary confession, and a declaration from both of them that it was an 'accident' would be their best chance for a reduced sentence.

"Have you heard anything from Huxton," said Annabel, putting her tea down as she discovered it was too hot. Silas shook his head.

"He'll come around," he said, "I know it. His wife is already convinced he should come clean, it's just him that's holding back."

"What if he doesn't confess everything?" she said. "Without him you can't show that McCabe was Ernest's killer."

Silas smiled knowingly, and she punched him on the arm. It seemed to be her favourite way of shaking loose information.

"I contacted his daughter from his first marriage," he said. "Told her enough to get her to lean on her father."

"Sophia?" said Annabel. "The one with her name on the Rotoma property deed? You sneaky sod. How old is this poor girl?"

"Late twenties," said Silas, "and she's got a masters in business studies. Seems she didn't inherit any of her father's movie skills. Very level-headed woman, and we had a long talk."

"She'll bring him round?" said Annabel, and Silas nodded.

"And you have a back-up plan if she doesn't," said Annabel knowingly. Silas seemed to think of everything.

Silas smiled but said nothing. Annabel lifted her hand and made a fist, but then she thought of something else, and put her hand down.

"You wanted to know about Donovan and Flynn," she said, as if she had been waiting for the right moment to talk to him. Silas turned his head sharply to look at her. When she wasn't immediately forthcoming, he gave a little nod. He was interested.

"I only know about this," she continued, "because I managed to get her nephew to focus enough, despite the pain after his motorcycle accident, to take on a rehabilitation course. There are very few people who know what I'm about to tell you, so you have to keep it strictly confidential."

Silas nodded, but that didn't seem enough for Annabel. "Look," he said, "I learned how to keep my mouth shut during my job, same as you I expect, but there's more to it than that.

"It looks like Flynn is going to be my boss again sometime soon, and I wouldn't undermine him in any way. He backed me on the murder cases when other inspectors wouldn't have, and that means a lot. He's also got a bigger picture of policing than most commanders in the force, and I want to work with him on that.

"So I'm not going to say anything about him and Tracey. Is that good enough for you?"

She smiled and nodded.

"They met early on," said Annabel, "and they both knew where they wanted their careers to go, even then. She rose to prominence quickly as a lawyer, and switched to police prosecution because she saw too many felons getting off on details. Meanwhile, he was rising rapidly through the ranks in policing. They had both grown up in this area, and they both settled back in the area.

"Yes, they were lovers, and probably still are, but you can imagine defence lawyers having a field day with that. They would accuse Flynn of planting evidence to support a case that his mistress was conducting.

"So if anybody asks, Silas," she said severely, "you have never seen them act in any way toward each other except to be rather critical. Which, by the way, is how they do behave toward each other in public.

"It's been a rocky road for them for other reasons too," she said. "Donovan doesn't want kids, and I don't know what Flynn thinks about not having children."

Donovan had always looked well maintained to Silas, always fit, and if anything a little too severe. It fitted the profile Annabel was laying out for him.

"Then Flynn developed prostate cancer," she said. "He's had the necessary surgery now, but they can't guarantee he'll live more than the next ten years. Of course he might be lucky, and the cancer might never come back. But the situation made him think about his future."

She paused, choosing her words carefully.

"That's where you come in," she said. "Donovan and Flynn both want you to hear this from me first, though I'm not sure why. Flynn will get around to confirming it when you're back in uniform."

That piqued Silas' interest. Anything that affected his position as a senior constable was important.

"Flynn can see the way policing is going," she said, "and it's common for ambitious officers to do a few years as chief of a quiet country station to advance their careers.

"He knows that it upsets the locals and demoralizes the front line officers, and he wants to bring back the old style of policing. That was when local knowledge was king, and officers were generally promoted through the ranks rather than bringing in outsiders."

Ambitious officers from Auckland, just like that goddamn idiot Billingham, thought Silas. It was one of the reasons he had left policing after Ian Findlay's death.

"Flynn doesn't want to see that happen when he eventually steps down from the top job," said Annabel, "which is why he is going to mentor you into the position."

"What?" said Silas, sitting up abruptly. "I'm an investigative officer, not an inspector. I'm no good at running a station, and I certainly do not want to be making statements to the press!"

Annabel was smiling now. "Donovan said you would say that, and neither of them is talking about tomorrow. You'll get tired of investigative work eventually, and then you will want to see good policing done in your area, and that's when you'll step up for the top job.

"That's what Flynn said," she continued, "according to Donovan. Flynn said 'the person to put into a position of power is the one who doesn't want it,' which I think is very true. He called the ones who crave the limelight some very rude names."

I'm with him on that, growled Silas to himself. Then his exasperation boiled over.

"Does everybody have my life mapped out for me?" he said tartly, making a show of mopping his brow. "Between you and the inspector, I'm surprised I've got enough spare time to pee!"

She laughed, and locked his fingers inside hers.

"You would be a fine inspector," she said, and shushed him when he tried to disagree. She picked up the remote to start the movie again, but he closed his free hand around hers on the remote.

"You asked me something once," he said, "and I think I've got an answer for you now."

She looked at him, pursed her lips, and raised her eyebrows.

"You asked me how it felt to know you were dying, if you were alone. You said the people you see as a nurse are okay if family are around, or even if there are doctors and nurses nearby, but what happens to someone who has to die by themselves."

Annabel remembered the moment. "Yes, I did say that, didn't I," she said.

"When I was in the lake at the quarry," he said, "and I couldn't get to the surface because of the weights, and it looked like there was no way forward through the rockfall, I knew there was a good chance I would die, but I didn't mind."

She looked at him with interest.

"I was okay with it," he said. "I figured there would be a moment of shock when cold water flooded my lungs, but everything would be peaceful after that.

"I'd fought the good fight, and done my best. There was no shame in dying at that moment. There wasn't any fear, if that was what you were asking. I had been working hard, trying to get up that underwater slope, and being exhausted might have something to do with it.

"I think nature has had a long time to prepare us for dying. If we go with it then everything will be fine. If we have our own ideas, and we fight it, then I think we might feel desperate or confused. But even then the body shuts down unhelpful feelings like that early on, as far as I can see.

"Does that make things clearer?" he added.

"You know, it does," she said. "I hadn't thought of drowning as an example, but I see what you're saying, and you were okay with it when it happened to you. Thank you for telling me this, Silas."

She squeezed his arm, and aimed the remote at the screen.

Epilogue

"It's kind of you to put us up," said Penny, as Mereana brought a plate of home-made biscuits to the table for morning tea. There was Penny and Maric, and Silas and Annabel, and Mereana, sitting around the kitchen table. Devon was busy completing his hours of community work for the weekend.

It was a Saturday morning, and Penny and Maric had been based in Mereana's home in Tokoroa for the best part of a week. They had found the spare bedroom very comfortable, and Silas had shown them the sights around Tokoroa and Tawhiti whenever he was free. They were getting very well looked after by Mereana, and some of the time they took off on expeditions of their own for the day.

""You were there for Silas when he needed you," said Mereana, looking especially at Penny, who accepted the words of gratitude graciously. Silas had been able to talk the investigation through with Penny on an almost nightly basis, and she was glad to have been of help.

"I wasn't of much use at all in the end," said Maric, impressed with the way Silas had taken to the rough-and-tumble of confronting McCabe and his underlings when it was required.

"Are you sure you don't want to try out for the SAS?" he continued, "We can always use a man with your experience," though he didn't think Silas would take him up on it. Part of the reason was his love of police work, and part of the reason was the no-nonsense nurse, Annabel, sitting beside Silas. The two of them were very close, and he could see that Silas would be able to discuss all the details of his investigations with her. That was a huge advantage in his line of work.

"I'm so glad we've come to have a look around this part of New Zealand," said Penny, and explained her origins in Flagstaff, Arizona. It meant that most of her adopted country was still new to her.

"I was disappointed when Maric cancelled a weekend away that we had planned a few weeks ago," she confided to Annabel. "You know how it is, it could have been the first sign that he was going off me," and Maric said that could never happen, putting his arm around her waist and drawing her close before he released her.

"But he told me he had something better planned," she continued, laughing, "and I'm so glad he did."

"These men of ours are hard to keep track of," said Annabel with a laugh, meaning Silas and Maric, "and you never know if they're going to come home in one piece!" which brought a nod from all the women present.

"When you see those occasional movies about military wives, they could be you and me, Penny," she went on, and Penny knew then that they were going to be great friends.

"How's Devon taking to his new freedom?" said Silas, and Mereana looked at him over the top of her cup. Devon's charges had been greatly reduced when it was clear the Devil's Outlaws had tempted him into their world at a difficult time in his life. Everyone has to take some responsibility though, and he had been lucky to get community work as a first offender. That was where he was today.

"He seems to be obsessed with his year 12 exams," she said. "Never thought I'd see the day! The one-on-one tutoring at the youth justice residence has made something click. He realizes he can learn this stuff now, it's just a matter of perseverance."

"How long until the exams?" asked Silas, and learned they would start in five weeks.

"I've hired him a tutor who can teach him maths and tidy up his English essays," said Mereana. "She was a bit of a find and lives nearby. It's expensive, but it's not for long, and I want to give Devon every chance I can."

"Good for you," said Silas, marvelling at the way parents would do anything to give their children a good start in life – but then, that was how he felt about Gords. It was good to know that Gords' flat was back to normal as well.

"Has Eli settled back into his chippie job?" he said, and Mereana nodded. Silas knew that Eli had a good head on him, and wouldn't have let the disruption of the last few weeks slow him down.

There was a lull in the conversation, and Mereana looked at Silas.

"Have they said goodbye yet?" she said quietly, and Silas understood at once what she was talking about. He wondered how she knew.

"Ella left as soon as I took the pendant from Luke Matto," he said, "and Stodge just wasn't there one morning. A day later I heard that Huxton had agreed to be a witness to Stodge's murder by McCabe. Stodge must have left the moment Huxton spoke to Flynn.

"I didn't realize they were constantly with me," he added. "I just knew it when they were gone. Weird, huh?"

Mereana nodded, and Penny looked at Maric. They hadn't been told all of it, but apparently the ghosts of Silas' cases stuck around until he solved the case, which was a concept they were still trying to get their heads around.

"So that's the end of it?" said Silas hesitantly. "I mean, I knew Stodge, and I felt like I knew Ella after poring over the story of her death for so long, and carrying it around in my head. So they came to me because I knew them, right?"

Mereana shook her head.

"You have the ability now," she said, "it's awake in you. When you're back in the police force and start taking on cases again, you'll know the feelings and opinions of those who have been murdered."

Silas didn't look too happy about that, and Mereana looked annoyed with him. "You have a gift, Silas," she said, "and you're on the side of the good guys. What more do you want? There's something bigger going on here than what is convenient for you, don't you understand that yet?"

Silas saw it all right, but he didn't want to go there. Good versus evil was too diaphanous a subject. It all depended on who you were and where you stood. Too subjective. But if he was going back into the police force he was going to come across murder cases, so he guessed he better get used to the victims hanging around.

"It's okay," he said, reaching over and taking Mereana's hand. "I think I can live with the 'inconvenience' as you call it. Most of all, though, I want to thank you for guiding me through the experiences I had. I might have gone mad otherwise."

She smiled, and squeezed his hand in response.

"Don't let Annabel see you holding hands with another women," she said, "she will skin you alive!" and Annabel laughed.

"That is so true!" she said, waving an admonishing finger at Silas.

"When are you going to marry the poor woman, anyway?" said Mereana, and Annabel's face crinkled into a smile.

"Well," said Silas, leaning conspiratorially forward on the table, "I did ask her, but she said she wasn't that stupid. She said she would wait and see what sort of creature I turned into once I was back in uniform. I guess she's got a point, she's only ever known me when I was resigned from the force."

"You only need to ask me what he was like," said Mereana, turning to Annabel. "He was fine when he was working, it gave him something to do with that inquisitive mind of his."

Silas laughed out loud. It looked like his future was going to be worked out for him by people who loved him and wanted the best for him. He supposed it could be worse.

Then he wondered for a moment if being an investigative officer again would be too tame, after cracking an international drug ring and a spate of murders. But he shrugged his shoulders, and settled back in his chair to enjoy the morning, and enjoy the company. In the afternoon he would make his way back to Annabel's place, and they had a social event lined up for the evening. What more could he want from life?

Then he thought about what Mereana had said. His 'abilities' weren't going to go away, and she had said he was now a tohunga kehua, an elder experienced in the presence of the dead.

Good grief, he thought, what did that mean in everyday terms? And how was he going to put up with it? But it wasn't all bad. Part of him could see how his new abilities were going to help him in his role as an investigative officer.

But he shoved any ideas of becoming the next inspector, when Flynn retired, to the back of his mind. Taking up his old job in the police force, and getting used to his new abilities, was quite enough to worry about for the moment.

THE END

~

~

The Dogged Detective

Copyright © June 2023 Casey Swan

9 798227 693877